To my younger self:
I'm sorry that I didn't know any better.

The

Delusion

of Cinderella

The

Delusion

of Cinderella

A NOVEL

KYM WHITLEY

JOYCE'S JOY PUBLICATION

ISBN 978-1-7323659-8-8

Library of Congress Control Number: 2018946378

Published by: Joyce's Joy

Encino, CA

First Edition: Men and Sex - Power, Pleasure, Pain

December 2010 by C. Mikki

Cover Design: Carla Simone

Cover Design Layout: BrainStreetDesign.com

Interior Layout: A Reader's Perspective

Proofread: EBM Professional Services

Printed in the United States of America

...one day you will kiss a man you can't breathe without
and find that breath is of little consequence...

−Karen Marie Moning

That One
A poem by Jade Hall

Blinded by his light, I see him.
Love. I feel him.
Lust. I taste it.
Pray. Let him be mine
beyond the ending of time.
But if he should ever have to go
his pleasure I know.
That one. Yes that one.

Death of Cinderella
Jade

My earliest sexual memories were the sounds of my mother experiencing her daily after-school orgasmic explosion at the home of her very married boyfriend, Mr. Frank. I was seven years old and I knew that something was happening to her, something that made her beg for more. My mother and Mr. Frank would keep me busy by giving me new toys to play with, but the Barbie dolls were my favorite. I had amassed a collection of dolls that lined the top of my dresser in my bedroom and I named them all.

Of all the boyfriends that Mother had, Mr. Frank was like Prince Charming. He had a kind voice and a bright white smile, and was always dressed like he was heading to church.

We went to Mr. Frank's house almost every day after I got out of school, but this day was unique. He gave me a Cinderella version Barbie doll. I didn't have this one and I'd never seen her in stores. She was the prettiest doll I'd ever beheld. Her dress was puffy and white, with sequins along the rim of the dress. He tapped me on my nose and bent down in front of me. "She's a special doll and not many people have her, but you are special, so take good care of her." I nodded, eager just to open the box.

"Go on," Mother said. I obeyed her command to sit down, be quiet, watch TV, and play with my new Barbie. I sat in the living room quietly and tried my damnedest to block out the sounds of my mother's moans. The sounds echoed in my mind as I tried to figure out if she was in pain. Years later, I would understand what Mr. Frank meant when I heard him ask her, "Whose is it?"

I named all of my dolls after each letter in the alphabet and this one I called Yolanda. With just one more doll, I would have the entire alphabet, from A to Z. After unpacking Yolanda and admiring her, I darted for the candy jar, grabbed all the candy my little hands could hold, and sat in front of the television to watch *The Proud Family*. The television was beside the door and I scooted closer to it, hoping the noise would drown out the high-pitched screams and moans. I hid the candy wrappers inside a fake ivy plant right next to the television so my mother wouldn't know I had eaten so much junk. The show was almost over and I was gathering all of my candy wrappers, shoving them in the plant, when I felt a tap on my shoulder. I jumped as a beautiful woman with long, black hair and big brown eyes said, "Hi."

"Hi." I tried to rub off the chocolate stuck to my teeth with my tongue.

"You must be the little one eating all of my candy." A single tear traveled down her face. Her voice shook as she knelt down beside me. "Who gave you this doll?"

12

"Mr. Frank." My heart pounded.

"Cinderella. My little girl has the same doll."

Still trying to clear the chocolate from my teeth, I didn't know what to do but sit there quietly. I recognized her as the lady in the pictures on top of the television, but I had never seen her in person. As quickly as she'd appeared, she was gone. Within minutes I heard yelling, shattering, thumps, bumps, and shrills of pain. I was terrified. I crawled into the corner between the TV and the door and curled up as tightly as I could, burying my face between my knees. The thuds, thumps, screams, and bumps continued, and I started to cry. I squeezed my Barbie doll as close to me as I could and told her, "It's okay. Don't be scared."

But I was frightened. I didn't want to open my eyes. After what seemed like forever, I finally heard nothing. Silence. It was as if the world had paused. Oddly enough, the silence was as scary as the noise, but I still didn't open my eyes. I squeezed them tighter, clutching Yolanda underneath my arm.

Suddenly I felt a hand grab my arm, propelling my entire body into the air like a rag doll. "Jade, let's go." Mother's voice spoke calmly. I was still terrified to open my eyes, but I did, only to see my mother covered with blood. Her new white bra that she had just bought the day before looked like an artist took a paintbrush filled with red paint and flung it against her. She reached for the door and then stopped to grab a jacket that was lying on the edge of the couch. She let my hand go, put the jacket on, and made adjustments to herself as if she were on her way to work or church.

Mother grabbed my hand again, opened the door, and walked sedately toward the car. She tossed me into the passenger side of our Chrysler LeBaron convertible, her purse flying into the backseat, and she calmly got into the driver's seat and slid a key into the ignition. Not once did the expression on her face change, emotionless and blank. Just as she put the clutch into reverse, the woman came outside. I pressed my back against the passenger seat, watching my mother's eyes shift upward. The woman's perfect ponytail had turned into a teased-out mess. Her face was covered in a mix of blood, snot, and tears. I could hear her high-pitched voice calling my mother words I'd never heard before.

Afraid of what was happening, I looked over at Mother as a slight smirk creeped across her face. I don't remember exactly what the woman said, but she suddenly kicked the front of the car. My mother didn't react right away; she just sat there, staring at the ranting woman. She moved the clutch from reverse to first, revved the engine, and took her foot off the clutch. The car moved forward. The woman's hand slapped down on the hood of the car and then both hands flew up into the air as her body took a baptismal dive backward.

My body jerked forward. I gasped and tried to raise up high enough to see the woman, but my mother moved her arm in front of me protectively. She barely glanced over the steering wheel as she backed up. She didn't seem to be at all upset or surprised by the woman's disappearance. I hid my eyes in my hands and closed them tightly, afraid of what I would see. I felt the car go into reverse and then forward. My doll Yolanda lay on the floorboard. My mother drove to our apartment and started packing without saying much of anything to me. We carried everything we could to the car. I had left Yolanda in the car and good thing I did because in the house Mother said there was no room for the dolls.

When we stopped to pick up my sister, Tracy, from a friend's house, Mother asked me to go get her. Tracy got in the car and I could tell by her slamming the door that she was upset, but no one said anything. Looking back on it, what would we have said? There were no words. Nothing we could have done or said would have made it any better.

We drove from Los Angeles to Houston, Texas, where my mother had grown up. She drove in silence for the first two hours, then she pressed the CD button. A song by Toni Braxton started blaring and Mother pressed the repeat button. She played "Breathe Again" over and over for hours. I even learned the lyrics and started to hum along. I turned toward the window clutching Yolanda and took a nap to Toni Braxton singing her pain and woke up several hours later to Mother banging her fist on the steering wheel, yelling at Tracy to hurry as a whiff of gas filled my nose. We had stopped to refill and I could only see read puffiness around my mother's piercing green eyes. She still seemed dazed by what had happened. Tracy finished pumping the gas and placed the nozzle back in the holder. Mother stared at me and I stared at her. I wanted to say something, something that would make her feel better, but I didn't know what to say. The pain in my mother's face became a look that I would never forget. I'd inherited my mother's green eyes but the redness now outweighed the green and she looked possessed. We stared at each other for a few minutes and I wish I knew what Mother was thinking about me at that moment.

We continued to drive. I was tired of hearing that same song but I didn't dare ask her to change it. The air was dry, the land was flat, and I was hot. I saw a sign that read WELCOME TO NEW MEXICO. I sat there, playing with my doll, when suddenly Mother turned to me with a sad face. "Cinderella is a mother-fucking fairy tale!" She snatched the doll from my hands and tossed her backwards out of the back of the car. I looked back watching Yolanda tumble from my view. I wanted to cry but I knew that I'd have to hold those tears for later. Mother didn't like for us to cry and I'd figured that if this is what people do when they fall in love, I should never fall in love.

More than twenty-four hours later, we arrived in Houston at my Aunt Robin's apartment on a hot Saturday morning. Exhausted and still emotionless, Mother made Tracy take me to the park. No sooner than we were out of Mother's sight, Tracy hit me on the back with her fist.

"Go play."

"I'm gonna tell Mother." I turned and took a swipe at her and missed.

"You better not." Tracy scowled.

I gave her the meanest look I had and walked away.

I ran toward the swings but stopped when I saw a little girl playing with a Barbie just like the one Mr. Frank had given me.

"That's your doll?" I asked.

"Yeah," said the little honey brown girl with long ponytails.

"I had one just like that."

"Where is it?" she asked.

Embarrassed to tell her what happened, I lied, "I left it at our house in Los Angeles."

"Los Angeles?"

"Yeah, that's what I said, ain't it?"

"Why you leave it?"

"'Cause I didn't like it. Can I play with yours?"

"I guess."

"What's your name?"

"Monica. What's yours?"

"Jade."

"Y'all just moved in?"

"Yeah, with my Aunt Robin."

"Miss Robin? I live next door to her." She smiled with excitement.

"Okay, we can be friends," I said.

"Will you be my best friend?" she added.

"Okay," I agreed.

I sat down beside Monica in the sand and we played until the streetlights came on. From that day, Monica and I were inseparable. We went to the same school, rode the same bus, and played together every day after school. We were best buddies.

Mother moved us into the apartment two doors down from Monica. She would spend the night often when her dad would drink too much and beat up her mom. As we grew older, Monica and I grew closer. My Cinderella dreams were damaged a little, but I had a new friend and that somehow made life a little easier.

Friendship
Monica

Growing up an only child was hard. I didn't have anyone that I could talk to, but most of all, it left me feeling alone until Jade showed up. If it hadn't been for her, I don't know that I could have survived. Jade wasn't only my friend but she became a refuge for me to get over the abuse from my father. The older I got, the more things seemed to escalate between my parents. My father was emotionally mean and I hated him for how he treated my mother. I never understood why she stayed with him. My mother had epilepsy and that kept her from working a decent job. Most times she would just cry and we'd go to the apartment or our neighbor, Miss Robin. Even when my mother would try to leave my father and get a job, we always landed right back with him.

My father's drinking was usually the catalyst for a session of violence. I would try my damnedest not to make him mad, even though he called me his precious Mo-Mo. He'd bring flowers, gifts, and all kinds of stuff filled with apologies. Over time, I learned to ignore them. He'd tell me how much he loved me but his love always hurt me physically. He'd tell me how I made him feel better when I would let him touch me. It made me feel gross inside and outside.

The day Jade moved in, my mother had ordered me to go outside and play but I was more interested in what she was talking to Miss Robin about. Miss Robin was single, had no kids, and could fight a medium-sized man on any day of the week. I was worried about what would happen because that morning, Miss Robin had slapped the shit out of my father. I had never seen a woman talk to him or treat him that way. He said he was sick and that he'd never do it again, but I knew he was lying.

It wasn't until I was older that I realized all fathers were *not* like mine. He made me believe that all fathers love their kids the same way.

Anytime my mother left the house she would ask, "Don't you want to go to Jade's house for a while?"

"Sure," I would always reply.

I asked Jade about the love that my father was giving to me and if her father's love hurt but she said that she never really had a father. By the time we were ten, my father's drinking had become uncontrollable and I almost lived with Jade. I would only spend one or two nights at my house. Less if I could. One night, my mom told me that we were going to be moving to get away from him. It made me sad that I might not see Jade again. She was like a sister to me. I cried as we packed up our apartment while my father was gone. I was in the kitchen packing the dishes when I heard a light knock at the door. I ran over to see who it was since it was so late. When I opened the door, there stood my father staggering and stumbling. He looked at me and smiled. I could smell the stench of alcohol on him as if it was coming out of his pores.

"Mo-Mo," he slurred, "miss me baby?"

I froze, unsure of what to do or how to answer, but I nodded in agreement, knowing that was the response he wanted.

"It's past your bedtime. What you doing up so late?" he asked.

"I fell asleep on the couch," I lied.

He pushed past me and staggered in.

My mother turned the corner and saw his face. She nearly turned white as a ghost when their eyes met.

"Monica, go to bed," she ordered.

He nearly fell onto my mother as he crossed the threshold. I stood back as he looked around and saw all of the boxes. I could tell that he was not happy. He pushed past her and looked around.

"What's all this?" he demanded.

"I can't take this anymore. We're leaving for good," she responded, but I didn't think she should have said that.

He reached back and landed a punch to her face that sent her spiraling to the floor, landing on nearby boxes. I stood there for a moment and then ran to the kitchen and grabbed the biggest knife I could find. I didn't think about what I planned on doing with it, but the piercing sounds of my mother's screams made me afraid that this was the time that he would actually kill her. I ran toward him, closed my eyes, and jabbed it. When I opened my eyes, I realized that I had connected with his shoulder. I just wanted him to stop punching her. Blood discharged from his shoulder like a waterfall and he reared back in pain. I let the knife go and covered my mouth.

"Monica, run!"

But I didn't want to leave her alone. I was frozen and unsure of what to do next. My mother got up off the floor and stumbled to her feet as he fell to his side. I could see the knife still sticking out of his shoulder as he failed to reach it. He begged, "Help me, Mo."

I couldn't make out the differences between my mom telling me to run and him asking for my help. I decided to get help, but as soon as I opened the door, there was Miss Robin holding a gun.

"Monica, go to Jade's house. NOW." She shoved me out the door and it slammed behind me. I ran to Jade's and banged on the door. Her mother came to the door and grabbed me, pulling me inside.

"Monica, what happened?" she said as she inspected my body. "Where's your mom?"

I couldn't speak. I just stood there and cried. The noise must have woken up Jade and she came toward me. Jade's mother thrust me toward Jade and started to leave when suddenly we heard a loud pop.

"Stay here and don't open the door." Jade's mother closed the door behind her.

The police and an ambulance arrived. They handcuffed my father and took him away. Jade and I stood nearby watching and I was afraid they were going to ask me what happened. My mom and Miss Robin did all the talking to the police and it was due to the marks on my mother's face that they decided not to press charges against her. After that night, I never saw him again, but I knew that no matter what was happening, Jade was there for me and that we were inseparable.

A Virgin...Damn
Jade

At the innocent age of sixteen, I decided I wanted to lose my virginity. Monica had fallen madly in love after her first time. I knew there had to be a better way of finding out what it felt like without falling in love. I was determined to figure it out. The best thing my sixteen-year-old mind could come up with was to have sex with someone I didn't really like but who was cute enough to at least kiss. I picked Eugene Collins. He was shy, quiet, and short. It turned out he wasn't just short in height, but short in other places too. Back then, I didn't know how important that was.

Eugene and I had gone to elementary, middle, and high school together. I thought he was the perfect person not to fall in love with because he would never hurt me emotionally and he wouldn't fall in love with me either. I wasn't sure how to tell him what I wanted without making it seem like it was a big deal, so one day, while having lunch off campus, I just came right out and told him.

"I want to have sex but I don't want any attachments."

I casually licked the salt off my fingertips from my greasy McDonald's fries as his mouth literally fell wide open.

"What do you mean?" he asked, exposing mashed hamburger in his mouth.

"I just want to know what it's like, but everyone that's done it so far has fallen in love, and I don't wanna be all sprung." I paused, then added, "On you."

What man can resist an invitation like that?

"When?" he asked eagerly.

"Whenever," I said nonchalantly, taking a sip of my drink and continuing to grub out on my fries.

It felt more like a transaction and business deal than a moment that should be filled with passion. We agreed on a date and time. In my mind, the next day would have been ideal, but that would have been Valentine's Day and under no circumstances did I want to attach my first time to that holiday, so we agreed on the following Friday.

On February 21, Eugene picked me up from the bus stop and drove to his house. His mom was at work, so it was cool. We rolled up to his house and I glanced over at him. His bottom lip was quivering. I didn't have time to ask why before he jumped out of the car and ran around to my side of the car to open the door for me, which was unusual. That's different, I thought. Didn't I tell him no attachments?

At that moment, it dawned on me that he might have feelings for me. The look on his face as he opened that car door made me wonder if he really liked me. We rushed to the front door since it was eight o'clock in the morning and we should have been in school. I looked around at the other houses to see if anyone was watching us as he fumbled so much with his keys that he dropped them.

"Hurry up."

He picked up the keys and finally got the door open. When I walked in the house, the smell of bacon and cigarettes filled my nose like a water hose. I looked to my left and, to my amazement, saw a pallet of blankets on the floor with rose petals sprinkled all around. I knew right then that he had put way too much thought into this.

"I didn't have time to clean my room and I really wanted this to be nice for you." His smile asked for my approval.

"I love it!"

I saw his chest fall as he exhaled in relief. He then walked over to the stereo and pushed play on his CD player.

"How sweet that you thought of music."

There was an awkward moment of silence as I stood there wondering, *How do we start?* Before that thought left my mind, he pulled me close to him. I'd never been that close to Eugene, but when I really focused on his face, I realized that he had some sexy ass lips. His smile made me blush. Out of nowhere, a warm, kind of tingly feeling moved through my body and landed in my pink polka-dot panties. I'd planned this around my period, so I was sure it couldn't be that.

It was like there was warm soap coming out of a dispenser trickling across my thighs. I made a mental note to have a discussion with my vagina about this. I was always intrigued with sexuality. My friends seemed more attached to needing the love of a person. For some, it was a baby, others, a man. I wasn't quite sure what it was for me. Mother had man after man so I figured that love had to be something different than just sex, but I wasn't sure they were connected.

I had started masturbating about two years ago, so I was

in touch with my vagina, or about as in touch as I could be at that age. Sometimes, you have to talk to your vagina to tell her what you need her to do. My many masturbation sessions led to me naming my vagina. Her name was Nita. I didn't want her to have a common label like everyone else's "coochie," "twat," or "pussy." Those were just so impersonal. But Nita was doing something very unusual that I hadn't felt before.

As Eugene pulled me closer and leaned in to kiss me, I realized that I had never kissed him before, so it felt very awkward. I pulled back.

"Are you nervous?" he asked.

I nodded my head and thought about how I'd perfected the art of kissing on my teddy bears and pillows. Kissing was damn near spiritual for me—not that introducing Nita wasn't a special moment as well, but I didn't understand sex that way at sixteen. I wanted my kisses to be similar to those on the soap operas, with soft lighting, and this was not it. He seemed to be uncomfortable with kissing me, and I think he realized that I wasn't going to be kissing him, so he went toward my ear. That was the most disgusting sound I had ever heard in my life, like someone was slopping around a wet mop in my ear. I had to move my head again in hopes that he'd move on. I didn't say anything, but I was thrilled that he finally went to my neck. I figured that if he didn't get that right, I'd have to take control, put him on the floor, and just get this over with.

There he was, kissing my neck, and he was doing pretty good when, suddenly, like a rabid dog, he bit me!

"Ouch!"

I yanked my body away from his. He grabbed me back quickly, as if we were playing ping-pong with our bodies and apologized as if he had stepped on my toe. I could only think that this was going nowhere. If my girlfriends were going through all this, where the hell was the part that they get sprung on, because so far this was some bullshit! I needed a minute to get myself together.

"I need to use the bathroom. I'll be right back."

He let go of my body and I huffed away, pissed off.

"Okay, I'll be right here," he said with anxiousness in his voice.

I opened the bathroom door and caught my reflection in the mirror. Why was I doing this? I found myself more worried about him falling in love with me instead of it being the other way around. I decided I had better check my panties as well to make sure Nita hadn't sprung a leak.

Satisfied that my period wasn't starting, I checked my neck to make sure that he hadn't made a mark on my light skin. Genetics had given me my father's skin tone, so I had to be careful not to get a hickey, but if I did get one I'd be able to cover it with my long black hair. Although happy that there were no marks on my neck, I dreaded the walk back to the living room. I looked over to find Eugene under the covers, his underwear tossed in clear view, so that I would know he was naked.

He flashed his seventeen-year-old smile and motioned for me to come to him. His innocent smile invited me to forget the last few minutes and start over. Hmm...he was really cute. His goatee perfectly shaped those sexy lips of his and invited me to want to finish what I had started. I had dressed appropriately for the occasion. I wore my lime green skirt and lime green shirt from Forever 21. I had this now-faded vision that there would be this passionate lifting of my skirt like on the soap operas. That didn't happen and here I was now, just taking it off as if I was about to have a bath. I quickly removed my clothes except my bra and panties. I wasn't ready to unleash Nita just yet. Nita was rocking the afro during those days, but I didn't think

Eugene cared. He looked at me in amazement and I started to wonder if this was his first time too.

He had told me that it wasn't, but so far, nothing was going right. If I wasn't his first, I was definitely his second. As I lay down next to him, he pulled the covers over me, which made me feel more ashamed about what I was about to do than I had before I lay down. He slid my panties down and crawled on top and immediately started humping on me.

I couldn't believe it. What the hell? I didn't get it. I could feel his penis trying to meet Nita, but she wasn't having it and neither was I. Nita never even opened the door. I lay there, still, legs squeezed together.

"Jade, relax," he said.

I figured if *he* wanted me to relax that meant I should be tenser.

He did about thirty fast dry humps and the faster he went, the more he groaned. So I started groaning and that seemed to make him even more excited. Nita wasn't reacting and she wasn't in pain. My friend Nadia had told me that it would hurt and that I might bleed. I was waiting on the pain, but it never came.

Then his dispenser spilled a soap-like substance all over my thighs. He let out the longest continuous sound I'd ever heard. His face looked like a skunk had shit in his nose and then he fell on top of me.

"Ooh, Jade, I'm so sorry."

I knew that this wasn't what it was supposed to be like, so I helped his ego and played stupid.

"Sorry for what? That was just what I wanted."

I wish I hadn't lied to him. He smiled as if he was proud of what he had not done, rolled over, and lay there with his hands resting behind his head. I looked at him, angry that my mother didn't tell me how to tell him that he was awful. I hoped he wouldn't go through life thinking that he just pleased me because I was pissed, but Nita was safe.

We got dressed and he drove us to school. I was angry the entire day. I never spoke to Eugene again after that.

About three months later, he wrote me a long-ass letter, saying that the sex wasn't worth our friendship. He was right, but I didn't know how to look at Eugene without wanting to slap him. He also wrote that he had feelings for me and wanted to see if we could start back with the great friendship we had. He thought that we might be meant for each other and he loved me. I never wrote him back, but there was something about that letter that initiated my warped view of sex and love. In the end, I was just glad that Nita was safe and I was still a virgin…damn!

Instant Gratification
Jade

After my episode with Eugene, I put a hold on Nita and increased my masturbation frequency to twice a day. Two years after my failed attempt to lose my virginity, I graduated high school and moved to Los Angeles. I had been accepted into the UCLA Department of Communications, but I only wanted to get out of Houston and away from my mother. Mother had remarried an older man that I called Mr. Gregory, but I think she married him because he had a nice house and a little bit of money. Leaving home was hard but only because I missed Monica. We had planned to go to UCLA together, but when her mom had a stroke, Monica stayed to take care of her. Nadia, one of my goofy classmates, was the only person I knew from home, so we decided to be roommates.

Nadia was the type of friend that I had only because we had grown up going to school together, but I didn't really like her. I agreed to live together under the assumption that having someone from home as a roommate would make it easier for me to transition to college. Plus Nadia was really smart when it came to books, though stupid in everything else. She had extremely low self-esteem and would lie about all kinds of shit that made no sense at all. I was still pretty mad at her for lying about how good sex would be when it was nothing like that. After my episode with Eugene, I didn't believe anything else she said to me.

During the first few weeks of college, Nadia began bragging that she had met this incredible man who was blowing her mind sexually and mentally. Now, Nadia was short, fat, and had small tits with no ass. Standing next to her, it was easy for me to be mistaken for a supermodel. Even though she really wasn't a close friend of mine, she didn't have a lot of friends and part of me felt sorry for her. Every day I had to listen to Nadia's stories of her man, Dre. The funny part was that I had never seen him pick her up from the dorm or any of her classes. That was usually the first indicator that Nadia was telling a lie.

She'd always claimed that he drove up just as I was walking off or that he had just gotten on the elevator or left the room. The journalism major in me was curious about this mystery man that was so good to her that I started to probe. The way she described him, I couldn't imagine a man like that wanting her. She described him as deliciously dark-skinned, with a body like Michael B. Jordan and a sexy smile like Idris Elba. I often asked her when I would get the chance to meet this delicious piece of manhood. Her response was always the same: "When we not spending time fucking." Then she smiled. Each time she would sound more and more annoyed. I knew she was lying and I was gonna prove it.

Nadia and I had an eight o'clock English class together. One Thursday morning, I overheard her telling Chandra, her study group partner, that Dre worked as a DJ at Club Z on Thursday nights. Thursday was 21 and under night and this Thursday would be the perfect night to go because Nadia was planning to stay home and study for her chemistry exam. Normally I would be bothered that she'd be in the room because I wouldn't be able to masturbate, but this time it gave me the perfect window to meet the man myself. That night, I put on my low back, ultra-sexy, black, tight, super-short minidress and headed to Club Z. Doors opened at seven. I didn't want to be the first one there, so I showed up around a quarter past nine. Since I was going alone, I didn't want to stick out as being dateless. I made a beeline for the bar as soon as I got there. Although they didn't serve alcohol, my calculus tutor, Slim, was the bartender and for five bucks, he'd spike all my drinks. Only problem was I never knew what Slim had on him, so it could be anything from Ciroc to Smirnoff.

Like most clubs, it was already hot inside. I sat down at the bar and scanned the room for the DJ booth. No one was there.

"What's up, Jade?" Slim smiled as he wiped off the counter.

"Not much. What's up with you?" I rummaged through my purse for cash.

"Just trying to graduate, you know," he replied. Slim was in the last semester of completing his bachelor's in biology. He was known for telling his life story, so I quickly changed the subject. I was on a mission and not in the mood to hear about his baby mama drama.

"Hey, who's the DJ tonight?"

"Oh, I think it's my boy, Dre." He pointed to the DJ booth. "Have you met Dre? He's real cool."

"No, I haven't," I replied.

"Oh, okay. Next time I see him, I'm gonna introduce y'all. He's real cool. Real cool."

"Actually, I wanted to request a song. If I ask him to play something, do you think he will?"

"Fo' sho. Just go up there." Slim pointed toward the staircase that led up to the booth.

"Cool." I made my way to the DJ booth, walked right in, and there he was. I guess Nadia wasn't lying. He did exist, but he wasn't as good looking as she said. He damn sure wasn't as fine as she had described him, but then again, this was Nadia telling the story. I wanted to make this quick, just in case he told Nadia that some girl said something to him.

"Hey, I'm Jade, Nadia's roommate. She told me to holler at you when I got here. Would you mind playing—"

He cut me off. "Who? Nadia? Who's Nadia?"

"Nadia Young," I said louder, thinking that maybe he couldn't hear me.

"I don't know Nadia, but okay…what song do you wanna hear?"

"I'll come back!" I yelled. I was so shocked by what he'd just said that I couldn't think of a song off the top of my head.

"Cool," he said and turned his back to me.

I closed the door and felt a surge of gratification that Nadia was again lying. This time, I planned on confronting her.

By the time I hit the dance floor, my favorite song came on and I was ready to shake my ass all night long. I was so happy about busting Nadia's trifling ass, I celebrated with three rum and Cokes, two Captain Morgans, and three Long Island Iced Teas. DJ Dre wasn't Nadia's man but he was my boy that night. He played every single song that I loved and I danced and sweated. It was pure celebration for me to know that I would finally be able to prove that Nadia was lying. When I requested a shot of vodka, Slim slid me a cup of ice water and suggested I take a break and get some air. He was right. It was hot, and

I needed some air. I decided to go outside. I grabbed the ice water and looked for the exit sign.

"Be right back, Slim." I hopped off the barstool, careful not to expose my thighs. I spotted the bright red exit sign and steered myself carefully through the club toward it.

As the crowd of sweaty girls and boys parted like the Red Sea, there, leaning against the door, was the sexiest brother I had seen all semester long. My eyes locked into eyes that were sleek and mysterious. Although I preferred my men like chocolate, he was creamy and caramel like a Sugar Baby. His lips were full and plump like Chance the Rapper and his eyes were soft with just enough edge to make me intrigued. I couldn't tell what his hair looked like because he was wearing a hat, which had a warm colored pattern that complemented his skin tone. The low brim made it hard to see above his eyebrows. He stood maybe 6'3" in a black V-neck T-shirt and jeans that made it apparent he spent time in the gym. The closer I got to him, the more the lights above him revealed his enticing eyes and high cheekbones, giving him a mysterious air that beckoned me. He smiled slightly, just enough to allow me to see his straight, white teeth and God-placed dimples, accentuated by a perfectly trimmed goatee. I knew I'd had a lot to drink, but he was captivating. Something about his aura drew me closer. I flashed my smile coyly, acknowledging that I had seen him and wanted him to see me.

Before I could extend my hand to open the door, he opened it for me. I reached toward the door anyway to show my personal independence and noticed the muscles in his extended arm. Slick as a gazelle in the woods lacking affection, I purposely brushed my body lightly against his, hoping to catch his scent. This man was so enchanting that I had forgotten all about Nadia. I had planned on leaving after having my cigarette, but this man changed the game. I wanted him.

When his body aroma slid into my nose and blood vessels, I understood what Nautica cologne was supposed to do. Men don't realize it, but it's not about the cologne. It's about how the cologne reacts to one's natural chemistry, and this man's natural aroma agreed with his chosen fragrance. The lavender and honeydew mixed scent was a perfect fusion of sexiness. Within seconds, euphoria tantalized my mind and sent an unfamiliar tingle to Nita that was strong, causing an interruption in my stomach.

As I stepped out the door, I turned to him and said, "Oh, please don't close it all the way. I do want to come back in." I smiled again, issuing an invitation with my eyes.

"Don't worry. I'll let you in. But I am more concerned about a beautiful woman like you being out here alone. I hope you don't mind if I join you," he offered politely in a deep, raspy voice. When our eyes met, there was depth to his deep set, dark brown eyes that captured me and caused me to stare just a little too long. I had to snap out of it.

"Sure, but only if you'll protect me from the good, the bad, and the ugly guys," I answered jokingly.

"I'm a good guy. Should I protect you from me?"

"I don't know. Do I need to be protected from you?"

"Depends on how you determine what's good and what's not."

There I was, within the first ten seconds of conversation with this man, and I was ready to have an orgasm. I laughed to lighten the conversation because I could see this going in a direction I wasn't sure I was ready for. My original plan was to have a cigarette, but I really wasn't a serious smoker and only did it when I went out with my friends. With him standing there, I didn't want to smoke because I was worried that my cigarette smell would turn off his intoxicating aroma. I wanted to be intoxicated and drunk with his scent. I took a sip of my water, hoping it would calm my nerves a little.

"So what's your name?" he asked.

"Jade," I answered as I watched him lick his lips.

"Jade. That's beautiful."

"My mother told me when she saw me that my green eyes reminded her of Jade."

"Interesting. Jade is a precious stone derived from the Spanish phrase *piedra de ijada*."

I didn't know what the hell he said, but I had never heard my name sound so sexy.

"I didn't know that," I replied. "And what does that mean in English?"

"Bowel stones."

"Are you serious?" I asked incredulously. "My mother named me after shit stones?"

He laughed. "No, no, no. It was believed that jade could prevent bowel distress."

"I don't know if that's making me feel any better." I laughed with him. "What's your name?"

"Darnell. It doesn't mean anything."

"Oh, that's great. I get shit stones and you get nothing."

He laughed again, then gestured toward the club. "Hot in there, huh?"

"I just wanted some fresh air." I wondered if he knew I was coming outside to smoke.

"Oh, okay. Most people come out here because they want to smoke. So which is it? Are you smoking or hot?" He flashed his melting smile. Suddenly there was that warm, tingly feeling again. I tried to laugh it off, but I got distracted by the sight of the small patch of freckles on his face in the moonlight.

I chuckled, struggling to recover. "Well, what if I say both?"

"Then I'd tell you that you shouldn't mess up that pretty smile with cigarettes." He laughed and lightly grabbed my chin.

His touch sent coolness down my back and set a sizzle to my stomach.

From that moment, we laughed and talked and talked and laughed. Soon we found ourselves walking from the Santa Monica Promenade all the way to the beach. I hadn't looked at my watch and had no idea what time it was, but I didn't care. I just knew that I was enjoying his company.

"So what's your favorite song?" he asked.

"Do you really want to know?"

"I do." He smiled. "I can tell a lot about a woman by what her favorite song is."

"Well, I guess it depends. Are you talking about like favorite song of all time or favorite song right now?"

"Either."

"Well, in that case, my most favorite song to just chill out, pop a bottle of red wine, and relax to would have to be anything by Etta James."

He tipped his head back and laughed. "You're kidding! Mine too!"

"Bullshit!"

I was fully aware that this was not the type of music favored by my generation.

"No bullshit."

Suddenly he stopped walking and grabbed my hand, squeezed it, and tilted his head to the side just a little. We bantered play-fully back and forth, discussing several of her songs. He knew all the words and so did I. It was amazing. Never in my life did I think I would meet a man who had love for Etta the way that I did. At the end of each song, we would giggle because neither of us could sing, but we sang enough songs to prove that we both knew the words. Even though I was still somewhat drunk, I felt completely sober. We continued walking by the full moonlight and he grabbed me around the waist as we strolled and sang, as if I belonged to him. We sang songs by Marvin Gaye, Billie Holliday, and then Nina Simone. "Do I move you, are you willin'? Do I groove you, is it thrillin'? Do I soothe you, tell the truth now . . ."

"You're the first woman I've ever met who knows all the lyrics to a Nina Simone song."

"And you're the first man I've ever met who knows the words to that song."

"Okay, who else do you like?"

We both loved many of the greats of old and the greats of new, all the way from Phil Collins to Kendrick Lamar. We both wanted to try skiing, but neither of us liked the snow. It was the most simple and easy conversation I'd ever had.

There was some kind of connection between us that had taken ahold of me and wasn't letting go. It was as if I had known him all my life, creating a strange level of comfort that was familiar. It felt good. I didn't mind that he was holding my hand or grabbing me around my waist. The sound of the waves sounded very similar to the way we were both feeling at that moment, like a silent crash, and I loved every moment.

We stared out at the ocean. I hoped that the silence would lead to a kiss, but we started talking again and again. We began sharing more personal parts of our lives. We sat there for hours and hours. We were even from the same city. I shared with him that my sister had married and moved away as soon as she was eighteen. Mother and I hadn't seen her in nearly seven or eight years. He told me that he was raised by his mother and that his dad had left when he was really small.

"One day, I came home and he was gone. My mother told me that I was the man of the house and that was it."

I glanced over at him and he seemed to be reliving that day at that very moment. After a long pause, he started again.

39

"After my dad left, my mom kept a lot of men around that were abusive to me and my sisters, so when I was old enough to fight back, I did. She put me out. I didn't see my sisters for years." After a few seconds, he snapped out of his trance-like state. He stood up abruptly and reached for my hand to help me stand.

"Let's go," he said and smiled. Once I was on my feet, he grabbed me around my waist and we started walking fast. He paused for a moment and gazed at me in amazement. "You're pretty cool."

The night air was perfect. The moon was full and the stars seemed to be shimmering in the ocean. Waves crashed against the shore in a rhythm that was almost erotic. I knew it was well after one o'clock because we could see the lights of the beach police coming toward us from the distance. He grabbed my hand and we ran toward a dimly-lit house. The feeling of his hand was electrifying. It was hard running in sand, but we made it to the side of a house before the cop car reached us. He pressed me against the wall and stood in front of me with his hand across my waist as if he was shielding me.

"You know how they get with us college kids."

I laughed as the rush of running and laughing tickled my head. He put his finger to his mouth to quiet me. Moments later, we watched the cop car pass. He removed his hand from my waist and turned to face me. The seriousness in his face and my shortness of breath clued me in that something marvelous was about to happen. He grabbed my hands in his and raised my arms above my head, then leaned in to kiss me but stopped before reaching my lips. He sniffed around my lips and cheeks quickly, yet sensuously. He pressed his firm body against mine enough to let me know that he was in control.

Nita was leaking like a faucet. He sniffed near my earlobe and licked the hair near my neck that I didn't know I had, then he used one hand to bring mine together and held my wrist above my head. With his other hand he pulled my breast out of the top of my dress. I had never felt such a flow go through my body. My legs began to dance as if I had to urinate. Nita felt warm, then very, very hot. He caressed my breast with his mouth, circling my pulsating nipple with his tongue, then released my arms and cupped one hand around my other breast. My hands felt handcuffed to the wooden siding of the house and I didn't move. He slid his slightly sharp fingernails down my arm, slowly past my elbow, trailing a tickly path along the inside of my underarm toward my armpit. Never in my life did I think that I would have tingles from someone passing fingertips over my armpit, but here I was, with the pulsation of sensuality going through my body.

He continued to travel down my arm and over my rib cage, then he made his way to my thigh and reached up beneath my skirt. His nails signaled Nita to get ready. While he was lifting my skirt above my thighs, he continued to lick my breastbone and collarbone. He bit down on my collarbone ever so lightly, sending me shrieking down the wall.

I caught the scent of my own sex—a smell I had never smelled before. With his left hand under my skirt, he moved his right hand from the nape of my neck to pull my head back, using my hair like a rope pull. As my neck relaxed, my mouth opened and I took in a deep breath. It was as though I could taste the air. I panted so hard, I feared I would hyperventilate. My body and mind seemed to be estranged. I couldn't stop my own hand from helping him remove my panties. They were soaking wet and I didn't care. Wiggling my hips, I let my panties fall to the sandy ground. I grabbed his face between my hands and tasted his full lips. He was being so good to my body that I wanted to mimic what he'd done to make my body quiver.

After all, shouldn't we do unto others as they do unto us?

I wanted him to know that he was pleasing me, but my moans of pleasure undoubtedly alerted him to that fact. I was only able to kiss him for a few moments before a whimper escaped. I couldn't focus on enjoying what he was doing to me while trying to do it to him, so I decided to let it be all about me. Suddenly he stopped and pulled back. I knew I looked a mess, but I didn't care. My body crawled against the wall like a snake looking for an escape route. Although he was no longer touching me, my form still quivered as if he had never broken contact. My heart was racing as fast as if I had just run five miles on a treadmill. I was sweating and for the first time in my life, I was high. The most euphoric feeling rushed over me as he gazed into my eyes with a devilish smile. His look went straight to my heart, which was opening wide.

Without warning, he dropped to his knees like a boxer who'd been punched in the stomach. He grabbed my waist, lifted my shirt, and lightly grazed his lips across the hairs on my stomach. He licked across my belly button like it was ice cream. After exploring my entire stomach and rib cage with his tongue, he moved his hands up my thighs and shifted my skirt above my waist to reveal Nita. Lifting one of my legs, he positioned it on his shoulder and enjoyed my free-flowing fluid.

This was beyond any feeling I had known during any of my masturbation sessions. I had never let anyone meet Nita face-to-face, but I wanted Nita to use her lips to kiss him back. The moment I felt his tongue part Nita's lips and reveal my bloom, I wanted to cry. My body had never felt that good. I shook, my heart raced, and I grew dizzy. The last thing I remember…blackness.

I opened my eyes to the sound of seagulls squawking and the smell of fresh ocean air. I could feel a hand caressing my hair. My head rested in Darnell's lap.

"Hey, you okay?" he asked with concern.

As I raised my head from his lap to look at him, I was ashamed to ask what had happened. Was it a dream?

"Yeah, yeah, I'm fine. Where's my car?" I felt dazed and confused.

He shrugged.

"What happened?" I asked.

"You passed out." He laughed.

"I did?" I was so embarrassed I could only cover my face in shame and shake my head. "I'm so sorry."

He placed his hand against my cheek. "Jade, it's okay. It tells me a lot about you." As I sat up straight, he put his hand around my shoulder and pulled me toward him to comfort me. I felt safe in his embrace. I dreaded knowing that I was going to be hurting in my 8:00 a.m. English class.

"Are you ready to go?" he asked.

"How long have we been here?"

"Not long."

"Darnell, I'm sorry. Thanks for staying with me."

"Of course."

We strolled slowly back toward the Promenade. We made a slight shortcut through the adjacent parking lot and arrived at a candy apple red BMW.

"Let's have brunch. Are you hungry?"

"I am, but I have to go. I have to get to class."

"Okay, just tell me where your car is."

When we arrived at my car, he got out to open the door for me. Still feeling somewhat dizzy, I leaned against his car to keep my balance. Trying to regain some of my dignity and coolness, I smiled at him and gave him a coy wink.

"So Jade, when can I see you again?" he asked.

"That depends," I answered.

"On what?" he asked quickly.

"On if you give me your number."

"Sure."

He leaned through the window of his car and pulled out a piece of paper, wrote on it, and handed it to me. I glanced at the paper, then did a double take, gasping in surprise.

"Dre?" I exclaimed. "I thought you said your name was Darnell!"

"It is. Andre Darnell Scott, but most of my friends call me Dre."

"Oh, okay," I said, trying not to seem shocked as I realized what I had done.

"What?" he asked suspiciously.

I stumbled over my words, searching for the ones that would make my answer sound believable. "Slim had just said that he was gonna introduce you to me, that's all. Were you in the DJ booth earlier? I thought Dre, I mean, you DJed on Thursday nights."

"Oh, that was my boy Marcus. He's doing Thursday nights now. Some weird fat girl was hanging around all the time bugging me, so I decided to switch nights with Marcus for a few weeks."

I gazed up at him and it struck me, at that moment, that this was the most incredible man I had ever met. I leaned in to give him one final kiss, determined to make Dre mine. I could still smell Nita's sap on his lips and enjoyed the flavor.

"Well, Dre, thank you for a wonderful night and day."

"Thank you, precious Jade."

I gave him my number, bringing our rendezvous to a close. Barely able to walk straight, I got in my car and drove away. When he was no longer in my rearview mirror, I lit a cigarette and drove down the 405 back to school. I barely remember floating back to my dorm room. My mind was locked on the ecstasy that Dre had brought to my body, giving my skin tingles with every thought.

As I turned the key to unlock the door to the room I shared with Nadia, I realized what I had done.

"Oh shit!"

I had never deceived anyone like this before, but then this was different. I couldn't think about Nadia now. All I could think about was how Dre made me feel. How could a man do that to my body? I didn't know, but what I did know was that I wanted more and I intended to get more. Only next time, hopefully I wouldn't pass out.

De-ranged
Jade

5:47 a.m.
Some days, everything that can go wrong will. Today was one of those days. From the moment the damn fire alarm went off, it started all wrong. Carly, the hall monitor, came banging on my door like a crackhead.

"What the hell?" I yelled. It turned out that my neighbors, Katie and Jamie, had come in tripping on ecstasy. A couple of very spoiled rich girls with too much money and too little common sense were so high on that shit they thought they were witches reincarnated from the 1800s. They were trying to prove that they could control flame, so they got naked, poured rubbing alcohol from one end of the hall to the next, and lit it on fire. The puff of flame freaked them both out and when Katie couldn't "control the fire," she ran up and down the hall screaming. Jamie got scared and pulled the alarm—the part where I got annoyed.

The water put the fire on Katie's ass out but her hair had gotten a little fried. That was funny as hell to me.

Housing staff evacuated us and we had to stand outside while the paramedics got the two of them under control and the fire department conducted an intensive search to ensure those crazy nuts hadn't set any other fire traps. That took forever.

8:13 a.m.

Finally, we were allowed to go back inside, and I headed straight to my bed. No sooner had I laid my head on the pillow then the phone rang. I jumped up quickly. It might be Dre.

"Hello?" I answered, trying to sound pleasant in case it was him.

"Where the hell were you last night?" the voice screamed on the other end. Mother.

"Huh?"

"You heard me. I called your room at eleven last night and Nadia said you weren't there and you hadn't been there. What were you doing? No decent, respectable woman has any business out that late at night. Only prostitutes are out past ten. Are you a prostitute?"

My mother had a way of making anything an issue. "I was at the library, studying." I'm nineteen years old and I still have to lie to my mother about where I've been and what I'm doing. I wanted to tell her that I was at the beach getting sexed up, but she might've had a heart attack.

"Just for that little stunt, I'm not sending you a dime this week. You go get ya pimp or whoever you were with to give you money!" she screamed.

"Mother, I'm not a prostitute!"

"Do you know I was so worried about you I called the police?"

"Why did you call the police?" I asked angrily.

"Because I care more about you than you do me. Why do you treat me this way? You don't respect me or the fact that I brought you in this world. Jade, are…are you on drugs?" she stuttered.

I didn't feel like dealing with Mother. All I wanted to do was sleep, so I did something that I knew I would pay for—I hung up. I turned the phone over and switched it to OFF, grabbed the covers, and pulled them over my head.

9:23 a.m.

I was awakened again by Nadia coming into the room, slamming the door and all but yelling, "Hey, girl! Where the hell were you all night?"

There were two moments where you didn't want to mess with me—when I'm tired and when I'm hungry. I flung the covers back and glared at Nadia.

"Do you not see that I am sleeping?" I yelled and yanked the covers back over my head.

"Well, excuse the fuck out of me," she snapped.

I could hear her shuffling keys, then her book bag dropped to the floor. I flung my covers back.

"What the fuck are you doing?"

"I'm out of cigarettes."

I reached down beside my bed and flung my purse across the floor toward her. "Just get one out of my purse."

I flopped down on my pillow and threw the covers back over my head.

"My Precious Jade, thanks for a yummy night? Dre 310-691-6920?"

Nadia picked up my purse and threw it across the room onto my bed. It hit me in the back. Makeup and coins flew everywhere.

"You bitch!"

I flung the covers from my head and jumped out of the bed, ready to fight. "What the fuck is wrong with you!"

"You fucked Dre!"

It took a minute for what she said to register.

"I did not!"

She tossed the flyer at me. "You a fucking liar. Why, Jade, why? Are you that jealous of me? You can't get a man, so you go after mine?"

No this fat, dumpy bitch didn't.

"Nadia, first of all, I didn't fuck Dre, but I could have if I wanted to."

"You think I'm stupid. Then what the fuck does 'thanks for a yummy night' mean?"

"None of ya fucking business. I don't have to tell you shit! Besides, ya stupid ass running up behind somebody that don't even know you."

"You so jealous of me because I have a man and you don't. Bitch, you don't know nothing about me and Dre."

"Nadia, for once in your life, tell the truth. You don't even know Dre and he don't know you!" I should have stopped there, but I couldn't. There are times in your life when you just know that you're about to go too far. This was my moment. "Let's just get a few things straight, you little fat fuck. First of all, the only reason that I let you hang around me is because I felt sorry for ya fat, dumpy ass. Nobody in high school liked you, but I tolerated ya trifling ass 'cause ya mama and my mama are friends. I don't even like you. I moved all the way to California to get away from ya lyin' ass. But no-o-o…you followed me out here. Hell, I'm surprised you've been able to stop sucking on your mom's titty long enough to make it through a full semester. You can't dress worth a damn and your breath always smells like you been eating burnt shit bread. Ya hair is nappier after you get a perm, which I never understood. And to top it all off, you have the nerve to get mad at me for letting a man that you've never even met eat my pussy? You just mad 'cause nobody would ever wanna eat ya nasty cat! Get the fuck outta here."

Nadia snapped. Her bright yellow skin was tomato red and tears streamed down her face. She lunged at me and we both fell backward onto my bed in a knockdown, drag-out brawl. We cursed each other, pulled hair, and both got in some serious licks. I felt my nails dig into her back as her fist smashed into my side. We tussled from the bed, to the desk, to the floor as Jamie and several girls from other rooms ran in. It took five girls to pull me and Nadia apart—three just to hold me back. Blood was everywhere. Nadia's nose was bleeding and I had a cut on my forehead. Both of our clothes were torn.

"Fuck you, Jade! I hate you!"

"Yeah, yeah, go fuck yourself, ya fat cow."

I turned back to sling more insults at Nadia as the three girls pulled me out of the room. She was crying uncontrollably. I didn't really mean all that stuff I said to her, but when I start, it's like I can't stop. I'd said some things that I couldn't take back and I knew it was too late.

Several thoughts went through my mind while I stood in the hallway. The foremost question in my mind was, *Did I just fight over a man?* I had rules about doing shit like that. I don't fight women over men, and I also had other rules, like I don't fight before noon.

It was too early for this shit.

I was called to the dean's office to explain what had happened. I admitted that I had provoked Nadia and it was my fault. I told the dean I was willing to take the harshest punishment as long as he wouldn't call my mother.

As soon as I let that slip, he picked up the phone. I had to listen to my mother yell for thirty minutes about how stupid I was. She was even more convinced I was on drugs. She threatened to take me out of school and demanded that I be put on probation. I also had to take an anger management class and see a counselor. I couldn't believe I had all these repercussions for a man I'd only met once. But if someone would have asked me if it was worth it, I would have said "yes." It was that good. I'd relive that night again anytime.

The rest of my day went just as bad. I was late for my eleven o'clock class because I had to be monitored in my room since Nadia had gone back up there to pack. She wanted to move out, which was fine with me. I fell asleep in my Marketing 101 class and while I was dozing, the teacher decided to give a pop quiz. I failed it.

I dragged myself to the school café and ordered an omelet and fries. It looked so good that I nibbled on my fries on my way to the register. No sooner had I walked away from the counter, some goofy white boy ran into me. My cheesy omelet and fries went flying into the air like confetti. I was pissed, but I figured I better not trip since I was already in trouble with the dean. I let it slide and got back in line to get another omelet and fries and began snacking on the fries again. I got to the front of the line only for the cashier to tell me that my card had been deactivated.

"But I just came through the line like not even five minutes ago," I said hastily.

"Sorry," the cashier replied while reaching for my plate. I pulled the plate close to my face, stuck my tongue out, and licked the omelet. She snatched her hand back.

"That's nasty."

She was so grossed out that she told me to go. I finished my lunch and headed back to my room to try to get some more sleep. When I got there, Nadia was gone and so was all of her stuff. There was a stack of clothes on my bed that she had borrowed. On top of the stack lay two cigarettes neatly on top of the Club Z flyer, next to my phone. I saw a missed text on my display that read: "Hey, you. It's Dre. Call me."

His voice sent signals straight to Nita. I locked the door and went into my panty drawer to look for Chuck, my vibrator. Chuck had become my lover shortly after that Eugene fiasco. I decided I'd give my virginity to myself. Chuck didn't talk, cheat, or say stupid shit right before my panties dropped. I attributed not having sex with those consistencies in men. I replayed the message five times before pushing all the clothes on the floor and climbing into bed.

"Hello, Dre."

Lovingly looking at my vibrator, I pressed the button to check the batteries. Before last night, I hadn't gotten that close to any man. With thoughts of Dre on my mind, I closed the curtain and crawled under the covers with Chuck.

As I lay on my back, imagining Dre was there touching me in all the right places, I caressed my own breasts and gave each of them a slight tug at the nipple the way Dre had pulled them with his teeth. I touched Chuck to the tip of Nita to allow her to get warmed up. With Dre on my brain, she was ready within seconds. I enjoyed Chuck working his way in for several minutes. Taking control, I rolled over on my stomach with Chuck in place and began to pleasure myself. An uncontrollable feeling overcame me and I called out, "Dre, Dre, Dre...aaaaahh." I squeezed every muscle in my body until I had expelled all of my energy from inside of me. My stomach actually felt better right after I finished. I was about to get up when I realized that I wanted more. I wanted him and so I masturbated again and again and again.

The Beginning of Power
Jade

After four climaxes, I knew there was something special about this man. The phone rang. I jumped. I was so excited that I did a nosedive to the phone. "Hello?"

"Jade?"

Free flowing like air, my stomach curled up.

"Hi."

"It's Dre."

"Oh, hey, what's up?"

"Not much. I wanted to know if I could see you today."

"Sure!" I tried to mask the excitement in my voice a little. "Come on over."

I gave him directions to my dorm and prepared myself to see him again by masturbating two more times before he got there.

3:58 p.m.

A knock at the door signaled to Nita that Dre was near. I had cleaned my room as best I could and tried to fix my hair. Nothing mattered once I opened that door. He stood there, looking like a caramel-coated candy apple. Delicious as ever. He wore a Polo shirt, jeans, and Bass loafers with a UCLA hat that was tattered around the edges like he had worn it too much. He held a drink from the local gas station. As I moved closer I envied the straw in his mouth. Much more casual than last night, but still sexy as ever. As soon as our eyes met, a smile rose from my face like the sunshine in the morning sky. Two words from him would send signals from my brain to Nita.

"Hey, you."

"Hey."

He pulled me close to him and leaned into me. As I prepared my lips for his kiss, he moved his head to the side and gently kissed my cheek. I closed my eyes for that brief moment and inhaled the scent of Nautica for Men exuding from his skin. His fragrance alone drove Nita into a tailspin. Between the sight and scent of him, his touch, the kiss, and his words, Nita had soaked my underwear.

"I was thinking...let's go to Magic Mountain," he suggested as he moved past me into the room.

"You mean Six Flags?" I asked in amazement. He wanted to leave and I was horny. I wanted him. He felt so good to me on the outside; I could only imagine what it would be like to have him inside of me.

"Yeah, why not?"

"I don't know? I guess I just wasn't expecting you to say Six Flags." I was a bit angry at the thought of not being able to spend any private time with him, but it did sound like fun. "Okay, let me just put a little makeup on." I walked over to my purse and rummaged through it for my lipstick. Suddenly, I was twirled around and hoisted up against the wall. The slight jolt as my body connected with the wall made me inhale quickly. My head fell back and my legs felt like jelly as they struggled to keep me standing up this time. Nita was pleased when, like a vampire, he bit down on the right side of my neck and I dropped my purse.

I could feel his arousal through my clothes, and I was sure he could smell mine. He started to kiss me and I tasted mint on his tongue. His lips wrapped mine like candy in a wrapper. I closed my eyes. Just as Nita started to leak again, he backed away.

"Go shower," he commanded.

Without hesitation, I collected my shower things. I was calm getting out the door to go shower, but as soon as I closed the door, I sprinted down the hallway. I took a shower unlike any shower I had ever taken before. I made sure to clean my neck really well. Not like I hadn't before, but I scrubbed right up to my hairline. I cleaned every inch of my body as if I was in quarantine. I was glad that my toes were looking nice and I had worn my shower shoes so I could keep my feet clean on my way back to my room. I made sure to scrub Nita extra clean.

When I opened the door to my room, Dre was sitting on the edge of my bed watching TV. "Wow, that was quick!" As he smiled at me, Nita began to flow again. I wanted to drop my towel and jump on him, but I needed to get dressed. I smiled, walked to my dresser, and opened the top drawer to select the right panties. I pulled out my sheer black ones, but I didn't know how I was going to get them on if I had to drop my towel. Intent on finding my matching sheer bra, I was relieved to see it appear. With my back to him, I shifted my towel to my waist and put on my bra.

I knew that he was looking at me and I could feel his eyes going right through me. I never heard him get up from the bed. Instead, I felt a rush of air on my neck that caused the hairs to rise.

Whispering, he said, "You are so beautiful." I blushed as he turned me around to face him. He leaned into me, grabbed my face, and kissed me as if the oxygen that I was breathing was going to save his life. I put my arms around his neck. He picked me up with both hands like a doll and carried me over to my study desk. He stopped and sat down in the chair to my desk, lifted my left leg, removed my flip-flop, and kissed my toes, giving each one special attention. I looked at him as he made his way around my foot with his tongue.

This can't be real. Lord help me. Is this what love feels like? *I think I love this man,* I finally admitted.

Moving upward from my foot, he wrapped his hands around my ankle and brought it to his lips. The intensity in his face told me that he was enjoying this moment. My breathing became heavy with anticipation. He inched his fingernails up my leg, stopped at my knees, and caressed them with his lips. My leg quivered as he turned each one just enough to gently bite the underside of my left leg. His bite sent electrical orgasmic rhythms to my soul. Just as I thought that he would continue to go up my thigh, he moved my right leg, then started over. From my toes to my kneecap, he paid attention to parts of my body that I didn't know needed attention.

Nita was in heaven. He scooted his chair closer and pulled my body to the edge of the desk. He slid his fingernails down my inner thigh, prompting my thighs to open farther. I was amazed by the way my body responded to his slightest touch and did anything he wanted. I opened my legs, pressed my palms down against the desk, and closed my eyes. He kept me in place for fifteen minutes. At the moment that I knew I was about to climax, I grabbed his head and screamed in pleasure.

"Oh, yes," he uttered, never once moving during the entire climax. After I stopped he said only, "More?"

I couldn't speak; I could only nod in agreement. His tongue opened Nita's lips and out came her bloom. He blew a gentle flow of air from his breath on Nita and it was the most erotic feeling of coolness. He rotated his tongue so gently that it was feather-like. One hand occupied my thigh as the other slid up my stomach between my breastbone. His hand felt the quiver within my stomach and the shutter of my rib cage. The wetter I was for him, the more he seemed to tease me. He reached up and pulled down the cup of ice water he had brought with him. He removed the lid and put a piece of ice in his mouth. The touch of his cold hands on my thigh excited me. He began to blow air toward Nita again, only this time the chill of the air was a sexual stinging that made me arch back to get ready for more. He would alternate his hands sometimes, using them both to keep me on the edge of the desk. I kept scooting back, wanting to climb straight up the wall. Using his tongue to go in and out of Nita's entry, he would suck on Nita's flower and let the ice lie on his tongue, providing Nita's flower a comfort. Again, I climaxed. I moaned his name.

"What are you doing to me?" I asked in a whisper. He paused for a moment, looked up at me from between my thighs, and put his index finger over my mouth. No words were spoken as he reconnected with Nita. Another ten minutes came and went and I came two more times. He moved my legs to his shoulder and I purposely pushed my body forward. I wanted more of him. I removed my legs from his shoulder and reached down to grab his arms. I pulled him to his feet.

"Insatiable," he whispered softly.

I wrapped my legs around him and pulled him close to me. "I want you. Please, I need you," I begged. He kissed me.

"Let me get a condom," he said, but I wanted him and I didn't care about a condom. The glistening of Nita surrounded his nose and the flavor was fresh. He unbuttoned his pants and let them drop to the floor, exposing his boxers. I could see his manhood waiting to greet Nita, and she was ready to make friends. He pulled me close to the edge of the desk. I could feel him going in.

My body froze, and he pulled back and asked, "Are you a virgin?"

Feeling ashamed, I answered, "Yeah." There's nothing like virginity to ruin the moment. I thought about Eugene for a brief second and I wanted to whip his ass.

"Oh, baby girl. You don't wanna do it like this." He pulled away, but I grabbed him and pulled him back close to me.

"I want you," I said, looking in his eyes. "Please. I want you to have me. I want to be yours." My eyes started to tear up, thinking he was going to walk away, thinking that love was going to leave me.

He held me tight and said, "Okay."

He lowered his boxers. He held his manhood in place and slowly worked it inside of Nita. His strokes were slow and seemed to get a little deeper each time. Suddenly there was a sharp pain inside of me. I grabbed his body tightly to find protection from the pain. He went in deeper and it was as if he had moved beyond a wall inside of me. I wanted to scream but I held the voice in until I couldn't hold it anymore.

"Oh. God!"

His continuous stroke began to work its way inside of me, creating a heat that I had never felt before. I could sense excitement in his body. He started to hold me tightly, closed his eyes, and climaxed inside of me. He never made a sound. I wanted more of him, but I couldn't take it anymore.

He stood there with his arms around me. "Are you okay?" he asked.

"I'm perfect," I answered.

"I didn't hurt you, did I?" he asked sincerely.

I shook my head, although it was somewhat painful. I was afraid to let our bodies separate. I wanted to hold him close and he knew that. He held me and it was so comforting.

As he withdrew his body from mine, I looked down and saw that Nita had bled all over the towel underneath me. I quickly covered it, feeling embarrassed and emotionally connected. He picked up the face towel that was lying beside me and started to wipe off the traces of my soul. I had given all of myself to him. I had released everything into him. I had given him the remote control to my heart, the key to my soul, and Nita belonged to him. I knew I would never be the same. I could never return to a place where my virginity could be reconnected to my self-esteem. This was the beginning of power.

Blissful Bubble
Jade

There's that point in our lives when we know things will never be the same. Sometimes, change can send us spiraling out of control. Having Dre in my life sent me swirling around like a fairy high on pixie dust. I had never felt so incredibly loved and complete.

In the past, there were some occasions where my mother would start to drink and tell me things that may have been her true feelings. I remember once she told me that in order to have a fulfilled relationship, there are three main components that every woman thinks she needs to be complete.

"Honey, if you can find a man that will stimulate your mind, arouse your body, and evoke emotion within your soul, then maybe you've got something."

I had found all of that in Dre, and we were inseparable. We would party together and drink 'til the sun came up. His favorite drink was Crown Royal and so was mine. He especially liked to pour it on Nita and lick. I learned to return the favor and Chuck was out of my life for good after that. Dre always surprised me with where we were going to make love. One night, we were on our way back from Magic Mountain and decided to stop at a park. We played like two little kids at recess. We jumped off the swing to see who could go the farthest.

Since we were both fiercely competitive, it was a barrel of fun. The merry-go-round was Nita's favorite. I would lie down in the center and spread my legs, and Dre would spin the merry-go-round as fast as he could. Then he would jump on and give pleasure to Nita while I held on tight. Spinning around being pleased was the most exhilarating feeling I'd ever experienced. The best part was that he wouldn't stop until the merry-go-round stopped.

We would kiss as we swung on the monkey bars. We would stand on the bridge connecting the jungle gym and he would take me from behind. Beyond the lovemaking, Dre and I could enjoy doing nothing. We would have that comfortable silence that felt right. We were so connected that when people saw us together, we were never aware that anyone was watching. We lived in a bubble that only the two of us knew existed.

Dre taught me so many things. He taught me how to drive a standard shift car. He taught me how to cook his mother's infamous pot roast. Together we learned how to surf and rock climb and we even drove up to Big Bear for my birthday in November to ski. That was the best birthday in my life. He had rented a cabin for us but we made love outside in the snow. He would make me candlelight dinners at his apartment on the patio. He would wake me up to see the stars in the sky that were in new constellation patterns. He even named a few of them after our future children he sometimes talked about.

With little resistance, he convinced me to shave the afro off of Nita to heighten her awareness. He taught me that my body could respond to so many different stimulations I didn't even know existed. Everything was erotic, from the back of my neck to the top part of my ankle. He would bathe me; yes, physically bathe me in lavender and vanilla. We spent six continuous months in bliss, and no one was allowed in.

For Valentine's Day, Dre and I took the ferry to Catalina Island and had the most romantic time ever. He had rented a hotel for one night, using his savings for the past several weeks. I had never been to a hotel and it was perfect for my first time. We couldn't afford a fancy dinner, so we kept it simple, but that didn't matter to me. All I wanted was to be with Dre. He went to the store and bought everything for us to have a picnic on the beach. He even bought two little cupcakes to celebrate with.

Perfect.

We got back to school that Sunday evening after Valentine's Day about a little after six. I was exhausted and asked Dre to take me back to my dorm. I think the ferry ride back over made my stomach queasy and I just wanted to lie down. Dre dropped me off and made sure that I got to my room okay. He needed to leave so that he could start packing up his place. His roommate, Marcus, had graduated and Dre had found a new roommate, but that also meant that he had to move. I told Dre I would come over later around eight-ish, if I felt better.

"Take your time, baby. I have a lot to do and the noise will bother you," he said as he kissed my forehead. I crawled into bed and rested on my pillow.

"Jade. I love you. You know that, right?"

I nodded. "I love you, too, baby."

"Get some rest. I'll see you later."

"Okay."

I pulled the cover over my head and closed my eyes.

I must have been really tired; I woke up the next morning at 6:45 and still wasn't feeling too good. I looked over at my phone and saw that there were no messages.

"Hmm, that's odd."

Rubbing the sleep from my eyes, I picked up the phone to call Dre. It rang three times and a recording came on: "We're sorry, the number you have reached is no longer in service. Please check the number and try your call again."

Convinced I had pushed the wrong contact, I tried again, but the same woman's voice told me the same thing. I suddenly felt scared, and I got out of bed to go check on him. I hoped he was okay. It wasn't like Dre not to call or at least leave a message. I kept trying to call as I threw on a pair of shorts and a T-shirt. I didn't remember him telling me that his phone would be cut off today. I quickly brushed my teeth and washed my face. I was sure that he was fine and I was probably overreacting. I grabbed my purse off the desk and headed out the door.

I wanted to take the elevator, but there was too much adrenaline in my body to wait. I ran down the hallway and down the staircase to the courtyard. When I turned the ignition, there was a clicking sound and the engine wouldn't start. My battery was dead. Dre had promised to fix it for me. I beat my purse against the steering wheel and let out a frustrated cry. I got out of the car, slammed the door, and ran all the way to the bus stop within a half mile from my dorm. Even though his apartment complex was only three miles away, it seemed longer. So many things went through my mind. Had he been in an accident? Was he in the hospital? Was I just being paranoid and he was fine? I could almost hear him saying that I was overreacting and his smile would warm my heart. I couldn't check his social media because he didn't believe in it.

I arrived at his apartment and I jumped off the bus in haste to get to his apartment complex. I could see his bedroom patio from the street. I walked inside the complex and across the courtyard toward his apartment. Fourth one on the left. When I walked up to it, I could see right through the entire apartment.

Empty.

I banged on the door and jiggled the lock, hoping that he was inside. He hadn't told me where his new apartment was, so I had nowhere to look, no place to call. I went to the next door neighbor's and banged on his door. I had met him once. I thought his name was Anthony, a really cute guy with a really ghetto girlfriend. Speaking of the devil, Tasha furiously opened the door, probably thinking that I was his other woman. "Who are you?" she said as she chewed her bubble gum, looking like she had just come from a strip club.

"Is Anthony here?" I asked. My voice shaky.

"Who are you?" she asked again, ready to fight.

"I'm Dre's girlfriend, next door. Do you know where he is?" I asked.

Anthony came to the door to see what was going on.

"Oh, hey Jade. What's up?"

I could tell he was relieved that it was only me. He moved his half-dressed girlfriend to the side. Frantic, I asked, "Have you seen Dre?" My eyes started to well up with tears.

"Oh, he's gone. He left around ten last night," Anthony said nonchalantly.

"He did? Where did he go?"

The pity in his eyes told me that the next thing to come out of his mouth would change my life forever.

"He left. He told me that Shelly, or Shelby, or somebody was back," he said as he looked at me pitifully.

My body went cold. My chest tightened. I swallowed my breath hoping to slow down the racing in my heart.

"Oh, okay, okay. Okay thanks." I held my breath.

I turned my back to walk away, finally exhaling, but when I heard Anthony's door slam shut, I jumped. I walked back to Dre's door and just stood there looking at the numbers on the door—114. He told me he knew I was the one for him because my birthday was 11/4. He told me we were destined to be together. I stood there and as my lips dropped down and began to quiver, the tears met the corners of my lips and connected at the base of my chin.

I started to bang on the door again, thinking this had to be a whacked-out dream. I looked through the window, hoping to behold his black leather couch that we made love on eighteen times. I could still mentally see the blue recliner chair that we had fallen asleep in twenty-two times. There was the red spot from my failed attempt to balance a cup on my head like Miss America.

I kept banging on the door and soon started to scream for him. "Dre! Dre! Where are you?! Where are you?! Why…why…why? Oh my God oh my God no please God no. Please, no!"

I begged God as if He were right there in front of me. I didn't care who heard or who saw me. I was alone without Dre and I didn't know how to move. He had guided my every move over the past six months, eight days, and twelve hours. Thinking I needed a cigarette, I turned to walk outside to smoke when my eye caught a visual at the end of the hall. It was a brown box and sticking out of it was a stuffed animal that resembled Daffy Duck's feet. I walked to the other end of the hall and there he was. Daffy Duck, head first in a box that read TRASH on the front of it. I knelt down and tore into the box. Inside were all the poems, letters, and cards I had made for Dre.

For our first month's anniversary, I had made a bottle of sand and inside was our first picture. We took pictures together in one of those cheesy booths on the pier where we made love the night we met. The box had everything I had given him and even things that we had bought together. Magnets, shot glasses, T-shirts from Magic Mountain, even our Lakers jersey, all of it was right here in a box labeled TRASH. My body trembled as I stared at the word. I put everything back in the box and cradled it in my arms. I carried it back to the other end of the hall delicately as if it was a newborn baby. The hallway seemed long and endless.

As I passed the door, I felt that tingle inside of me as I remembered how many times we had made love on the other side of that door. I dropped the box, fell to my knees, and knelt down like I was praying at the church altar.

"Oh, God, please don't do this to me. Please don't do this to me, please," I begged again. I lay in front of the door feeling vulnerable and alone. Anthony must have heard my cries and came outside.

"Jade, you alright?" he asked.

I didn't respond. I couldn't speak.

My body was numb and felt weighted, and I couldn't stop shaking my head in utter disbelief.

"Come on," he said as he picked my lifeless body up off of the floor. "Come on, girl. You're okay, come on." He tried to help my legs work, but they wouldn't. I tried to support myself and one glance at the box sent me into hysterics. I flung my arms and screamed like the Holy Ghost had touched me. Anthony did the best he could to control me. I couldn't stop screaming. I couldn't stop crying, and I only wanted Dre. Only he could help me, but he was gone. He was really gone.

"He told me he loved me…he told me he loved me… he…told me he…loved…me!" I cried. The screaming and hollering exhausted me. Anthony held me up by my arms and, without notice, I vomited all over the floor and collapsed.

"Call 911!" Anthony yelled to his girlfriend.

As my head and body fell backward, my eyes rolled back into my head and I vaguely saw a body running toward me.

It was Nadia.

Depressed
Monica

When I got the call that Jade was in the hospital, I honestly didn't want to believe it. Nadia was so notorious for lying that I wanted to pretend that she was making this up for some stupid reason. I had to check for myself. I reluctantly called.

"Fourth floor, can I help you?" the female voice said.

"Hi, I'm calling to check on Jade Hall."

"Are you a family member?"

"Yes," I lied, knowing they wouldn't tell me anything if I wasn't, even though I was her best friend.

"Your name?"

"Monica Hall, her sister."

"She's stable."

"Stable?"

"Yes, that's all I can tell you."

"Tell her that her sister Monica is on the way please."

"Will do," she replied.

"Thanks." I hung up the phone and leaned back on my sofa to think for a minute. What the hell does "stable" mean? What are the other options? I watched *Grey's Anatomy* enough to know there are three primary condition—critical, stable, and dead. I thought those were the only options you get. Regardless, she was my homegirl and I needed to get to her as quickly as I could. I knew my 2001 Honda Civic wasn't going to make the drive from Houston to Los Angeles, so I had to find a faster way. The only person I could think of was Reggie. He'd always had a crush on Jade and he could get his hands on just about anything.

"Reggie, what's up? It's Monica."

"Monica, what's up, girl?" He sounded happy to hear from me.

"Hey, I need to get to LA. Jade is in the hospital."

"What's wrong? She aiight?" I could hear the concern in his voice.

"I don't really know. They just said she was stable."

"Stable? Shit, that's just somewhere between dead and damn near dead."

"Reggie, you not helping me feel any better. I know that. Do you know anybody that can get me on a buddy pass?"

"Hell yeah. When you wanna leave?"

"As soon as possible."

"Cool, pack ya stuff and I'll call my sister to hook you up. You gonna need a car too?"

"Yeah, probably."

"Aiight, cool. My sister's girlfriend works for one of them car places right outside the airport. Don't even worry about it."

"Sheila's gay?" I was surprised to hear.

"Yeah, you know, she moved out there and that L.A. life got to her. Damn, I hate to hear about Jade. You know I always had a lil' crush on her fine ass, with that long black hair and them pretty green eyes."

"Okay, so I'll pack and hit you back."

"Do that. I'll get you hooked up. Give me about two hours."

Reggie was always good for doing what he said he was going to do, and I knew his attraction to Jade would seal getting me the ticket. I hung up the phone and knew I needed to start packing, but I just sat and made myself a drink. I asked Aunt Robin if she would check on my mom while I was gone. I lied and said that I was going to L.A. to visit Jade for the weekend.

Less than an hour later, Reggie had a buddy pass for me, just like he said he would. With Reggie, every hookup came through and I landed in L.A. the same night that I got the call from Nadia. Reggie's sister, Sheila, gave me directions to the hospital, and even though I was tired and hungry as hell, I drove straight there. I knew Jade would do the same for me. When I arrived, I truly didn't know what to expect, but I didn't care. I took the elevator to the fourth floor and went straight to room 412. I peered through the glass pane to see if I was at the right room. Part of me was hoping that this was all some sort of joke and Jade wouldn't be there, but she was.

I slowly opened the door and saw her lying there, sleeping. As I got closer, I noticed restraints on her hands, keeping them tied to the side of the bed. I was at a loss for words, trying to figure out what the hell had happened. I didn't know what to say or do. I leaned in close to her and put my hand in hers. She opened her eyes to see me and neither one of us had to say a word. There was so much that I wanted to say and ask, but I didn't know where to start. A few seconds went by and we both started to cry.

"Jade, it's okay. Don't cry. I'm here," I said, wiping the tears from my face. "We will get through this. Whatever it is, I'm here for you." This was more serious than I thought it was going to be, and I couldn't bear seeing my friend like this. Jade was more than my friend, she really was like a sister to me. We had grown up together and I had never seen her so fragile. It was like she was a totally different person.

She tugged at the restraints. "Monica." She smiled and tried to reach for me, but the restraints on her wrists stopped her. Panic ran across her face and she looked at me.

"They tied me . . ." she said softly and didn't have to say anymore. I started to pull the slipknot to untie her without hesitation. I knew Jade and it was wrong to have her tied down like she was some kind of animal. As soon as I unbuckled both of her hands, she reached up and embraced me. I held her and she cried like I had never heard her cry before. Her tears began to wet the side of my shoulder; I could feel her body tremble and I knew that my friend was hurting. I didn't know what to say, so I just held her. Several minutes passed and I didn't let go until she let go. She fell back on the bed as if her body had used every ounce of energy just to sit up.

"Jade, what happened?"

"I don't want to talk about it."

"Okay, you don't have to. Are you okay?"

"It's dead," she cried.

"What? Who's dead?"

"All of it." She sobbed.

"You're not making any sense, honey. I don't know what you mean."

"Our baby. It died."

"Baby!"

She hadn't mentioned to me that she was pregnant. Jade and I hadn't really talked a lot over the last six months, but I would have thought that she would have told me something like this.

I knew she had a guy she was wrapped up into, but I didn't know much more than that. I assumed that she had at least four or five different men since then. Jade typically dropped dudes every weekend, so this couldn't be because of a boyfriend.

She wouldn't tell me more; she just kept saying that it was dead. I didn't know what to say, so I stayed silent.

Jade slept off and on the rest of the night. She would wake up panicking and I was there to hold her.

By morning I managed to get in touch with Nadia, who'd been leaving her study group when Jade collapsed. Nadia helped calm Jade and she told me that Jade kicked and spit on everybody like a crazed dog. She was cussing and knocking things over. One of the paramedics asked her if she was pregnant or if she had been raped because she was bleeding from her vagina. Jade told them no, but by the time they got her to the hospital, they discovered that she was eight weeks pregnant. When they told her they were trying to save the baby, she reached for a pen and stabbed herself in the stomach. That's when the restraints came into the picture. Listening to the story still made it hard for me to imagine; this was so unbelievable.

The next morning, I was standing by Jade's bedside when a nurse entered the room. "Hi, I need to take some tests, so if you don't mind staying in the waiting room I'll come and get you when she's ready."

I felt Jade grab my hand tighter and she looked at me with fear in her eyes. I leaned in close to her.

"I'm not going anywhere." I squeezed her hand tighter and gave her peace. Without saying a word, she nodded her head in agreement as much as she could move. I knew she wanted me to stay.

"You're very pretty," the nurse said.

"Thanks," I responded.

"You should be a model," she said as she took Jade's blood pressure.

"She's always been beautiful." Jade turned to me and smiled. It was good to hear her voice.

"Only as beautiful as you."

I turned my head away from her to look toward the window when I noticed the box on the floor with Daffy Duck slumped over, smiling at me. The box said TRASH on the front of it. Apparently Dre had told Jade that when they had kids the room would be in all Looney Tunes characters, so they had started a collection of toys for the baby, starting with Daffy Duck. I didn't know that yet when I so easily asked, "What's up with Daffy Duck?" Jade's face scrunched up and with every breath her body jerked as she began to cry.

"What's wrong? Is it the duck? What the fuck's wrong with the duck?" I walked over to the box and put it inside the closet.

"Okay, okay…fuck the duck!" Carefully watching her calm down, I hurried back over to her. "Oh my God, what did he do to you?"

The nurse walked to the side of the bed and put her hand on Jade's forearm. "Jade, you're going to be just fine, okay? The doctor is on her way to talk to you. I need to take a few X-rays of your stomach. Is that okay?" she asked with a concerned look on her face.

As the nurse lowered the bedsheets and lifted the gown, it was as if Jade went numb. She just wasn't there. She was somewhere else and I needed her to come back. I heard the door open and saw the doctor walk in. Her face showed genuine concern.

"Good morning, Jade. I'm Dr. Keating. I'm glad to see you're awake. Has anyone talked to you about what's happening?" she asked. Jade didn't respond. She just looked off into space.

"Are you okay with her being in the room?" she asked Jade.

"I'm her sister," I quickly added.

Jade nodded in agreement.

"You had a miscarriage. I'm sorry." She paused and gazed at Jade with sympathy. "Were you aware that you were pregnant?"

Jade moved her head to say "no."

"It's going to be okay. I know this is a lot to tell you all at once, but I just want you to know that this doesn't mean you won't have children at some point and have a completely healthy pregnancy. Now, if you need to talk to someone, we have people here that you can talk to. Just let us know," she said as she smiled at Jade with reassurance. "Are you okay?" she asked and waited for a response.

Jade didn't answer.

"Well, let me know if you need to talk and we'll get someone for you, okay?" Jade still didn't respond. "We'll need to see you in a few weeks for a checkup." She rubbed on Jade's leg. "We are gonna have someone come talk to you because of what happened and I'll check on you again later."

I straightened her blankets and covered up the restraints with the bedsheets. Jade took a few deep breaths and relaxed. I just held her hand and sat next to her. She barely moved or spoke more than five words for the next several hours.

I dozed off and then I heard the door open again. A handsome, tall young man walked in. I got up out of my chair, ready to fight because I didn't know if this was Dre or not.

"Hi, I'm Anthony. I live across the hall from Dre." He reached his hand out toward me.

"Hi, I'm Monica, Jade's best friend," I said, shaking his hand and trying to be less groggy.

"How's she doing?"

"Okay. I tried to make jokes, but nothing's working. She's

been pretty quiet since I got here." I paused, trying to figure out where he fit into the picture. "So you know Dre?"

"Unfortunately I do. I feel so responsible for this."

"Why do you say that?"

"Because Dre told me what was going on, but I didn't think it would have this kind of impact on her."

"What did he say?" Just as he was about to tell me, Jade started to wake up.

"Dre?" she muttered.

Anthony walked over to her.

"Hey Jade, it's me, Anthony."

"Hey. What are you doing here?"

"I just wanted to check on you." He grabbed her hand and sat down.

"Thank you for what you did."

"Don't thank me. I feel like this is all my fault."

"No, not at all."

"Well, just let me know if there's anything I can do."

"I will, thank you."

"I can't stay long. Tasha is in the car, but here's my number and, umm…just call me." He leaned over and kissed Jade on the forehead.

"Thanks for stopping by."

Jade tried to sit up and the blanket fell over, exposing the restraints. She quickly tried to push them back under the cover, but it was too late. I knew she was embarrassed by her stuttering.

"I'm…this is…umm . . ."

He shook his head and smiled. "Hey, no worries. Just get better and when you do, I'm here."

She nodded in agreement and he gave her a hug as she held back the tears that eventually came down. Her head was buried in his chest and she held onto him tightly.

After Anthony left, it was time for dinner, but Jade didn't eat. She didn't eat breakfast the next day either. The nurse continuously asked about Jade's mom but I knew that calling her would only make Jade worse, so I lied to them.

"Her mom isn't going to come and Jade doesn't want to see her."

I called Reggie and he had a cousin who lived in L.A. named Keisha; she let me stay at her place so I could go back and forth to visit Jade. The hospital would only keep Jade for another two days and then she'd have to go home. I knew Jade wasn't ready, so I called the school and they transferred me to a counselor. Her name was Dr. Wheeler, but she wouldn't give me any advice, she only said that it would be up to Jade to make the call if she needed therapy. I wasn't sure how likely it was that Jade would go to a therapist, but I kept her number just in case.

The day we left the hospital, we had to take the bus to Jade's dorm. The entire ride, we didn't talk much but we held hands. Jade cried off and on, but I never asked her any questions. When we arrived in the dorm room, Jade made a beeline to plug in her phone. It had been dead for days. When it finally came on and the messages display said she had five missed calls, she suddenly had a smile on her face. But they were mostly messages from friends in her dorm, and she just kept rolling her eyes as she skipped them. But there was an unknown number where someone had just hung up.

"That was him. I know it was."

Helplessly, I sat beside her on the bed, wondering what she was talking about.

"Listen, I know a lot has happened. I'm not sure all of what exactly happened, but whatever happened, honey, you've got to move on. This isn't the Jade I know. It's going to be okay, I promise," I tried to say convincingly.

She jumped up and put her finger in my face. Had she not been my friend I would have broken it off.

"You think so! You really think so, because I'm not so sure! I'm not sure that I can make it! I met a man who gave me everything I wanted, more than I knew that I needed and ecstasy beyond my own dreams. So when you say it's going to be alright, I'm not sure that it's gonna be okay!"

She was slightly laughing, but it was that twisted, losing your mind kind of laugh. Sure enough, the laughter turned to rage.

"What the hell would you know about love? We were in love. We talked about getting married. We talked about having kids and we talked about going to the fucking Olympics in Canada! Have you been to Canada? Have you? Well, neither have I and now I'll never go! Now what do I do? What the fuck am I supposed to do?

"Tell me, Monica, since you got all the fucking answers. How do I move on? How do I just keep breathing every day without him! How do I deal with not going to Canada?" She picked up the phone and threw it against the wall.

Since I'd never been through anything like this before, I didn't know what to say. I didn't know how to respond. So I just said the first thing I could think of.

"Jade! Have you lost your mind? You have, haven't you? You've completely lost your mind behind a busted-up dude that fucked you up and then threw all your shit out without so much as telling you bye."

Jade fell to the bed and held her head, crying uncontrollably, but I didn't care about her tears. I cared about her heart.

"Jade! You want me to feel sorry for you? I don't, okay? There you have it. I don't feel sorry for you. I feel sorry for him! And most of all, you should feel sorry for him. If he didn't realize the type of woman that you are, then he's a damn fool. Come on, seriously, do you hear yourself right now? All of a sudden, you don't know what the fuck to do? You can't breathe? What kind of shit is that? And for that matter, you're an even bigger fool if you're gonna sit here and let your existence depend on a dog that didn't give you the respect as a woman to be man enough to say that he doesn't want you. That's just what it is, honey. He don't want you and he doesn't deserve you! The moment you get that in your head, you will get over it."

I walked over and knelt down in front of her. I moved her hands away from her face. She had been crying so much that her eyes were as big as cotton balls and red as wine.

"You can breathe. You're doing it right now and he's not here."

I reached up and hugged her. I held her tight, hoping that she knew I loved her. "Don't let him get you like this. Don't, please don't. No man is worth this." I got up to get her a tissue and just as I stood up, the cell rang. Jade sprinted to the phone to pick it up.

"Hello?" she answered anxiously.

"Jade! What the hell is going on with you?" The voice on the other end shouted loud enough to be heard beyond the receiver.

"Mother," Jade said disappointingly. She pushed the speakerphone button and put the receiver down.

"The school called and told me you were in the hospital."

"Do you care?"

"I called you, didn't I? If this is your way of getting my attention, it's not working. You are not going to make me lose my job, trying to play games with me."

"Thanks for the support, Mother."

"Support! I'm about to show you support. GROW UP!"

Hearing Jade's talk with her mother let me know that things

were probably not going to get much better for my friend. I called Aunt Robin and explained what really happened, then apologized for lying to her.

I knew that this was going to require more than just a quick trip to LA, and Aunt Robin suggested that I stay with Jade for a while. I called and quit my job at Foot Locker and took the little money I had and found a cheap apartment. Aunt Robin said she would send more money to help me out later. I knew that Jade wouldn't be able to stay by herself in the condition she was in so I moved her things out of the dorm and into my place. It wasn't much but it was better than her going back to the dorm.

The following two months were long and hard. The school had a program of counseling for students with posttraumatic stress. Even though breaking up with a boyfriend wasn't always considered major stress, losing a child was, so I was able to get her into the program that way. I made sure she went to every appointment and I sat up with her many nights, letting her cry herself to sleep in my arms. It was like she had stopped living. She stopped brushing her teeth, taking showers, combing her hair, and eating. Jade dropped from a healthy one hundred and thirty pounds to ninety-eight pounds and she smoked cigarettes daily. I had to control her pain medication by hiding them. She would take three and four Valium at once and wash it down with Crown Royal.

I managed to get her off the Valium, but I couldn't get her to stop drinking countless bottles of liquor. Some days I needed a drink my damn self. I didn't want to push too hard because Dr. Wheeler said she might be like this for some time. After the first month, she would only wake up and sit up to watch TV. She barely even went to the bathroom. Sometimes she would have Anthony drop off Crown Royal for her, but then she would put him out. She said it helped her sleep and I understood that.

Summer was near and the school was having a Cinco de Mayo party. I thought it might be a good time to try to get Jade out and about. That day was no different than any other day until lunchtime. Jade had gotten to the point of getting back into a daily routine of at least brushing her teeth and washing her face.

"Okay, now…I'm going to go down and grab us something to eat. I'm starving." I laughed. "What do you want?" I asked, expecting the usual answer.

She replied, "I want a double cheeseburger, fries, and a root beer." I was so shocked that Jade said more than two words and she wanted real food.

"You do?"

I was surprised that she had spoke more than three words.

"Yes, I do."

"Cool, I'll be right back." I grabbed my purse and keys and walked out the door.

Rebirth of Power
Jade

Monica walked out the door, but she reopened it and peeked her head around the corner. "You okay?" she asked.

"Yeah, I'm okay. I'm hungry," I answered, but I wasn't okay.

"Okay. I'll be right back." She smiled and left. I lay back and grabbed the remote to the TV and turned it on BET. They were playing old school videos when suddenly, there it was—Toni Braxton, singing the love song that my mother played over and over during our long ride from Los Angeles to Houston. It wasn't until this moment that I would actually understand what the words meant.

Listening to her song probably wasn't good for me and it was really fucking me up right then, but I felt every word. With my arm extended, I wanted to press the channel button to change it, but I couldn't. The song had taken me in already. Everything she crooned was so true. I didn't even know where to begin to get over this. I positioned my body to get out of bed and as I let my feet touch the cold floor, I felt afraid. So I pulled my legs back up to sit Indian style on my bed.

I soon found my thighs wrapped in my arms and all I could do was cry, rock back and forth, and breathe. As the song came to a climax, it was harder and harder to not want to scream. Anger and pain filled my soul but it had nowhere to go. I held myself tighter and tighter, but it wasn't tight enough to squeeze Dre out of my heart. I reached over to grab my pillow to scream and as I put it against my face, there was his scent, Nautica for Men.

I sprang out of the bed and screamed, "Fuck Nautica and Toni Braxton." I was pissed! I started thinking, *Why don't I know where he is?* I stood up and looked at that pillow like it was Dre. I kicked it, stomped it, and tore it apart. My cheap pillow burst and feathers exploded around the room as I banged it against the wall and let out an angry wail that had been held up inside of me.

It wasn't fair that men could just up and walk anytime they wanted to. Did they listen to Toni Braxton and freak out?! Was Dre even thinking about me? And who the hell was Shelly anyway?

I didn't know what happened, but it was like I snapped and my mind went to a new space of anger. I stood by the window, out of breath as feathers continued to fall around me. I saw a few couples walking down the sidewalk and I made a declaration to myself and all the women who had been scorned.

I would take the power that I had as a woman, add in the sexual pleasure that Dre taught me to make men fall in love with me, and then I would dump them. But I wouldn't dump them until they were completely in love with me. I would leave them when they cried. I would make them buy me things, things I would throw in the trash. I had the power. I would make them desire me and make them beg for me. I had the power. I would make them trust me, which I could use to make them give me their souls. I had the pleasure of wanting sex, anytime and anyplace. I would mix all of it together to make myself invincible, make my heart impenetrable. I would do it until they were ready to cry for me, beg for me, die for me. I was in control now of who I helped and who I hurt. I would help them by letting them feel the pain that women felt. It was the perfect plan.

"Oh shit. Now I gotta clean up all these fucking feathers."

Later that night, I looked up the word "whore" in the dictionary and was fascinated by what the definition was. It said, "an offensive term for somebody who is willingly setting aside principles or personal integrity in order to obtain something, usually for selfish motives," or "an offensive term for somebody regarded as being sexually indiscriminate." I had no plans on setting aside my principles, but I was looking to obtain satisfaction.

My view of a whore was someone who used sexuality with internal hopes of gaining affection. Every girl that I referred to as a whore was really just someone who wanted to be loved and used sex as a tool to acquire that love. The funny part was that she never got it. I couldn't think of one ho that found true happiness. Ho, being a term primarily used for women who just give it up to anyone for no reason at all. Then, by that rationale, if a ho couldn't find true love despite compromising herself, what chance did I have at finding true love? I had given Dre everything and that didn't turn out so well.

Monica had returned home and as the summer passed, I realized that Dre really wasn't coming back to me. When school started I knew that I needed to get it together. I spent the summer going to makeup classes and meeting with my counselor to try to get my head right. I couldn't go home because I knew that my mother would just terrorize me to no end. So I stayed at school.

I was really glad when the fall session started. I felt like it was going to give me a new start. I'd meet someone new and hopefully forget all about Dre. I wanted to move on, but it was so hard not to think of him. When I would think of Dre there was so much to process in my mind. Not only was he not coming back, but I hadn't heard from him and no one seemed to know where he was. I didn't care. I had to move on with my life.

I appreciated Monica moving to L.A. and finding a place for us. She really helped me get myself together but I was also hurt that she saw me that way. I found myself watching lots of movies in our apartment. Most Friday nights started out at the local Redbox. It was fascinating to watch men and women interact with each other. I would watch couples argue about which movie to select while other couples had that blissful look of connection when they selected the same movie. That was something that I understood. Dre and I had that connection and yet there I was standing in Redbox all alone. All of a sudden I felt like I had a flashing sign on my head that rotated with streamers coming out of it that read DUMPED...DUMPED...DUMPED!

I walked away and into the Walgreens. I headed toward the counter to grab a pack of cigarettes. I immediately noticed Jasmine, a girl from school, checking out people. But I didn't want her line. She had seen Dre and me in the store countless times.

"Hey, Jade. Haven't seen you in here for a minute. Where you been, and where's that fine-ass man of yours?" she asked.

"Oh, he's in class."

"Girl, you better hold on to him because he is fine." I wanted to knock her ass out. So far, I had gone an entire three minutes without thinking about Dre.

"I'll remember that." Why in the hell was the Walgreens girl in my business? I had to wait on the bus because Mother had stopped making payments on my car and it had been repossessed. I hated it because the route to Monica's place would pass Dre's old apartment anytime I had to go somewhere. Each time the tears would come. Some days were easy and some days were hell. I was doing the best I could not to cry in public…I refused to cry in public. I kept tilting my head back, trying to get the tears to stay in my eyes, but it wasn't enough. One of my tears escaped and I quickly wiped it, hoping that no one saw. I couldn't wait to get off the bus and walk as fast as I could to my room. Despite my newfound freedom, I still anxiously checked my phone, hoping that Dre had called, but he hadn't.

Monica wasn't making enough money to keep up the apartment and we got a roommate since she didn't think I should be alone all the time. Her name was Missy. Missy was a very naïve eighteen-year-old girl from Kentucky. The way she carried herself just screamed country virgin. Missy was about 5'6"—a dark-skinned girl with a thirteen-year-old's body. She walked with her books close to her chest and her head down all the time. She didn't wear makeup and her hair always looked like it was in shock. She never said much to me and I didn't say much to her. All Missy did was study all day and all night.

Monica had promised to watch a movie with me, but she called and said she had a date with some new guy she met named Shawn Devereaux. He was from a wealthy family in Los Angeles, and soon I didn't see her as much. Since I didn't have anyone else around, I thought I'd ask Missy.

"Wanna watch a movie with me?"

"Nah, I have an astrology exam," she said, not making eye contact with me as usual.

"When's the test?" I plopped down on my bed and just stared at her in amazement.

"Next Wednesday."

"Next week, Wednesday? Girl, please, it's Monday. Come on, don't you wanna take a break for just an hour?"

"Well, what did you rent?" she asked. That's when I realized that I didn't know what the hell I had. I had to lean over and look at the box.

"Ooh, *Boomerang*." I was excited.

"I've never seen that."

"YOU'VE NEVER SEEN *BOOMERANG* with Eddie Murphy, Halle Berry, and Robin Givens? Shut the fuck up. You're joking, right? It's a classic!"

"No. My dad's a preacher and we weren't allowed to watch TV," she calmly explained.

Did she realize I could take her black card for that? Who the hell hasn't seen *Boomerang*?

"Well, even more reason for you to watch it." I jumped off the bed and put it in the DVD. Missy liked the movie so much, we watched it three times. I hadn't seen the flick in a while, but during the second time around, I realized that I had been the Halle Berry character all this time. I was the weak but cute, crying bitch. Screw that shit. I wanted to be Robin Givens' character, Jacqueline. Even though she got dumped, you knew that she would just go and tackle another man. My favorite part is when Eddie's character, Marcus, sees Jacqueline for the first time. He stops, tilts his head to the side, and the sound of a dog is played in sync with his movement.

Woof! That was classic.

The home phone rang and Missy reached to answer it. It was Slim, the bartender. He wanted to know if I would go to a movie with him. I knew he was just trying to get me out of the house, so I agreed. When Slim came to pick me up, I hated the pity I saw in his eyes and heard in his voice.

"How you been, Jade?" he asked.

"I'm fine. How are you?"

I wanted to tilt my head as we headed toward the lobby exit.

"I mean, how are you after everything that happened with Dre?"

"What do you mean? We broke up, that's all. It happens."

We had made it to the car, but as soon as we sat, I stopped him from putting the key in the ignition.

"I'm sorry if I seemed rude. I just hope that you aren't taking me out because you feel sorry for me or anything."

"No, I just—"

"Just what?"

"I like you."

"Good. I like you, too." I didn't need to know anything else so I crawled on top of him and gave Nita some much needed relief. Slim wasn't good and he wasn't bad, but he was just what I needed that day. We never made it to the movie. After I climaxed, I crawled down, fixed my clothes, and got out of the car. I could feel his sense of confusion and maybe even hurt but either way, I didn't care. I never even looked back.

Every day was like starting over. Some days it would be easy and some days it would be hard, but I would eventually get up and remember my mission. The fall session would be starting soon and I hadn't really gone to many of the parties. I wanted to shed my "I got dumped" look and put on a fresh face. I decided it was time to get out again.

I purchased a new bra and panty set and a fresh cut like Rihanna. Even Nita got a little design. I trimmed her in the shape of an "N." I went out with my confidence on. Even though I was only 5'4", I was walking like I was 6'4". I was on the prowl and brothers were checking me out left and right. I knew it was time to start on my journey.

As I walked to my calculus class, I scanned the area to see who would be my first victim.

"Jade!" a voice yelled. As I turned around, I saw a skinny, tall, honey-brown brother running toward me. I didn't recognize the face initially, but the way he ran was similar to a baseball player.

Woof!

Holding on to his backpack, he jogged toward me.

"What's up, Jade?" He smiled. "It's me, Curtis. Curtis the Cutie."

"Oh, Curtis, hey, how are you?" Curtis the Cutie was a year younger than me, but we went to the same high school together. I heard that in his senior year, his mom was killed by a drunk truck driver that worked for some big company. They paid Curtis handsomely for her death. He was such a little cutie-pie. In school, we called him Curtis the Cutie-Pie, but now he was all grown up.

"Wow, I barely recognized you." I reached up and gently pulled on his barely grown-in facial hair as I gave him a coy wink that meant yummy victim number one. That was all it took; he was hooked. Curtis the Cutie asked me out on a date and I, of course, agreed. That night, he picked me up in his fly-ass Ford Explorer. I was glad because I had wanted to drive one. His car smelled like French vanilla pie or something. Very surprising for someone so young to care about the scent of his car. I was also surprised to find how nicely dressed he was. I assumed he would have on baggy pants and a big sloppy shirt, but he didn't. It was refreshing to look at a new piece of meat.

After a nice dinner and a movie, I directed Curtis the Cutie to a quiet place near the beach. He thought we had parked there to talk and soak up the night air. Little did he know I hadn't had sex in nearly five days and Nita was struggling! I imagined that the only way I could get over Dre was to start seeing and fucking other people. I didn't know what Curtis the Cutie was talking about, but I leaned over and started to nibble on his earlobe. His deep inhale told me that he wasn't expecting that to happen. He started breathing so hard that I thought he was going to nut just from that. I went from his earlobe to straight down his neck. He reached over and started kissing me.

Yuck. He couldn't kiss. That's okay; I wasn't there for kissing him anyway. Keeping him distracted with kissing, I tinkered with his pants and he quickly helped me unbutton them. I hiked up my skirt and climbed my tiny frame over the gear shifter to sit on top of him. He was hard and that's all I needed. I started kissing on his neck and he started to pant like a puppy in heat. He stopped to let me know something that made this moment sweeter.

"Umm, Jade, I'm a virgin," he admitted. I could sense his embarrassment and that made me even hornier.

"Oh, baby boy, then you don't want it like this."

In some weird way, I viewed myself as Dre, and that felt powerful.

"No, it's not that. I just don't want to disappoint you."

He hung his head down, trying not to make eye contact with me. I took my hand, lifted his face, gave him a gentle kiss, and said, "Then I'll make sure to take it easy on you." I smirked. I closed my eyes and pretended that Curtis the Cutie was Dre. I swooped toward his neck to lick it like it was ice cream. I wanted him to taste like Dre, but the Nautica cologne mixed with the taste of his skin was no comparison. So I kept my eyes closed and in my mind I made him Dre.

"Hold it straight up for me," I commanded him then I raised my body up and wasted no time to slide down on him. His penis felt more round than I was used to with Dre. Nita and I were on the same page and we both needed this. I rode him like a show pony for about three minutes and without notice, he grabbed me and held me really tight and started screaming like a five-year-old girl.

"I'm sorry."

I rose up and moved back to my seat.

"You should be." I laughed.

"Huh?"

"Don't worry about it." I shifted my skirt. "Let's go."

"I'm sure that wasn't what you expected."

Oh, lawd, I hoped he wouldn't start crying. I managed to calm him down and reassured him that it was fine, but it wasn't. Nita and I were both pissed, but I knew it would crush him if I told him how I really felt.

Poor Curtis the Cutie was so embarrassed that he barely uttered more than two words to me on the way back to my apartment. When we pulled up front, he just stopped the Explorer and pushed the electric lock to open the door. I opened the door and then reached for his hand.

"Curtis, I want you to know that I'm so glad that you shared that with me. Maybe it will make you feel better if you know that you're only the second man that I've ever been with."

I wasn't sure why I was telling him that bullshit, but I enjoyed it. He looked up at me with joy.

I reached over and kissed him on the cheek. That seemed to make him happy, so I decided to add to it.

"Curtis, I don't want someone who's been with a thousand girls. I want someone who will only want me."

"That's exactly what I want," he said and then he grabbed me tight to kiss me. The ear-to-ear smile on his face told me that this made him really happy and that made me horny. He was hooked.

"Will I see you tomorrow?"

"Sure, baby." I had no plans on seeing Curtis again, but he didn't know that. I looked at the clock in his car and realized that I was about to be late for my next date with Luis the Linguist.

Luis was an international student from Paris that I had asked to help me with my Spanish class. I really just wanted to see if men from Paris were great lovers like I'd heard.

"Listen, baby, I have to study. My tutor will be over in about ten minutes." I had one leg out of the car and just as I was about to take the other one out, Curtis grabbed my hand.

"Jade, I really dig you. I always have. You the kinda girl I could fall in love with."

"You don't love me, you love my coochie." I laughed and got out of the car, slamming the door behind me. I waved to Curtis the Cutie and walked seductively toward my apartment. I knew that Curtis was all mine. When I walked into the lobby, I saw Luis sitting in front of the TV snacking on potato chips. Before the night would be over, I wanted to introduce those lips to Nita's lips. Before we could even figure out what chapter we were on, I was on him.

And with that, the rebirth of power began. And so did the list.

Black Fantasy
Jade

Over the summer, I had gotten a part-time job since my twisted, evil-ass mother had decided she wasn't sending me any money. It also helped me to focus on what to do in the mornings rather than think about Dre. I was working as a receptionist at a graphic arts company and every day I would have the delivery packages ready for the super cute pick up guy who happened to be white.

I'd never been attracted to white boys, but Rob was a very different kind of sexy. I wondered what the difference would be between Rob and Luis. Luis had a nice tan to go along with his sexy lips and accent. Rob was pretty boring in terms of just being a regular guy. The phones didn't ring very much, but Curtis the Cutie had been calling often. I would ignore the phone when I saw it was him. Besides, every day at 4:30, Rob would come pick up packages from the delivery company.

Rob had a short buzz cut with dark brown hair that had just enough curl to make you think that he had a little black in him. His eyes were very young and boy-like, with a certain innocence to them that invited you to look at him. His nose wasn't super thin and it wasn't big. It was just in the middle to make it cute as a button. He had the perfect lips for a white boy. The top lip was thin and the bottom lip was just juicy enough that he might have been able to do something with it. Most white boys that I'd seen all had the super tiny lips and that wasn't attractive to me. His body wasn't anything to die over, but for a white boy, I was willing to work with it. Rob was just "Rob, the white guy" on my list. He didn't talk black when he was talking to me, and I liked that. He was just who he was. And I'd heard that not all white boys had small penises. Rob seemed to make it obvious that he was well-stocked in that area. Every day he would jump out of that big truck and I would watch him glide his cute ass in the door.

"Hi, Jade."

"Hey, Rob, how's your day going?"

"Good, now that I'm here." He flashed his boyish smile. "So Jade, it's Friday. What do you have planned for the weekend?" he asked curiously.

"Nothing, really. What are you up to?"

"Well, I'm singing tonight at a little club downtown and I wanted you to come and check me out."

"Oh, wow, I didn't know you sing."

He broke out into a song of his own. "I sure do...I love... love...to sing," he crooned in his soprano voice.

I couldn't believe my ears. "Damn, you can sing for real."

"Thanks."

"Where and what time?" I asked.

"You're going to come?" he asked excitedly.

"Yeah, I'll come."

"Cool."

He seemed really excited that I'd agreed to attend the show, so I figured I should definitely go. He wrote the name of the club down on a piece of paper and almost seemed to skip out the door. When I looked down at the paper, I realized that his gig was at Club Z. I hadn't been back there since Dre and I had vowed never to go back. Rob must have felt the thoughts going into my head, because he turned around and came back inside.

"Hey, I'll put you on the list so you can get in free."

"Okay." I smiled and waved goodbye to him. He did a slow trot back to his truck and kept turning to look back at me before finally driving off.

That night, I got dressed in a short skirt and a really cute halter top. I didn't feel like doing a lot to my hair so I just pulled it back into a ponytail. I stood looking at myself in the mirror and thought, *What if Dre is there?* I would want to be looking my best. I took out my curling iron and spent the next thirty minutes perfecting it. When I arrived at the club, all I could do was stand and look at the area that Dre and I had walked when we first met. Memories flooded my mind and my stomach felt nauseous. I hadn't even been back to this part of town. I had to try to move past the thoughts of Dre and on to Rob. I at least had to enjoy the night, so I gritted my teeth and walked to the door.

"Hi, I'm a friend of Rob's."

The burly bouncer at the door seemed to be about 6'5" and well over three hundred pounds. "Your name?" he asked while leaning down to me.

"Jade."

"Oh, Jade, okay, follow me." He grabbed me by the arm and moved me behind him. I held onto the bouncer and stood there waiting to get my hand stamped when I noticed that inside women were screaming. I could hear a voice singing. It was smooth like Brian McKnight's and sultry.

I stood on my tiptoes and tried to see Rob as I walked toward the front of the stage area. I was surprised to see him sitting at a piano. As soon as he noticed me, I saw him sit up a little bit straighter. Our eyes met and he gave me a wink. He sang about wishing for someone to love him no matter his color. When the bouncer made his way to the front, he guided me to a seat that had a rose laying on it.

I was surprised by the amount of thought that Rob had put into this. I noticed that all the white women around me were truly excited to be watching him perform. I was the only black woman in the crowd. I wondered why Rob was so interested in having me there, especially when there were plenty of women already clamoring at the sight of him.

For the next two songs, he kept his eyes directly on mine.

I was thrilled about my last-minute decision to look my best. As he finished up his songs, I found myself clapping and screaming right along with the other women. Just as he started his fifth song, he asked everyone to have a seat. He sat at the piano and started to play a soft melody.

"I call this song, 'Notice Me?' I wrote this for a special lady that I want in my life but she doesn't know it." He looked directly at me. The girl next to me leaned over toward me.

"Oh, this is a really good song. I wish he was singing it about me." She flipped her blonde hair and sat up taller in her chair. I sat there and decided to pay close attention to what he was saying. The lyrics to the song talked about how he wanted a woman to love him for who he was and not be worried about what he has or doesn't have. The hook particularly stuck out to me.

"If when you looked in the mirror and I looked just like you, would that change how long it took for you to notice me?"

He sang that song until he was kicking over the chair to the piano. He got up and sat on the edge of the short stage in front of me and sang the hook.

"Notice me, 'cause I notice you."

I could feel the white girls around me looking at me, wondering why he was singing to me. He eventually put the microphone aside, jumped down to the floor area, and knelt down in front of me, cupping my face in his hands. It was as if the sounds all around us had gone away and we were the only two in the entire room. He didn't kiss me, but he got close enough to my face that I could smell the spearmint-flavored mouthwash that he must have used before the show. There was a euphoric feeling about that moment, and I decided that I would enjoy it while the feeling was there.

A part of me wished that I could have shared this with Dre.

When the show was over, the enormous bouncer came and got me and took me backstage. He told me that Rob wanted to see me. I had never been backstage anywhere before, but I felt like I was getting the celebrity-groupie treatment.

The space wasn't as glamorous as I thought it would have been. The room was being shared by various other groups, so the experience felt more like chaos than a celebrity event. As soon as Rob saw me, he jumped up from his chair and hurried over. He gave me a hug and then placed his hand on my cheek and started to kiss me. I was in such shock, but I was in even more shock that he was able to kiss. Before I knew it, I had put my arms around him and was enjoying kissing him back. That bottom lip turned out to be as juicy as it looked.

When he finally stopped kissing me, he whispered to me, "That was everything I knew it would be."

Part of my mother's paranoia started to creep in and I had to ask myself if he was trying to kill me as part of some sort of skinhead initiation or if he just wanted me to be his black fantasy. No matter what the answer was, I waited for him to get dressed and invited him to come to my place. I was intrigued by the kiss and I wanted more.

"Do you mind if I take a quick shower?" I asked.

"Not at all. I'd prefer to have you fresh."

I felt like he was going to eat me alive. I laughed and thought, *That's exactly what I'm going to do.*

That night, Rob and I fucked in the shower, on the floor, against the wall, outside against the building, in his car, and at McDonald's. We were so tired, but we finally had one last round in the bed. I was exhausted, but I still wanted more.

The next morning, I was tired and hungry, so we decided to go out and eat. We made our way to a restaurant that had outside seating. I hadn't noticed anyone around us until we sat down. The table was close to the door and was small enough for only two people. Rob was such a gentleman, opening the door for me and pulling out my chair.

"I had an amazing night."

"So did I," I replied.

After we settled at our table, Rob was looking at his menu as two black men walked past us. One of the men tapped the other on the shoulder and pointed back toward me. The other man turned and looked at me. He looked back at his friend and they both shook their heads. I couldn't believe what had happened. At that moment, I felt like I was betraying my race by being on this date with Rob, but what was I supposed to do? Black men date white women all the time and he was a really great guy and I was enjoying his penis' company.

"People can be so ignorant," I complained.

"What do you mean?"

"Those two black guys just pointed at us. I guess they don't approve."

"Well, that's okay. I don't approve of them either, but I do approve of you. I think you're amazing and making love to you was like heaven on earth."

I wanted to jump up and do the touchdown dance. I had officially been compared to heaven.

"If I had known that lovemaking would be like that, I would have saved my virginity for you." The look on his face told me that I could officially add him to the list. Dre the Demon, Slim the Bartender, Curtis the Cutie, Luis the Linguist, and now Rob the White Guy. After our delicious breakfast, Rob asked me to come back to his house. But I'd had more of him than I needed, so I told him that I wanted to go to the store but I really wanted really wanted to drive his dope ass car and drive by to see if Troy the Trucker was home. Troy was a truck driver that I met at a bar one night. Troy the Trucker was a half-black, half-white guy who was married to a passive-aggressive black woman and had three perfect kids. I knew that I wouldn't have to worry about him wanting to marry me.

Troy lived in Gardena, which wasn't too far from where I had left Rob. Troy told me to pass by the house and if the curtain was open, that meant his wife was home. If I drove by and the curtain was closed, that meant park across the street and come to the side entrance. I didn't have to guess because I actually pulled up just as his wife was pulling out of the driveway. I slowed down to let her back out and followed her to the next street. I waited to see which way she turned and I turned the opposite way. I made my way around the block and parked across the street from Troy's house. I was happy when I saw that the curtain was closed.

When I walked in the door I realized that I should probably shower. I excused myself to the bathroom to wash Rob's scent off of me. As soon as I opened the bathroom door, Troy grabbed me and we made our way the living room couch.

103

"Tired?" he asked.

"You know what? I really am."

"Do you know how beautiful you are?"

I parted my lips to say thank you, but he put his index finger to my mouth. Nita was feeling like a bad girl. I licked his finger just enough to wet the tip. He grazed his finger across the rim of my lips. When he had circled my entire mouth, he leaned in to give me a kiss. From there it became one of the most sensual moments I'd had since Dre.

He reached for my breast, his wet tongue circling my nipples and his moans informing me that he was enjoying himself. I knew that he was becoming more and more horny as the moments went on. Not since Dre had a man taken his time to move across each part of my arm as if he were looking for imperfections. He kissed and stroked and caressed each part of my body as I lay on the couch.

"You have no idea how much I want you," he confessed.

That was exactly what I wanted him to say. Finally, I had become so incredibly horny that I wasn't able to wait on anymore sensuality, I just wanted to fuck and now. I tugged on his pants and he helped me get them down. We were well past the pleasantries of love-making. Finally, he was down to his boxer shorts and I had already moved my legs so that I could be open and ready for him to enter. He grabbed his pants quickly, reached for a condom, and sat down on the floor to put it on. Curiosity made me stretch my neck over the edge of the couch to see what Troy was working with.

And there it was. The size was just right. It didn't look too big and it sure wasn't too small, but the color! Oh snap, it was white. White enough that I could see his blood vessels and that just grossed me out.

What was I doing? Did I really want this uncooked piece of sausage to be inside of me?

"What's the matter?" he asked.

He could tell that something was wrong but I didn't know how to respond.

"If you're not ready, we can wait. There's no rush. I don't want you to feel rushed. I want this to be good for both of us. I want it to be perfect."

So I said the first thing that came to my mind. "I'm not sure that I'm ready for this. I just got out of a bad relationship and I've only been with one man my whole life. Besides, you're married." As those words rolled out of my mouth, I wondered why I kept telling that lie. I jumped up from the couch and pretended to be upset. He pulled up his boxer shorts and looked confused.

"We don't have to do anything that you're not ready for. I'm sorry if you felt rushed."

I was thinking, *Okay, is this really happening? A man is actually apologizing for doing something wrong?* And he hadn't actually done anything; I just wasn't ready for the lack of color of his penis. Rob and Luis had some kind of tan to theirs, but his was just raw looking. He hadn't done anything wrong. He could kiss, he was cute, married, and emotionally unavailable. I didn't have any other choice but to like him.

Thoughts of Dre suddenly filled my mind and everything started to go downhill. Remembrances of Dre were more overpowering than any of the other images in my mind. Maybe it didn't have anything to do with color, maybe it had everything to do with Dre and that was starting to damage my ability to move on.

By Monday morning, I didn't want to see or hear from Curtis, Rob, Luis, or Troy, and so I changed my number. If anyone stopped by, Missy would tell them I had moved. Sure, none of them deserved what I was doing to them, but I didn't deserve what Dre had done to me, and I didn't think that I could truly be interested in anyone until I was completely over him.

A Penis in a Blanket
Jade

The Kappas were having a party and I definitely planned on attending. I had met Keith the Kappa at a barbeque cookout the week before. He looked just like me—green eyes, black thick curly hair, and a pretty smile. I had never dated anyone that had green eyes like mine. I agreed to go with him because I needed a ride, but I had no intention of being his arm candy for the night. Once a girl becomes Kappa candy, it's almost impossible to get a date for a while and that wasn't what I wanted.

I will admit that stepping out of Keith's BMW was a great intro for me and a great way for me to start training Missy. I promised I would teach her a few things about how to find a man. She was shy, but I knew there was a freak inside.

When Keith the Kappa picked me up, he seemed a little disappointed to see Missy dragging behind me. The distraction of my new, tight-fitting, red miniskirt and white halter top was enough to calm his nerves.

"Hey. Keith, Missy; Missy, Keith." I got in, slammed the door, and turned to look at him as he drove off. The frustration in his face was obvious, but I quickly got him to remove that when I leaned over and gave him a kiss on the cheek while grabbing his penis.

"Hey, thanks for coming to get us. The party is at Yellow Jackets, right?" I asked.

Yellow Jackets, a new club, was the hottest spot for all of us who were still under twenty-one to have a good time. Slim had told me about it, but I had avoided going 'til I figured things had calmed down between him and me.

When we arrived at the club, I could hear the music nearly a block over. As we were walking, Keith kept trying to hold my hand. Each time, I would reach for my phone or wave to someone. I wasn't having it. I had already passed up about three different men who piqued my interest. I had accomplished the first part of my goal, which was to get to the club. I had no intention of hanging around with Keith the Kappa all night. Besides, his breath stunk.

I needed a reason to walk back to the car, so I used the one thing that no man wants to talk about.

"Oh shoot, I need to get my purse out of your car. My tampons are in it. Can I borrow your keys? I'll meet you at the door."

"Sure," he eagerly said as he reached in his pocket and gave me the keys. I could have asked him for a kidney and he would have given it to me.

"Thanks."

As I turned to walk away, I heard Missy say, "I'll wait with Keith."

"No, come with me."

I grabbed her hand and started walking in the opposite direction. Hesitating, she came with me.

"What are we doing?" she asked.

"I'm not hanging with Keith all night. Do you see all these fine-ass men around here? This is a Kappa party. There's going to be the best selection of cuties here. You could line them up and pick your pleasure."

I could tell that Missy was enamored and in awe by the way she stopped in her tracks and grabbed my arm as if she had seen a celebrity.

"Wow, he's really cute, the one in the navy blue shirt coming toward us."

Woof!

"Hmm, yes he is."

I tilted my head to the side.

"I wouldn't mind meeting him. What should I do?" she asked.

This brother had a body that was well-maintained. He was a high-yellow brother, which meant he might be one of them Creole boys. His hair was jet black and slick looking. His blue Polo shirt and tan slacks complemented his frame well. Just a hint of muscles protruded through his pants, giving a glimpse of his thighs.

He had a confident walk, and I liked that.

"A girl like you would never get a man like him. I'll take this one."

Well, that must have pissed her off.

"I saw him first," she whined.

"And what do you think he would want with your boring ass? Have you ever had an orgasm? Do you even know where your G-spot is?"

She was speechless.

"Exactly." I continued to walk toward him. I started thinking that was mean and I should apologize to Missy, but I would fix that later. As he got closer, I locked my eyes into his and captured him with my beauty. It was as if there was no one else within our paths.

Just as he and his friends were passing, Missy whispered a pitiful, "Hi."

I winked and kept walking right past him. I walked about another five steps when I realized that Missy wasn't with me. Perfect! She was helping and didn't even know it. She gave me a reason to turn around.

"Come on." I yelled to Missy but his eyes perked up and he pointed to himself. I shook my head in agreement and smiled.

He started walking toward me anyway, and Missy was still standing there like a puppy about to pee on the floor. She snapped out of it as he walked right past her toward me. He and I exchanged pleasantries, introducing ourselves. His name was Ben Boudreaux, a sexy Creole brother from New Orleans, Louisiana. I was always amazed at how many Southern boys come to L.A. to go to school.

"Where you going? The party's this way, yea." His smile reminded me of Dre's perfect smile. The way his teeth sat perfectly together and the size of his lips made my mouth water.

"I left something in my car," I answered.

"Well, an attractive woman like you shouldn't be walking around by yourself. I'll come with you, if you want," he offered.

I agreed and we walked off together. I had no idea where Missy went. We made it back to Keith's car and I opened the door as if it were my own. I pretended to be searching for something. I made it a point to bend all the way over, exposing my thighs underneath my red mini. I searched long enough to give him a hard-on. I was pleased to see it when I turned around to face him.

"Oh, well, I guess I left them at home."

"What are you looking for?" he asked.

I wasn't looking for anything. I just wanted to get away from Keith and take that BMW for a ride.

"Well, you nosy as hell." I laughed.

I invited him to ride to the store with me to buy cigarettes. We picked up a bottle of vodka as well. We drove up to Fat Burger to eat and we chatted for what seemed like hours. When we finished our food, we sat in the parking lot, drinking from our bottle of vodka. I was still horny from my married lover and I had decided that Ben would be my next victim. Half drunk, we decided to drive around for a little bit. I knew that Monica wasn't home and Missy was at the party, so I drove him to our apartment. By the time we got there, we had drunk the entire bottle of vodka and were still laughing and talking, but I was only entertaining him, hoping to get what I wanted.

Sex. Sex had become a service to Nita like getting a car washed.

"Is this your place?" he asked as I fumbled with the keys.

"Yep. Come on in."

"Nice."

"Yeah, it's cool." I tossed the keys on the table. I grabbed him around his neck and pulled him toward me and started to kiss him. Finally, a good kisser, not like Dre, but good enough. And he smelled better than Keith. He didn't hesitate to oblige me with some kissing and fondling.

Fuck fondling; let's get this pony on the pedestal.

I guided him up against the wall and started to unbuckle his pants.

"Do you have condoms?" I asked.

"Yes."

"Good."

He pulled a condom out of his pocket. Barely able to continue standing, I backed up, waiting for him to drop his pants and when he did, there it was. A penis…in a blanket. He wasn't circumcised. It was like his dick was wearing a turtleneck.

Muthafucka! What the hell?! I had never seen anything like that before in my life.

"What the hell is wrong with your dick?" I asked.

"Nothing's wrong with it. I'm not circumcised. My parents are devout Catholics."

"What's that got to do with it? Can't you fix it now that you're an adult?"

"I don't need to get circumcised," he slurred and smiled.

"Well, you need to either get a new religion or tie that shit back. Get a rubber band and pull it back or something." Note to self, never date a Catholic guy 'cause his dick might look like a chocolate-covered anteater. This was some bullshit and he was definitely wearing a condom.

Hell, for all I knew, he could be storing food down in there or something. He tried to show me that it wasn't any different and that it was just foreskin, but when he pulled the skin back, that disgusted me even more. I was like, oh hell no! His penis popped out like a groundhog emerging to look for a shadow. I needed another drink if I was going to have sex with Ben the Blanket.

Nita was on a mission that night and I was able to let the groundhog get some. We had sex right there standing up against the wall. Nita and I both became frustrated when I felt him grab me tightly to notify me that he had expelled himself. So far, Nita and I had no luck in having an orgasm, but I wasn't going to let him off the hook that easy. I made him sit down on the floor and tried to ride him, but he was soft. He lightly pushed me off as if he was swatting a fly.

"I'm done."

"Good for you. I'm not." I tried to get him aroused again without getting angry. He pushed at me again. I pulled back and looked at him as if he were crazy.

"Are you serious?"

"Yeah, baby, what were you expecting?" he asked.

"I was expecting to get my rocks off. That's what I was expecting. Hell, I would think your groundhog-looking dick would be happy to come out and play for a little while since it's being held hostage in a little house." It was apparent by the look on his face that he did *not* expect that to be my response.

"What do you mean?"

I shot him a look of utter disgust and disbelief.

"Get dressed. I'll take you back to the party or home or wherever the fuck you want to go."

"What?" He was still in disbelief that a woman was talking to him like that.

"Look, put on…get your shit and let's go," I demanded.

I was so pissed that I stood at the door waiting for him to come back from taking a pee. We got in the car and didn't say a word the entire ride. I drove right up to the entrance of the party, which was a few blocks away, not thinking at all about Keith. Ben had the nerve to try to lean over and kiss me. I pulled back from him and sat back and waved.

"Bye."

"Maybe I can call you sometime?"

"For what? Boy bye."

I could tell his feelings were hurt as he slowly got out of the car. I turned around, ready to shoot an angry look, and there was Keith.

"Oops."

He came to the window and peered in.

"Who was that?" he asked angrily.

"That was just my homeboy. Shut up and get in."

"I didn't know you were gonna drive the car. Where have you been? I've been looking for you for the past four hours."

"Shut up and get in."

He did it. He got in the car and I sped off. I turned the corner and entered the parking lot of a gas station. I threw the gear into park and got out.

"You drive, I'm drunk."

As I made my way around the back of the car, he met me with a hug.

"Hey, don't do that again." He held me closely around the waist, hoping for a kiss.

RED FLAG! RED FLAG! He was tripping, but as if that wasn't enough he kept digging his own grave deeper and deeper.

"I was worried about you, baby. I really like you," he said as he smiled.

"Umm…okay." I patted him on the shoulder to indicate that I wanted him to let me go. Little did he know that was all I wanted and I would avoid Keith the Kappa and Ben the Blanket from now 'til three days after never.

I went back to my apartment and had to whip out Chuck to relieve some of the tension. My vibrator lover was back. Naked, I crawled underneath the covers and enjoyed myself. It was as close to Dre as I could get—for now.

The Hardest Part
A Poem by Jade Hall

Knowing I won't hear your laugh or get to see you smile,
That's hard, but that's not the hardest part.
Powerless to give you consent to be my sexual tour
guide for life.
Hmm, that's hard, but no, baby, that's not the hardest part.
Losing the resonance of your voice in my ear,
Hard, but not the hardest part.
Searching for the syllables that trace tingles into my
head,
Hmm, hard, but no, no, that's not the hardest part.
Searching for the mixture of fragrance and body only
To find that I'm furious to be free of your aroma,
No, that's not the hardest part.
Leaving my soul behind, barely catching it as it falls,
No, that's not the hardest part.
Not able to ever feel the embrace of your skin,
Hard, but not the hardest part.
Knowing I have to live uncovered, naked, and cold,
Unable to watch you sleep in contentment and peace,
Oh no, baby, that's not the hardest part.

No waking to lovemaking, thrusting and shaking,
Hard but not the hardest part.
The hard,
The harder,
The hardest part . . .
Is the wetness of my tears at your door,
Knowing you just didn't want me no more.

Disconnect
Monica

When I first came to L.A. to help out my girl Jade, I didn't really expect to stay as long as I did until I met Shawn Devereaux. I wasn't looking for a boyfriend since I had so many things to do to get Jade back on track, but I'd be the first to admit that I was lonely. Being lonely can cause you to do things that you don't think you will. Jade had a drawer full of vibrators and rabbits and plastic shit, but that wasn't my thing. I like real men and I just couldn't get with sticking something in there that didn't come with a warm body. I wanted conversation, love, and affection.

Shawn was like no other guy I had dated. His dad was the president at a financial firm and his mother was one of the executive producers at one of the major movie studios. He was well-educated, respectful, had no kids, and was on his way to finishing medical school. Shawn wanted to become a gynecologist and lived in an oceanfront condo that was breathtaking. He even had a maid and a chef. He was the perfect man for me, a dream come true. He was everything that every woman would have ever wanted in a man. He was nothing like the broke assholes back in Houston.

Meeting Shawn was like getting a breath of fresh air and it had been a long time since I even thought about having a relationship. Shawn and I met at a coffee shop and our chemistry was instant. I knew that it was destiny because he met me the day before I was about to go back to Houston. I was sitting on the patio reading a book about balancing my chakra. Dressed in a black tank top and a beige and black wrap skirt with an African mask printed on it, the cool breeze of the wind blew softly through my curly two-inch afro. As soon as he walked out of the café, I noticed him looking around.

"Are you looking for a seat?" I asked.

"Yes I am, but please don't leave because of me. I'll just wait."

"Why wait? Here, just sit with me."

"Are you sure?"

"Yeah, I don't mind." I smiled.

"That's very nice of you."

He pulled the chair out and sat with me. I couldn't resist his eyes. They made my heart flutter. I felt like destiny had landed in my lap. We sat at the coffee shop through lunch until it was time for the open mic poetry dinner. Talking with a man who was well-versed in James Baldwin and Zora Neale Hurston was impressive. I didn't really feel like I was on his level but he had done something no other man had done. He listened. Shawn was the first man who I felt saw something other than a pretty face. He saw me as a woman who really wanted more from life. I had never been on a date like this before and it was the most amazing day of my life. From that day on, we never left each other's side. I moved in with him after about three months, not because I thought it was a good idea, but because it felt so right. I had found my Prince Charming.

When I moved in, we were living like husband and wife. We made dinner together and would take short trips on his parents' boat in the marina. Shawn was big on education and moving forward in life. He always questioned me about what my plans were but I hadn't really thought about it much, so he suggested that I go to school and study nursing. He said that nurses were the best people in the world because they can always save a life.

"That sounds nice, but I don't have money for that."

"I'll take care of it. Don't worry about that."

"Shawn, that's so sweet, but I really want to be a model."

"A model?" He seemed displeased.

"Modeling. You know, *Elle, Vogue*."

He took his napkin and wiped his mouth.

"No wife of mine is going to be in a magazine."

It was the first time anyone had ever referred to me as a wife.

"Now, I'll support you going to school for a real job but not for some childhood pipe dream. Besides, I wouldn't be able to stand it knowing that men are lusting over my baby like that."

"I understand, but Shawn—"

He slammed his fist down on the table. The clank of the utensils scared me.

"Never mind. I'm sorry, okay...I'm sorry," I said, grabbing his hand. "You're right; it's a crazy idea anyway. You know, I was originally studying interior design. Maybe I can finish that," I offered, hoping that a change of subject would help to calm him down.

His momentary anger reminded me of my father.

"Nursing sounds fine. Besides, models are just self-centered bitches without souls who like to get dressed up and put on makeup."

I just agreed with him so I could enjoy the dinner.

The next morning I was sitting on the back patio enjoying the morning breeze, reading a magazine, and there was an ad for a modeling agency looking for fresh faces. The ad read, "If you are between the ages of 18-25 and are 5'10", we are looking for you." I kept reading and so many of the things sounded just like me that I was waiting for the ad to say, "If your name is Monica Thompson, please reply." I tore the ad out of the paper and stuck it in my pocket.

I kept looking at the magazine and suddenly Shawn was standing right behind me.

"Good morning, baby." He leaned over to kiss me. "I bought you coffee."

"Shawn, you're so sweet. Thanks."

"What are you looking at?" he asked.

"Just a magazine." I turned the publication so that he could see the front. As soon as he saw the cover, he snatched the magazine from my hand, rolled it up, and tossed it over the balcony.

"I will not be married to a woman who has her body spread all over the place." He turned and walked into the house.

I sat for a moment trying to understand what had just happened. I finally got up and went inside.

"Shawn."

"What!"

"I'm sorry."

"I'm sorry, too." He reached for me, but I shrank back.

"I love you, Monica, and you are so incredible that I don't want to lose you."

I listened to what he said but something just didn't sit right with me and a ball of nervousness started to twirl in my stomach. That same swirl would happen right before my father would start in on my mother, but I ignored it. I could only think of one person to turn to. Jade.

I hadn't been back to our apartment in so long, but nothing had changed. When I arrived, she was asleep or recovering from a hangover. She wanted to go grab a bite to eat but I had to be back at Shawn's soon so I told her I didn't really feel like going out.

Jade made coffee and I sat at the nearby kitchen table. I pulled the magazine out of my purse.

"Check this out." I said as I slid the magazine across the table. She picked it up and looked at it.

"So, you wanna be a model?" Jade asked.

"I don't know, but I've thought about it."

"Well, I think you should. People are always telling you how pretty your face is and I think you can do it."

"Well, I'm glad that I have one fan already. I'm just not sure Shawn would like it."

"Shawn? Who cares if he likes it?"

"Well, I care."

"Why?"

"Well, because I kind of like him and you haven't noticed that he's good to me and for me. He might be the one."

"Yeah, I can tell by the way you jump every time he calls. What's wrong with you? And when did this guy get so fucking important to you that you have to ask yourself if you're going to model? Hell, that's all you've ever talked about doing since we were kids and to think that you're considering not doing it because of what Shawn might think is just kind of fucked up." Jade flicked her cigarette toward the overflowing ashtray.

"Excuse me? Did you really just say that shit to me? Don't get to throwing shit all over the place because your shit smells a whole lot worse than mine, Jade. You have no idea of what love is. Hell, if it wasn't for you I wouldn't even be here. Just because you don't know how to keep a man, don't get mad at me because I do. For your information, Shawn wants to marry me. And you know what? It's a whole lot more than you have. At the rate you're going, you'll never get married because you just don't know what true love is really all about."

"Come on, Mo, don't be like ya mama and get your ass beat for the next thirty years for some earrings. Ain't this the same shit we watched your mama do?"

"Leave my mama out of this, Jade. I didn't say shit about your mama. Married a man who she probably doesn't even know his first name."

"You know what? If you weren't my best friend, I might actually get mad at you about that shit. Wow, this dude really got you sewn up by the way you're acting. Maybe you ought to talk to the therapist, Mo."

"Why? You're not learning a damn thing. Hell, after two months of therapy, somewhere in your warped brain you actually think Dre loved you. Hell, for all you know, he didn't even like you. Jade, really, do you think that what you and Dre had was real love? That was total bullshit. You got sprung over a dick."

"You don't know a fucking thing about me and Dre."

"Jade, you are being a real bitch! I don't need to know any more than I've seen. Hell, I'm here because he's not." I slammed the refrigerator door and made my way over to where she was sitting.

"Did you just call me a bitch?"

"Yes, bitch, I did."

"You are tripping."

"Nah, you trippin'. You probably need to take your medicine and take your ass to your room and masturbate to the thoughts of a motherfucker who left you."

"Fuck you, Monica." She picked up an empty soda can from the table and threw it at me. I ducked to miss the can flying at my head, but before I knew it I had picked up some magazines and threw them at her.

"GET OUT!" Jade screamed. "Get the fuck out."

"Jealous bitch!" I walked out the front door. This was the first time in the fifteen years that I'd known Jade that we had a disagreement. I didn't know what to do. I heard the door open and turned around thinking that Jade was going to apologize. Instead she flipped me the bird and slammed the door. It almost seemed unreal, and yet it was very real 'cause I had just driven away.

Depression
Jade

Monica and I had never had a fight in the entire time we'd known each other. When Monica left my place, I didn't know what to do, so I hopped on the first bus that came by and just rode. When the bus turned down the street that Dre's apartment was on, I decided to get off. I walked toward the complex and stopped in front of his window. Inside I could see a man walking around with a woman and a few kids who ran quickly back and forth in front of the window. I wanted so badly to go inside and lay on the carpet and cry. I started to get angry that those people were inside, putting their scent on his carpet. They had probably removed the stain from the floor, and all traces of the love that I had for Dre were gone.

My stomach churned. I had dreams of Dre almost every night. I dreamt that this nightmare called reality was just a dream and I would wake up in his arms. I tried not to replay every moment in my mind, yet that's all I seemed to be able to do, over and over again. I wasn't sure what went wrong and I wanted desperately to find out why he had left. I wondered if I would ever see him again. I loved him. I loved him more than my own self. I stood there, waiting for Dre to show up, but I knew I was fooling myself. I turned and walked to the nearby 7-Eleven to grab a pack of cigarettes.

When I went in the store, there was a cute cashier at the counter. I had seen him a few times around campus, but he wasn't really my type. There was something sexy about him though and I wanted him.

"Hi, may I help you?" he asked.

"Virginia Slim Lights, please," I responded.

"Hey, don't you go to my school?" he asked and smiled.

"Yeah, I've seen you around a few times. What's your name?"

"Charles."

"I'm Jade."

"Nice to meet you." He reached to shake my hand.

"Do you live around here?"

"Yeah, I live in those apartments right there."

"Oh, okay. What you doing later?"

"Not much. Just chillin'. What about you?" He smiled.

"Nothing, really. I was thinking about walking over to the Redbox and picking up a movie."

"Oh, cool. What are you gonna pick up?"

"Not sure. Got any suggestions?"

"Nah, I haven't been over there, so I don't know, but I'd love to watch it with you."

"What time do you get off?" I asked as Nita started to pulsate.

"I get off in about fifteen minutes if dude shows up on time. Do you want to wait for me?"

"Yeah, I'll wait."

"Cool. You can go in the back and chill if you want."

"Oh, okay. I'm gonna go smoke first."

"Too pretty to be smoking, but do what you do."

"Thanks, but I really don't need any more lectures today."

"You used to go with ol' boy downstairs, didn't you?"

"Who are you talking about?" I pretended not to know who he meant.

"Dang, I forgot dude's name."

"Well then, no, it wasn't me. I didn't date anyone over here. Anthony is my homeboy. I use to come and see him."

"Oh, okay. I just thought I remembered seeing you around with that cat who drove the red BMW."

"Nope, wasn't me."

"Oh, okay," he said and I walked out.

I walked outside because I really needed that smoke now. I walked around to the side of the building and lit my cigarette. My mind started to drift to thoughts of Dre as I stared in the direction of his old apartment. The more I thought about him, the hornier I became. I was miserable. I was so horny that my stomach was nauseous, and I knew that I either needed to get some or get home to Chuck. I turned and looked in the window at Charles and he winked at me. That was enough to turn me on.

I saw a man in a 7-Eleven shirt pull up and figured he must be Charles' relief person. I put my cigarette out just as he walked in and I trailed right behind him. Charles motioned for me to come to the back. I followed him and my walk would have indicated that I had other thoughts on my mind. Charles opened the door to the back room, and just as we entered, I pushed him against the wall and started kissing him. I tugged and pulled on his 7-Eleven shirt, trying to get it off. Thankfully he decided to help. I noticed a chair within arm's reach and I pulled it over and pushed Charles down in it. I climbed on top of him as if I were about to give him a lap dance.

I whispered in his ear, "Is the door locked?"

"Yes," he panted.

"Good...now fuck me."

Eagerly, he pulled out his penis and I wasted no time at all to sit down on it. After my previous failed attempts at any good sex, I decided I needed to take control and I did just that. I bounced up and down on him harder and faster, faster and harder. Within minutes, I was able to climax. I didn't think that he had, but I also didn't ask. I squeezed him tightly when the climax was over and got up.

"Damn, baby," he moaned. "Let me get some more. I've never felt a pussy that wet before." I had already started to pull my skirt down.

"Nah. I got what I wanted."

"What?"

I noticed that he was still at attention.

"Thanks and bye." I opened the door and walked out.

Guilt

Monica

Several months passed and Shawn and I had been spending every moment together. I had plenty of time on my hands since I wasn't taking Jade to her therapy appointments anymore. We hadn't spoken since the day of our argument and it bothered me, but she was wrong and I wasn't going to apologize. She owed me an apology and I intended to wait for it, which was fine with me because I could focus on my relationship with Shawn.

Shawn would take me to nice designer stores to shop for clothes. Most of my shopping had been in little alley stores and I never spent more than twenty-five dollars on a pair of shoes. With Shawn, the shoes were no less than $250. He often took me to fine dining restaurants. He bragged that his woman had to be looking good, so he would take me to Saks Fifth Avenue just to buy an outfit for dinner. He had even given me the key to one of his four cars. He had a black convertible that he drove on days he didn't feel like driving his Mercedes. He let me use his Mustang or Mercedes anytime I wanted.

Shawn loved having sex with me and often. He liked to do lots of pretend play and at first it was really fun, but it was getting tiring since I had to make sure that I was doing and saying everything that he wanted me to say. He'd pretend he was a cop and I was a prostitute, or he would be a doctor and I would be a sick patient. One of his favorites was that I was in jail and he was the keeper of the key to my cell. I'd have to give him head to get the key. I didn't always feel like playing the games, especially when I got out of a full day of school, but it made him happy. Since I had never had a man treat me the way he did, I owed it to him to at least keep him happy in that area.

Then one day, everything changed. I skipped my period and I found out that I was pregnant. I sat in our bathroom and watched the blue line turn into a plus sign.

"Shit."

I wasn't ready to be a mother and I didn't want to ruin what I had going with Shawn, so I took out some money from the checking account he had given me access to and scheduled an abortion that next Tuesday morning.

Tuesday seemed to come within hours of taking the home pregnancy test. When I woke up, Shawn was hovering over me, waving a piece of paper in my face.

"What the fuck is this?" he demanded. "What did you get four hundred dollars out the bank for?"

I was barely awake, so it took me a second to figure out what he was saying.

"What?" I asked, holding my face.

"Oh, you can't hear now? I said WHAT THE FUCK DID YOU GET FOUR HUNDRED DOLLARS OUT THE BANK FOR?" Before I could sit up straight, he tossed the paper aside and grabbed my face. He was so close that I could see the fine hairs on his cheekbones.

"Are you fucking somebody and giving them my money?"

"What!? No!" I was in complete disbelief that he was even asking me this.

His tone changed.

"If you don't answer me, I'm going to shove your ass right out that window." He grabbed me by my neck and held it tight. I tried to fight back by swinging my arms and kicking, even though I was terrified. I'd never had a man talk to me like that and I didn't know what was happening. I didn't want to tell him about the baby, so I made up the first thing that fell out of my mouth.

"I wanted to buy you a really nice anniversary present," I quickly answered.

He stood up, looked at me, and turned and walked out the door without saying a word.

It took me a minute to catch my breath, and then I got out of the bed and went into the living room where he was sitting on the couch.

"Shawn, why would you think I was with someone else?" I asked.

"Don't you know how much I love you?"

He didn't bat an eyelash or look my way. He just kept watching TV. I walked over to the couch and sat next to him.

"Shawn, talk to me. Please!"

He continued to ignore me.

"Shawn, look at me." I sat down next to him. "Baby, what's wrong? Why would you even think I would do that?"

"Because that's what my ex-wife used to do to me."

"Ex-wife? You never told me you were married."

"So you're judging me now?"

"No, I'm just saying. We've been together long enough that I would think that I would know that. Do you have kids?"

"No and I don't want any. I hate kids, so don't think getting pregnant will help you keep me because it won't. Do you love me, Monica?"

"Yes, baby, I do."

"Then give me a gift right now. Give me the gift of some head." I was confused as hell with his speed bumping over all of these major topics, but I also didn't want him to freak out anymore.

"Now!" He pulled out his penis as if he was about to use the toilet. I didn't flinch one bit, even though I was scared.

"Yeah, bitch, yeah," he moaned over and over. I gave him head until he was ready and them I swallowed him for the first time. I wanted to show him that I truly cared about him. I also hoped this would make him forget all about the four hundred dollars so that I could get the abortion in two hours. Sure enough, he was satisfied and I was free to leave. I told him I was going out to look for his present. I wasn't sure how I was going to pull this off, but I needed to figure out some way to get him a gift that cost nearly that much and do the abortion. I couldn't figure out both at the time, so I just went to take care of what I had to take care of.

When I arrived at the doctor's office, they had me fill out some forms and watch some really gruesome videos. Then a counselor talked to me about my options. I could keep the baby.

"No, I'm not ready for that and neither is my boyfriend."

I could put the baby up for adoption.

"No, I'm not ready for that and neither is my boyfriend."

I could still go through with the abortion and be prepared to experience some level of guilt. My life had become a game show of bullshit, but I was going to take the abortion for four hundred dollars because that was the option.

"You can keep the baby," the counselor said.

"I could but guilt will last longer than this moment of fear."

"Guilt? Why guilt?"

"Guilt would be placing a baby in my boyfriend's life right now. Guilt would be knowing that I could have taken care of this privately and kept him happy. Guilt would be hating this child for messing up my life and my chance for happiness. That's guilt." I didn't really know where any of that came from, but I knew this was what I had to do.

"Now let's get this over with. I have things to do."

Just as I was about to finish getting undressed and turn my cell phone off, it rang. It was Jade. I couldn't answer it right then because I knew what she would have said, but I figured I better answer so she didn't call the house next. Then Shawn would be asking where I was.

"What?"

"What are you doing?" Jade asked.

"Something for my man," I replied sarcastically. There was a long pause. "So what's up?" I was trying to rush her, but I knew Jade well enough to know something was wrong.

"Nothing, really, it's just that…today is…well…today is, umm . . ." She kept stuttering. I looked at my watch, wondering if I had missed her birthday or something, but I knew I hadn't.

"It's the 4th of November." She paused as if I was supposed to know what that meant.

"Okay, what's November 4th?"

"It's the baby's birthday."

"What baby?"

"The baby I would have had with Dre."

My heart sank when I realized what she was talking about. I stopped in midstream of taking off my pants and leaned against the wall. Tears started to roll down my face and I took a deep breath. "I…I, um…I gotta go."

"You know what, don't even worry about it. You changed,

Mo, and you know what? I don't like it, so fuck you and don't worry about what the fuck I need. I'm fine without Dre and I'll be fine without you." She hung up.

I had to really contain myself from exploding into tears, knowing what I was about to do and that Jade needed me. I stood there for a few minutes, trying to collect myself and follow through with what I needed to do. I was doing this for Shawn. *I'm doing this for him, I'm doing this for him,* I repeated to myself over and over. I kept repeating it until they took me into the room.

When I awoke, I couldn't believe what I had done, but I still knew that I had done the right thing for Shawn, that baby, and me. It took everything in me to drive myself home. I knew Shawn had class all day, so I could rest.

Missing
Jade

November 4th played out like a day from hell. I had decided
that I wasn't going to go anywhere. I was going to keep
my ass in my room, in the bed, and under the covers. I didn't
have much of an appetite and all I wanted to do was talk to Dre.
I knew that he didn't know I'd been pregnant, but I wanted him
to. I needed to find him. Hell, I needed him. With Dre, my life
felt right. Without him, life felt empty, and the love that I felt
with him was so real. More real than anything I had ever known.
Dre didn't believe in social media so there was no way to find
him and he convinced me to get off of social media because he
wanted to keep our love between us. I started thinking of all the
ways I could find him, but I remembered that he'd told me that
his mother changed their names. I wasn't sure if Scott was even
his real last name. I wasn't sure of much of anything.

I decided to go back to school and see if anyone there could help me find him. On my bus ride, I sat there cramping, and with each pain I held my stomach wishing I could feel our child inside of me, but I couldn't. I only felt emptiness. I couldn't handle what was happening to me and being without Dre. I probably should have gone to the records office, but instead, I took the little money I had and stopped at the liquor store.

I went inside and picked up a bottle of vodka. I went back to my apartment and didn't bother to mix the vodka with anything; I just opened the bottle and drank it straight.

I needed to talk to someone so I called Monica, but she was so wrapped up in Shawn that she didn't have time to listen to me. I drank until the bottle was empty, then passed out on the floor in my room. The cold floor felt comforting and peaceful.

Because I hadn't eaten much, the vodka didn't sit well in my stomach. I started to vomit, but I couldn't even move myself to get to the bathroom. I lay there with my face in my own vomit for an unknown amount of time. I couldn't move. I didn't think I wanted to move and maybe a little piece of me hoped that I would just lay there and die. I went in and out of consciousness, only to find more vomit on the floor.

Drunken dreams are like real-life nightmares with sound. In my blacked out state of being drunk, I had a dream that Dre and I were back together on Catalina Island. In my dream, we had a baby girl dressed in all pink with a head full of hair. Her hair had three puffy ponytails with little white barrettes that barely held onto her hair at the ends. She had my green eyes and his grin. She was so beautiful.

She had plump cheeks and a smile that could melt a frozen chocolate bar. Her little ears were pierced with tiny diamond studs. Her little arms were so chubby that she could barely separate them. She had a laugh that lit up a room. Her little hands played in my hair. I could smell her baby scent surrounding me.

Dre had a pair of black swim trunks with blood oozing out of them. I could see his tattoo of praying hands on his arm as he lay in the sand and our daughter, Destiny, patted his chest, and said, "Da-da."

"Hi, Destiny."

She looked over at me and a tiny amount of drool started to come from her mouth. She couldn't walk yet, but she was able to crawl. She climbed over Dre as he lay there in the sand.

"I'm going to let her play in the water."

He picked Destiny up and held her to try to help her walk, but the chubbiness of her thighs barely let her move. So he picked her up and carried her toward the water. He held her and let her feet touch the ocean. I was lying on my side in the sand watching them when suddenly they started to get farther and farther away. I panicked as I watched them leave me. I screamed for him and I screamed for her, but it seemed that the water kept pushing me back and they kept going out further and further.

Dre waved and helped the baby to wave at me. I tried to run after them and I screamed for help, but no one else was there. I looked all around and tried to run out into the water, but I couldn't get out any farther. It seemed like the water was pushing me back against the sand. I looked down at my feet and they started to sink into the ground, which was like quicksand. The harder I fought, the worse it got. I reached and reached for them, but they were soon gone. I cried until the throbbing in my body was too much to bear.

A drunken sloppy mess, I felt someone pick up my limp body and wipe my face off. I opened my eyes, hoping it was Dre.

"Dre, I knew you'd come back for me. I love you, baby."

"I know. I love you too, Jade," the voice said and I blacked out again.

The next morning I awoke in my bed with a cold towel on my head and a large towel underneath my face. Propped up on two pillows, I turned over to see Missy sitting on a bean bag eating noodles.

"Hi. Are you okay?" she asked.

"Yeah, I'm fine."

"You sure?"

"My head hurts, but I think I'm okay. Thanks for everything."

"For what?" she asked as she put a forkful of noodles in her mouth.

"Putting me in bed and cleaning up my mess. I'm really sorry about that."

"Monica been at her boyfriend house and hadn't heard from you so she asked me to check on you."

"And your helped yourself to my noodles?"

"Hey, everybody gotta eat, but I'm about to go."

I was immediately scared. Had Dre come and put me in the bed? Did I imagine that it was him? Was it really him? He had told me he loved me. But who cleaned up the mess? Where was the bottle of vodka?

My mind flooded with questions that I didn't know how to answer. Just then I looked over near my phone and saw a note taped to it.

"Dear Jade, I just came by to drop off a few things of yours that I had. Hope your day turns out okay. Call me when you get up. Anthony."

I reached for the phone.

"You gonna be okay?" Missy asked.

"Yeah, sure." I put the phone in my lap as I tried to sit up and call Anthony.

"Hello?"

"Hey."

"Well, hi there. How's your head?" he asked.

"Oh, I'm fine. My head hurts a little." I laughed. "Listen, thank you for everything. I'm sure I was a mess when you came by."

"It's cool. Just try not to drink so much."

"Anthony, I don't need a lecture from you, too."

"I'm not giving you a lecture, but if more than three people are telling you the same thing, you might want to listen."

"I'll think about it."

"Jade, listen, I know this Dre thing took you by surprise, but how much longer are you going to disrespect yourself to try to prove something to him."

"What are you talking about?"

"If you don't know, I can't tell you."

"Anthony, why do you keep coming around if you're so annoyed with my lifestyle? It's my life. You can stay out of it."

"I would, but somebody has to care about you."

"Fuck you." I hung up.

Dreams

Monica

After the abortion, I went straight home, crawled in the bed, and fell asleep. No sooner had my head hit the pillow than I was out like a light. I was glad that Shawn wasn't home. I don't know how long I was asleep before I started to dream. I could hear a baby crying. I was running through a forest, looking for the baby, but I couldn't find him. When I finally got to a crib, I ripped the blanket back and there was nothing there but a pool of blood. I woke up from that dream in a cold sweat.

The pamphlet said that I might have a bad dream or two for a few days, so I hoped that this was going to be the only one. It wasn't. I managed to go back to sleep and the next dream seemed to pick up where the last one left off, only this time I was tied to a tree in the forest and I could hear the baby crying. I tried to scream for help, but I had no mouth. Then I was talking to the baby and trying to make him stop crying, but I couldn't.

Suddenly, a wolf came toward us. I tried my best to get up, but I was stuck to the tree. One wolf appeared and then another and then another.

Soon we were surrounded and the wolves attacked the baby. All I could do was scream, cry, and watch. When they finished, they all came toward me with blood dripping from their mouths. I ran toward a house and burst in the door. I ran to the bathroom and looked in the mirror. I was the wolf. I woke up, completely covered in sweat.

By that time I was convinced that every time I closed my eyes I was going to have a nightmare, so I went to the bathroom and found some of Shawn's sleeping pills. I took two of them and was finally able to sleep without dreams. That night, Shawn came home and, lucky for me, he wanted to go out for dinner. Despite all I had been through that day, going out to eat put something normal back into my day. Shawn always took me to expensive restaurants so I could get used to dining the right way.

He constantly told me that he couldn't introduce me to his parents until I learned how to eat correctly. The places where we dined were so exclusive and upscale that I would try to drop my Southern accent and use proper grammar so I wouldn't embarrass him. Shawn had great taste in everything.

I stopped wearing my hair natural and had the best weave. It was silky and straight. Even though it was a pain in the ass to keep up, it was beautiful. I went with Shawn weekly to get a manicure and pedicure. I would always let him pick out the color so he couldn't blame me for picking something he didn't like. Even though I didn't like the bright hues, he did. I preferred natural nails, but the fake ones were fine. Eventually all of my old vintage throw-on, free-flowing dresses were gone and everything I owned had a label attached to it. I didn't own any browns and deep mauves.

The waiter came to our table to take our order, but I hadn't really had time to look over the menu.

"Hello and welcome to Oz."

"Bring us a dry white wine," Shawn instructed the waiter, not acknowledging him.

I didn't want to be rude, so I said, "Hi," but by that time the waiter had already left.

"You like the waiter?"

"Shawn, don't be silly."

"I saw the way you looked at him."

I tried to change the subject. "Honey, have you decided what you want for dinner?"

"I may have decided on an ass-whipping if you don't stop flirting. I don't know yet. What are you having?"

"I'm gonna have the pecan crusted salmon."

"Monica, can you please choose better words? And don't ever order anything you can't pronounce. It makes you look stupid."

He smiled.

I knew that I was embarrassing him, so I did what I would always do and attempted to change the subject. "I'll just have what you're having."

He smiled in delight. When the waiter returned, I kept my head down. I also said a quick prayer. *Lord, help me get out of this mess.* I've learned that when you ask, you will receive.

"Babe, I'd like you to meet my parents next weekend."

"You do?"

"Well, I just want you to know how much I care about you. I want to do the best I can for you because you've brought out the best in me. I want a real woman standing by my side for life and I think that woman is you. I see so much in you that makes me want to be a better man. Every day we're together is another day that I want to take care of you, protect you, and provide for you."

He grabbed my hand and looked into my eyes. "Monica, my life is nothing without you. I want you to have something." He caressed my hand. "I want you to have my last name."

He pulled out a tiny red box and opened it. Inside was a beautiful sterling silver ring wrapped in diamonds with a pearl in the center.

I didn't know what to say. I wasn't sure what to say. Something inside of me said to run but what came out of my mouth was, "Yes."

The next day, Shawn wanted us to go to his parents' house and I spent the entire day making sure that everything on my body was perfect, from head to fingernail to toenail. I had never seen a mansion, but I was sure that this was the definition of one. I immediately started to imagine the new lifestyle I would be leading with his family and I was more in love than ever. When we drove up to the house, the yard was manicured with all types of flowers and trees that I had never seen before. Various shades of greens, browns, and reds covered the ground. Shawn said his mother liked birds and there were hummingbird pods hanging from several of the trees. When we went up to the beautiful glass door, I felt like Cinderella who was about to meet the king and queen.

Along the rail to the house were orange blooming flowers that lead to the sprawling double doors. We walked up the stone entry and my heart raced inside of my chest. I knew how important this was to him. As soon as we entered, I could see the beautiful décor that made the space look like a model home. His mother came right up to me and gave me a big hug as if she had known me all her life.

"Oh, hello, Monica. I've heard so much about you."

She looked at me with skepticism in her eyes. I made sure

that I was conscientious of my grammar and word choice so Shawn would be proud of me.

"Good afternoon, Mrs. Devereaux. It is a pleasure to meet you." I shook her hand lightly. "I hope that you have heard how much I adore your son. Thank you for raising such a good man."

"Oh dear, a girl after my own heart! Finally, a girl that sees my perfect baby. Not like that dreadful Allison."

"Mother, we're still friends."

That was news to me, but I didn't dare make any kind of expression to show my surprise. I focused on being perfect all the way through our meal. I had even researched the right ways to eat a formal dinner and I was glad I did because it was a full course affair with a table setting just like I'd learned about. There was a fork and a spoon for everything. I did everything correctly and made all the right moves. I could get used to this.

After dinner was over, Shawn's father took him outside to show him the paint job on his new '67 Porsche. His mother took me outside. Initially she'd told me she wanted to show me around her garden. She took me out all right. Just as we walked past the door where I was able to see Shawn, she whirled around like the devil had possessed her and looked me directly in my eyes.

"So Monica, I'd ask you to tell me about yourself, but I know that there's nothing fantastic about you that you can tell me. You're poor and you see my son as a paycheck. Well I would rather my son be interested in a woman with more than just a pretty face and a big ass, but I'm sure I won't be seeing you around too much longer. He'll never marry the stupid one. You'll be lucky to be his mistress." She showed no emotion and simply walked away.

I had never been confronted by anyone that way and I couldn't think of what to say back to her. I just stood there, shocked as hell that this woman would even say something like that to me. I walked in the house and looked for Shawn but I couldn't find him. I sat in the living room until he finally reappeared.

The Whistling Fornication
Jade

Love is one hell of a drug, similar to cocaine or crack I assumed. I'd never tried either, but somehow I could relate to the nostalgic feeling that people must have when they experience that type of high. I'd heard that many people function on cocaine just fine. Crack is the kind of overpowering drug that takes control of everything inside of you. You can't do anything but think about the next time you'll get it. To fight addiction, you have to make an effort every moment of the day not to think about the next hit. I couldn't figure out if Dre was crack or cocaine, but I knew that I needed to fight my addiction to him.

Chuck was pleasing Nita, but Chuck didn't do anything for me. I needed the touch, the scent, the kisses, the shiver in my spine. I couldn't buy that in a store. I wasn't sure how to fight my addiction of wanting Dre to make love to me one more time. I wanted him inside me just once more. I just didn't know how to find him.

To start truly fighting my addiction to Dre, I did what they do in rehab. I gave myself lower doses of love by finding and fucking all the wrong men. It all got worse after November 4th.

I was in a tailspin over the date of the baby and felt like I needed to talk to someone.

I didn't have insurance and I wasn't in school any longer, so I couldn't go back to Dr. Wheeler. One of my friends told me about students who need hours for their psych degrees and were offering free counseling, so I figured, why not.

I went to the on-campus office and met Jan Silverman. She was very sharp and seemed intensely calm, which was kind of weird considering she was just a few years older than me.

"Tell me, Jade, how do you feel about the men you've been with?" Jan asked.

"I don't."

"You don't have feelings for the men you sleep with?"

"Hell no."

"When you're having sex with them, what's going through your mind?"

"Not much, really. Well, not all the time. Most times I think about the alphabet."

"The alphabet?"

"Yeah, I want to see where the guy will fit."

"I don't know what you mean by that."

"See, I give all my lovers nicknames. Names that help me keep track of them."

"Why do you want to keep track of them?"

"Because I need something to do with my mind besides masturbating and thinking about Dre."

"Tell me about the men in the alphabet. Do you love them?"

"Hell no."

"Do they love you?"

"Some of them, yes. Most times, I don't ask."

"How does that make you feel? If they love you?"

"I don't know. Empty, I guess."

"Why is that?"

"Because Dre is the only one who's ever made me full inside."

"And the other men make you feel empty."

I took in a deep breath, thinking about the number of men I had slept with.

"Well, you know many of them, but I don't think I told you about Gino the Albino. He was a thirty-five-year-old virgin. I fucked him just because of the way he looked. I wanted him to feel special. Ben the Blanket didn't call me anymore and neither did Curtis the Cutie or Charles the Cashier. Now, Don the Doorman is still cool. We would fuck occasionally. I like going to celebrity parties and he knows I won't get him in trouble. Ed the Eagle is an annoying asshole with a short fat dick. I never called him again. Oh, but Fred the Freelancer, I have lots of fun with him. He takes pictures of me naked and they always come out so good if I fuck him after the photos. Henry the Hermit was smart and he has the most interesting conversations but he's a boring lover so maybe I shouldn't count him. Max the Magnum was a load of fun. He could go longer than just about anybody, but I enjoyed Nick the Nasty the most. He likes to be tied up. Did I ever tell you about Willie the Weed-Man?"

"No."

"Well, Willie the Weed-Man smokes too much weed. I don't mind a little weed, but Willie smoked all day. Victor the Mixer was a DJ. He always had the best songs lined up for our nights together. I kind of liked him."

"Can you count them all?"

"Well, I'm drawing a blank on some of them, but I think I've almost made it through the entire alphabet."

"Jade, what's the purpose of that?"

"To fuck the pain away. What else?"

"Does the pain get better?"

I stood up and walked toward a small waterfall fountain on a table nearby.

"Yes. Each of them makes me feel a little bit closer to Dre."

"I'd like to give you a suggestion."

"More suggestions?"

"I'd like you to go back to the last place you saw Dre and write a letter to him."

"For what? I don't know where he is."

"Just write it and tell him how you feel."

Ding!

The bell that signaled the end of my session chimed three times.

"And in our next session, let's talk about the letter. I'm sorry, but that's our time for today, Jade. I'll see you again next month."

"Maybe." I laughed and walked out, slamming the door.

I rode the bus to the beach to just sit and think. Something about the sound of the water crashing against the shore was calming. I sat and thought about the letter idea. It wasn't a bad idea, I just didn't know if I really could write it. I sat there watching the waves crash and thinking about how I felt telling Jan about that long list of lovers. I sounded stupid and I didn't like that the list was the only thing I had going in life right now. After a few hours, sunset was approaching. I headed home. Just as I arrived, I remembered that there was a party that night. I hadn't planned to attend, but after my day that seemed like a great idea. I went into my closet and laid out my red mini dress that was super sexy and tight, and my black stiletto strap-ups that made me about three inches taller. I was feeling a bit dark, so I had chosen all of my darker shades for makeup. I hadn't put my dress on yet when the doorbell rang. I strolled to the door with my vodka in hand dressed in nothing but my black panties and bra from Frederick's.

Dre had turned me onto Frederick's. Everything I had looked like I was about to do an amateur pole dance. As I made my way to the door, there was a part of me that always hoped it was Dre, but of course it never was. If that moment ever did come, I hoped I'd be wearing this exact outfit, but I knew it was only Willie the Weed-Man. Willie was the cool dude that I could kick it with and he didn't care about having any kind of relationship with me, so he was exempt from being roped into my twisted world. He had become my homeboy and anytime I wanted to just have a good time, I could call him. I also knew that I could count on him to roll me a clean joint with no additives or preservatives. I turned on some reggae music and we blazed up. The main reason I liked hanging around him was because he made me laugh and I enjoyed smoking weed with him.

"Hey, what's up?" I walked away, allowing the door to swing open and he came in.

"What's up, sexy? You about to have company or something?" he asked.

"No, I'm going to James' NFL draft party," I replied. James the Jock was celebrating his NFL draft status and his birthday, and I had heard he was going to be throwing a hell of a party.

"Oh, okay. He had told me about that. My bad, I totally forgot." Willie made his way to the couch and sat down. He pulled a small baggie out of his right pocket and used my hardcover coffee table book to start rolling a joint. I turned the music down and looked at the clock. It was 9:34. The party started at around eleven, so I still had plenty of time to get high and low.

"Want to come with me?" I asked as I veered my head around the corner from my room.

"Nah, you know I don't go to that kind of stuff. Hey, did you cook today?"

"I have some leftover shrimp fried rice from Mr. Lo Mein's. You can have it."

"Cool. How much longer before you ready to go?" he asked.

"I'm almost ready. I just have to put my mascara and dress on."

"You gonna hit this joint with me since you almost ready?" he asked.

"But of course," I replied in a terrible British accent. "Hold on, let me put a towel under the door." I grabbed a towel from the cabinet and put a little water on it. With my comb in my mouth, I ran over to the door and placed it at the base. Standing there, still in bra and panties, I turned to Willie. "Blow me a shotgun."

He motioned for me to come to him. He was sitting on the couch and I sat on the table in front of him. I had to step over his legs to get to a spot on the table.

"Enjoy," he said as he leaned in toward me, turned the joint around, and gently blew a puff of smoke toward my face. I used my hands to capture the smoke and inhaled deeply. Willie took a puff and another puff, then passed the joint to me.

The best part about getting high was those first two puffs that give you the anticipation of satisfaction to come. Puff, puff, pass…it was my turn again.

Since I wasn't an avid smoker, it only took about two turns and I would be high as three kites, but I didn't know it. Puff, puff, pass. Willie was the best at smoking weed. I loved it when he would make the smoke curl over the top of his lip. Damn, his lip was kind of sexy. Hmm…I had never really looked at Willie like that until that moment, but—puff, puff, pass—damn his skin was smooth as milk chocolate. Willie the Weed-Man was looking quite delicious.

I think he started to notice that I was looking at him in a

more than "we cool" way. By that time we had smoked our perfectly rolled joint down to what's typically called a roach, and it was time to get the tweezers.

"I'll be right back. We need some tweezers. I'll get them." I stood up. I should have stopped while I was ahead and still somewhat coherent. I stumbled my way to the bathroom to look for tweezers. Since there were more than two hallways in my vision, I ran straight into the wall. Then it was ping-pong, back and forth, all the way down the hall to the bathroom. I couldn't find the tweezers because I didn't know where to look, so I made my way back up front. Willie the Weed-Man had left. I didn't even hear the door shut. Knowing Willie, he probably needed to make a run. I hoped he would come back because now I was horny and no one was around.

There was a knock at the door and I assumed it was Willie. Maybe he had forgotten something. I was pleasantly surprised to find that it was Anthony.

"What up!" I was so excited to see him.

"Hey, Jade…are you high?" He laughed.

"Am I hot?"

"I said, are you high?"

"What? Am I hungry?" I was laughing hysterically. He came in the door and closed it behind him. "Oh wait, you asked me if I was horny." I couldn't stop laughing.

"I actually got the answer to my question about a minute ago." He sat down on the couch and leaned back with his legs spread wide open. I stood by the door.

"Anthony, who thought of the word tweezers? What's a tweeze? You know somebody high came up with that word." I burst into more laughter. "I mean, why isn't it called a fucker? I mean a plucker? How did they go from plucker to tweezer?" And I burst out laughing again.

"Can you get dressed for the party or are you too high to go?"
he asked while I peeled myself from the wall and headed toward
the couch. I was about to walk past him when he grabbed my
hips and I felt my entire body come close to him. Still dressed in
just my panties and bra, I noticed that he was using his teeth to
pull on my panties. I grabbed the back of his head and pressed
it toward Nita to give him a proper introduction. Nita blew him
a shotgun of her scent, intoxicating to every man that has ever
had a whiff of her. Horny as a hooker on the fifteenth of the
month, I put my leg up on the couch and leaned in toward him.
He put his hand on the back of my thigh and the other hand
pulled my black satin panties down toward the floor. For a split
second, I had to question what I was about to do. Anthony was
my friend. This might not have been such a good idea, but by
that time I could feel Nita warming my leg. He moved the table
back and straightened my legs so that he could take my panties
off. I helped by stepping out of them.

My heart began to beat faster. Then it seemed as if I could
hear my heart beating. The blood in my veins boiled and
pulsated to my head, giving me a lightheaded feeling. I found
myself wanting to lick his chocolate skin, so I did. His smooth
chest was the perfect place to glide my tongue, going up his
neck. I placed his face in my hands and looked right through
him. His lips called for me to kiss them and so I did. I cupped
his rounded face, feeling tickled by his after-five shadow of
a beard. I moved my tongue down his neck and to his chest.
As I licked his muscular chest, I captured his masculine scent.
I wasn't sure what the cologne was, but it sure as hell wasn't
Nautica, and that helped keep my mind off Dre and allowed me
to enjoy the moment. He used his hands to peek underneath
my bra and let the twins out to play with them. He stretched his
legs out on the table and once my panties were off, he pulled me

up on the couch. I stood there and allowed him to maneuver my legs. I placed one on top of the couch and rested the other on his shoulder. With that, I watched his tongue leave his lips in the shape of the letter "U." He licked and licked, putting me into pure ecstasy.

I was in a blissful rapture of sensual passion, feeling him between my legs. I allowed my head to lean back, letting out a sigh of relief that someone finally had pleased Nita and me. The panting of my breath got stronger and heavier the more pleasure he gave to Nita until I let out a scream that could have been heard by every human and animal in a twenty-mile radius. That wasn't enough. Nita hadn't had enough and truthfully, neither had I. He used two of his fingers to take a sample of Nita's flow and allowed me to taste. I enjoyed the taste of Nita on his fingertips. I grabbed his head and pressed him closer to me.

Nearly ten minutes went by and Anthony was showing no signs of wanting to stop. It was as if he was hungry and I was going to be his last meal. Over and over, he played with me and teased me. The anticipation of Nita meeting his gentleman overwhelmed me. I decided that I would hold back the second orgasm for the introduction. The entire time I had my eyes closed, and when I opened them all I could see were the waves on the top of his head and it reminded me of Dre. It was the first time in that moment that I had thought about Dre at all. I began to get confused and mixed up about what was going on. When I couldn't hold it back anymore, I let out a much needed scream.

"Ahh...Ahh...ANDRE!"

There's nothing better than mentioning another man's name to fuck up a perfectly close orgasm. He stopped and looked at me.

"What? Did you just call me Dre?"

I was about three seconds from climaxing and he stopped.

"What difference does it make?"

I could see his manhood was at full attention and I had totally missed when Anthony exposed him and wrapped him up. Nita was so open that I was ready to slide down on top of him. Sure, I fucked up by saying another man's name, but I didn't care. All I needed was to finish the moment. Just as I reached the tip, he grabbed my arms and moved me off of him. Like a flimsy doll, he placed me on a nearby cushion.

"Okay, okay," he said as he adjusted himself, pulled the condom off, and buttoned his pants up.

"Anthony, I'm—"

Before I could finish, he raised his hand and waved me off. He had a sad look on his face that I had never seen before and I felt like I had hurt his feelings. I reached down to pick up my panties. I pulled on my underwear and made my way to the bathroom.

There, I caught a glimpse of my face in the mirror. My makeup had smeared from the sweating and my eyes could barely be seen. I reached for my lipstick and just as I was about to put it on, I could feel someone staring at me. I looked up and saw Anthony standing in the doorway.

"He really hurt you, didn't he?" Anthony said. The piercing look that I gave him told him that I was pissed and annoyed.

"What?" I asked, just to make sure that I'd heard right.

"He hurt you," he said again.

Without thinking, I picked up my hairbrush and threw it at him.

"Who the fuck are you, asking me any fucking thing? You can get the fuck out." I marched toward him, pushed him out of the bathroom, and slammed the door in his face.

Who was I? What had Dre done to me?

My heart was beating so fast that I thought I was having a heart attack.

My rapid heart rate turned to racing in my mind as I thought of Dre. I was addicted to him. I needed him and wanted him. I missed his touch and so far I hadn't found a good enough replacement. I stumbled to the toilet, slammed the lid down, and sat on top. My eyes stared off into space and I dropped my head down and cried. Anthony opened the door and came over to me. His initial touch startled me, but it was comforting. The same comfort I felt the day that Dre left me and Anthony was there for me. He raised me up off the toilet the same way he lifted me before I collapsed in the hall the day Dre left.

"He never deserved you," Anthony said as he turned me around and welcomed me into his embrace. His arms surrounded me and for the first time in a long time, I felt...I felt...safe. Anthony leaned his chin on top of my head and his chest felt warm and peaceful.

"I loved him. I loved him so much," I cried.

"I know, baby girl—"

I shoved him away from me and shot him the most evil look.

"DON'T SAY THAT! DON'T CALL ME THAT. I'M NOT YOUR BABY GIRL, I'M NOT HIS BABY GIRL. I'M JUST ME! I'M JUST JADE!"

I heard the phone ring, but I didn't have the energy to get it, the first time in a long time that the ringing phone didn't send me into a mad dash. I needed to let go in this moment. I didn't need to run to anyone or anything. I was right where I needed to be. I fell to the floor on my knees and all I could do was rock back and forth. My hyperventilating turned to a full-on release cry.

Anthony bent down to hold me, but I resisted him. The more I resisted, the tighter he held on.

"Anthony, I'm so sorry. I'm so, so sorry," I moaned.

"You don't have to be. You don't have to ever apologize to me," he said. I could feel his hands on my back.

"Why did he leave? Why couldn't he just say goodbye to me? I don't understand. I don't know what I did wrong. I mean, I tried to do everything right. I gave him everything. I gave him all of me and he just threw it away. I just don't understand," I cried. "Maybe I gave too much too soon. "

"Maybe some things aren't meant for us to understand," Anthony calmly said.

"Who's Shelly?" I asked.

"I don't know. Should I?"

"That day, you told me that he and Shelly got back together. Who's Shelly?" I could only wonder what was so special about her. Why wasn't I the Cinderella that he was looking for? He was certainly my Prince Charming. He was everything that I ever wanted in a man. He swept me off my feet and made me feel like Cinderella.

"I honestly don't know. I just happened to be coming down the hall that night and I saw him. But Jade, it doesn't matter who she is. What matters is who you are. You're beautiful. You're stronger than you know. It doesn't matter who Shelly is or even where Dre is. I'm here for you. I'm here to hold you."

"What did she look like?" I asked.

"I don't remember," he said, shaking his head.

"Was she black, was she white, was she short, was she tall, what?"

"Look, I don't wanna play this game," he said. "I don't know. I'm not gonna try to remember so that every tall, white, blonde woman you see you try to kill because you think she took something from you. Hell, there are enough black women mad at white women for no reason."

"SHE WAS WHITE?"

"I'm not doing this. You're worried about the wrong thing. It doesn't matter what she looks like. If that's who he wanted then that's who he wanted. Ain't shit you or Cinderella can do about it."

He got up and left the bathroom. The blood in my veins began to boil. I held my breath, wanting to scream. I clenched my teeth, closed my eyes, and felt every muscle in my body get tense. I stood up, slammed the bathroom door, and let out a scream that could be heard across Los Angeles.

Before I knew it, I began to obliterate my bathroom. I ripped the shower curtain off the hanger and threw it against the wall. I pulled all of my hair products off the shelves and threw them against the wall. I was my own personal pitcher and everything in my hand was a baseball. I threw the soap, shampoo, conditioner, towel, shower gel, and lotion. Everything I touched went up against a wall. I went over to the sink and completely pulled off everything on top of it—my toothbrush, toothpaste, hair spray, curling irons, deodorant, hairpins, lipstick, foot creams. Even the toilet paper wasn't safe from my wrath. Everything I could put my hands on, I squashed, flattened, or squeezed.

Exhausted, I paused with my handheld blow-dryer in my hand and looked in the mirror at myself. "A white woman? Really, Dre? Really?" I paused for a moment and smashed the blow-dryer into the mirror. I reared myself back as the glass shattered all over the sink. I didn't care. I picked up the toilet plunger and hacked away at the toilet and the cabinets behind me. I hit and smacked so much that the top of the toilet seat began to chip. I screamed. "THAT MOTHERFUCKER LEFT ME! SON OF A BITCH LEFT ME...MOTHERFUCKER!"

I hammered away on the sink. The plastic part flew off the end of the plunger and all that remained was the handle. Like a batter going for a world record of hits, I whacked away at the sink until the handle broke.

I stopped to catch my breath, realizing what I had done. I could feel blood on my face, but I didn't try to wipe it off and I didn't care. I looked around the bathroom. This was a lot worse than the feathers.

I opened the door to the bathroom and cried, "Anthony! Anthony! Anthony, help me!"

Anthony was gone. I was all alone. Maybe he was right. Fuck that Cinderella shit.

I went to the kitchen, grabbed my bottle of vodka, and drank it straight. I stumbled my way over to the couch and plopped down. The vodka hadn't hit me yet, so I decided to fire up the second joint that Willie had left on the table.

Breathe.

Breathe.

Breathe.

Return to Catalina
Jade

I needed to escape. Nearly two years had passed since my bathroom explosion and seeing Dr. Silverman was really helping. She kept me on as a patient even after she graduated and I hadn't paid her.

"Jade, the work you've done over the past two years has been great. You've made some great strides. When you first came to me, you couldn't do anything on your own. Now you're working and taking a class. I'm proud of you. What are you doing to celebrate your birthday this year?"

"I'm thinking about going back to Catalina"

Somewhere between the real world and "Dre-still-loves-me" world was a blur of pain. I hadn't told her that sometimes I still sprayed his cologne on my pillow at night to masturbate to. As time passed, I came to realize that while there was something nostalgic about the cologne alone, there was also a component missing: Dre's natural scent. It wasn't the cologne; it was how it smelled against him. It was that mixture that would bring me from dreamland into reality as his scent began to wash away from my pillow, my sheets, and, hopefully, my soul. I still had the box of things that Dre and I had shared together.

It was tucked neatly in the corner of my closet. I threatened to break my roommate's arms if she touched it and lied to myself about keeping it to remind myself of how he had dogged me out. The truth was I was keeping the box because it was all I had left of him. The thought that I would never see Dre again still didn't seem real to me, yet almost two years had passed since I had seen or heard from him.

In that time, I really had grown tired of pissing on every man I met and had fucked the alphabet two times over. There was no point to it. I tried to change things by going by astrological signs, a useless revenge tactic that wasn't working. Nothing worked, most likely because I knew that they all were nothing more than failed attempts for me to mentally get back at Dre. It was time for me to truly heal and move on, except I wasn't sure of how to do that. Going back to Catalina might help. I needed to do this for myself and by myself.

The next morning, I rode the ferry over to Catalina Island. I stood in the same place on the edge of the ferry where Dre and I had stood. I remembered the way his arms felt around my waist, the way he would trail his fingertips along the nape of my neck and tickle my hair, and I envisioned his eyes and smile. As I deeply inhaled the salty smell of the ocean, I searched the air for his scent, knowing that it wouldn't come, but I was unable to stop searching. I watched the couples blissfully in love and wondered if anyone knew I was alone. It was unusually crowded, but I noticed a couple staring at me with that same pitying look on their faces that I saw every time I went out to eat alone or to a movie and asked for one ticket.

"Yes, I'm alone," I snapped. At the same time I realized they probably now thought I was alone because I was crazy. I walked to the other side of the boat until the ride was over.

Part of me was embarrassed to be standing there by myself and then I remembered what my therapist said. She told me to be proud of me and learn how to love being with just me. I didn't know what she meant at the time, but now that I was standing here alone I knew I had to stand tall and exude confidence. My therapist also suggested that I do little things by myself that Dre and I used to do together and make new memories alone.

As the ferry pulled up to the dock, I thought back to the moment Dre had stood there, smiling as he held out his hand to help me off the ferry. He treated me like Cinderella and, delusional, I'd loved every minute of it. I grabbed the straps and held my backpack securely against my back, then walked calmly in the same pattern we had before, inhaling the air. As I exhaled, I imagined I was releasing parts of Dre and leaving him on that island. I could actually feel myself letting go.

I arrived at the hotel room with my head held high, checked myself in, and requested the same room that Dre and I had before, but it was already taken. As I stood gazing into the mirrored glass of the elevator door, waiting for it to open, I thought about Dre so hard that for a moment I thought I saw him standing there behind me.

The ping of the elevator door opening rescued me and I stepped in, remembering the slight push that Dre had given me just before he spun me around and pressed me up against the mirrored walls. I remembered watching my breath fog up the glass as he pressed up against me. He had lifted my shirt, exposing my cold nipples against the glass. I remembered feeling his other hand going inside my panties. I opened my eyes slightly and recalled watching the floor numbers go by, feeling lightheaded and euphoric from his touch as the elevator went higher. I had spread my legs to allow his fingers to enter Nita. I remembered feeling his kiss on my neck, the slight bite that sent chills down my spine. Removing his hand from my breast to the back of my neck, he had grabbed the back of my hair and pulled it slightly—just enough to let me know he was in command.

He had tilted my head back and my mouth had opened slightly to allow his tongue entry. He had licked my tongue and my teeth, then grabbed my tongue with his teeth and gently bit down. The pain was erotic.

The elevator had chimed again, signaling that we were going to stop. I remembered standing there, unable to move as Dre swung me around by my waist. When he'd realized that no one was waiting on the other side of the elevator doors, he had pushed me back against the wall, lifted my shirt again, and kissed me. By the time the doors shut, he was on his knees pleasuring Nita's flower bud.

As the elevator continued toward the fifteenth floor, he had licked and sucked Nita for the nearly five floors. I remembered being so thankful that the elevator hadn't stopped along the way. These thoughts raged through my mind as if they were happening in the present while Nita tried to relive the feeling as well. As I watched the elevator move from the fifteenth floor to the sixteenth, I remembered why I was here now and the feeling left just as quickly as it had come.

I exited on the sixteenth floor and looked up at the sign to see which direction I should go to find room 1605. When I got inside, I looked around. It was exactly as I remembered. I tossed my bag on the bed and walked onto the balcony as I had before. Back then, I'd opened the door to capture the breeze, but as I leaned over the balcony, Dre had come up behind me and made love to me from the back. His stroke that night was particularly long and slow. He teased me by giving me half, all, a third, and then all of him. We drank and smoked a joint and the contraband increased the euphoric feeling of floating while making love.

It was hard for me to focus on the fact that I was here to heal myself. It dawned on me at that moment how frequently we made love and that it was the lovemaking I was finding so hard to accept losing. I realized that here I was, birthday, still thinking about a man I hadn't seen or heard from in nearly two years.

I meant to go out to eat, but somehow I never left the room other than to get a bucket of ice. I put my forty-two-proof bottle of Captain Morgan's Parrot Bay Rum with natural pineapple flavor on ice and drank it straight, all 750 milliliters. The last thing I remember was sitting in the chair on the balcony.

The next morning, I headed out to the beach for a jog. As I made my way down in my green shorts, yellow tank top, and orange hair tie, I noticed a large group of people gathered on the beach.

As I neared, I saw a white woman with short, bouncy, blonde hair walking down the beach. The groom was black. His family was on one side and hers was on the other. Then I saw Anthony. What was he doing here and why hadn't he told me he would be in Catalina this weekend? I followed the train of the bride's dress up the sand and past her to see the groom.

Shit.

Motherfucker.

It was Dre!

I stopped jogging as my mouth hung open. He was so enraptured by her walking toward him that he didn't even see me. I chuckled. I was far enough away that I was able to catch a spot on the beach and watch them exchange their vows—until I felt my blood curdle in my veins. My mind churned with vicious thoughts.

He left me for an ugly bitch. Ain't this some shit? This motherfucker left me for a skinny, ugly bitch. He left this juicy pussy for that? Why? It ain't the dick sucking 'cause I could put some white women out of business.

I got up and walked over to the bar, sat down, and asked for a bottle of water from the waiter.

"You part of the wedding?" he asked.

"Yes I am," I answered calmly.

"Well, looks like you're missing it." He smirked.

"Let's just say I'm not fond of my brother marrying a white woman, but I guess I'll have to deal with it."

"That's a poor reason. That's your brother. Is that why you're not in the wedding?" he asked, puzzled.

He passed me a bottle of water.

"Well, yes and no. I'm an interior decorator and my brother wanted me to set up their suite but I forgot the room number. I was trying to get down here before they started so I could ask, but I guess I'm too late," I said nonchalantly and took several long gulps of water.

"Well, what are you going to do?"

"Not sure. Apologize, I guess." I laughed. "My brother is going to kill me. I just don't remember what room they have."

He punched a few keys on the computer.

"It's twelve 69," he answered, laughing. "You didn't get that from me."

I frowned.

"You're right, I need to be more accepting. Thanks for the room number. My brother's going to die when he sees what I have planned."

"Have fun." He smiled.

I sighed with resignation. "Oh, I will."

I firmly believed that every human being has the ability to kill. My mother taught me that. Otherwise, God wouldn't have put it into our commandments. There's something that can make each and every one of us capable of killing. I was there. I had snapped and at this point, there was no reason to turn back. I might as well go all the way.

I snuck into their room. I left two drinks for them on the table with a note of congrats and then I waited three hours. They walked in, ready to make love. The stupid bitch got all excited about how beautiful the room was. Candles, rose petals, a warm bath filled with more petals while the entire room smelled of lavender. I had placed enough Unisom in their drinks to knock them both out for hours. When they awoke, they were both handcuffed to the bed, naked with duct tape over their mouths. I made sure to put the room temperature at fifty-nine degrees. That was the lowest setting the thermostat allowed and I prayed it would be cold enough. I sat in a chair directly beside the bed.

"Hi, baby," I greeted Dre, and smiled. The duct tape over his mouth didn't allow him to speak. He didn't look so happy. He actually looked scared. I didn't want him to be scared. I wanted him to be happy to see me.

"Have you missed me, baby?" I asked. "Wait! Don't answer that. I know you have, because I have really, really missed you. I've missed you so much that I've had to go to a therapist to get over you. See, she advised that I come back to the last place we were and try to release you in my mind. And while I really wanted to do that, I think that seeing you here has really sent me over the edge. Just a little bit. Actually, I'm so far over it now that there's no point in turning back, is there? So, let me just give you a rundown of how this is going to go."

I took a sip of my Crown Royal.

"First, I'm going to take what is mine. I've been feenin' for it since the day you left. After we make love over and over and over again, I'm going to let your new wife smell my pussy because I want that to be the last thing she smells. Have you ever been up close and personal, watching someone fuck? Because if you haven't, this is going to be good!" I laughed and took another sip of my drink. "By the time they get to the two of you, I'll be long gone! I'll be in the forest of Barbados or maybe the polar caps of Antarctica. Somewhere where I can sit back and smile every day knowing that the two of you are scared to death that I just might show up again. But let's just ask Shelly if she's going to stay with you if you have no dick, Dre."

I turned and looked at Shelly. Somehow the fear in her eyes was making me horny.

"I've thought about peeling your skin off, but that might be too morbid and twisted. What do you think, Dre?" I asked. A tear began to roll down his eye. I walked over to him to see if it was real.

"Are you crying?" I asked. "You punk ass bitch!" I laughed, raised my arm, and swung, connecting with his face as hard as I could. I slapped him so hard more tears welled up. "You're crying!" I burst out laughing. "Tears? Now? DO YOU KNOW HOW MANY TEARS I SHED OVER YOU? DO YOU? You don't, do you? Well, let me just tell you. Four hundred eighty-five thousand seven hundred twenty-five...that's when I stopped counting how many times I cried over you, Dre. I loved you and I still do."

I leaned in close and licked his face where the tears had flowed.

"And baby, I have to be honest with you. I'm still a little bitter." I kissed the top of his head. He cried harder and I felt bad as he repeatedly shook his head. He was mumbling so much that I finally asked, "Do you have something to say?" He nodded and I ripped the tape off his mouth.

He stuttered so hard he was barely able to put words together, but he finally managed to say, "I'm sorry."

I looked at Dre and could see something in his eyes. What was that? Sincerity? My heart empathized with him for about three seconds. I knew that he was being honest and that there was some strange but irreversible reason that he wasn't with me. I pointed the knife directly at his heart.

"Do you remember the last thing you said to me?" He shook his head.

"You said, 'You know I love you, right?' And you left me, Dre. You left me. So I will ask you one question. Did you ever love me?"

I pressed the blade closer to his heart, piercing the skin. As I watched the warm blood slowly progress down his chest, I wanted to say something intensely mean or callous. Something that would let him know how much I truly hated him for what he had done to me, but I could only say one thing.

"I love you, Dre," I said and pierced his heart with the blade. I pushed it in as hard as I could. I heard cracking and a click-crinkling sound. I pulled the knife from his chest and saw the blood on my hands. Shelly began to scream and shake violently. I backed away from Dre's body, stood, turned, and collapsed on the floor.

I awoke to the sound of banging at the door. I was lying on the floor beside the bed. I looked down at my hand.

It was clean. There was no blood.

I picked myself up off the floor, but gravity was weighing heavily on my head. I groaned, afraid to turn around. I gradually pulled myself up, using the bed as a crutch and slowly looked around at the chair, the bed. No one was there. No Dre, no Shelly. The banging continued at the door. I walked slowly toward the door feeling a heavy pain in my head. I opened the door and it was Anthony. He looked extremely concerned, and I was confused as to how he found me.

"Hi," he said somberly. He walked in and planted a small kiss on my cheek. "Wow, you smell like the bottom of a bottle."

I closed the door and turned to look at him. He came in and stood there calmly.

"Listen, I really need to talk to you," he began, then stopped as he got a better look at me. "Are you okay?"

Slowly I turned and placed my hand over my head. "Yeah, I just...I don't know. I think I had the craziest dream ever."

"What? About Dre again?" Annoyance flashed across his handsome face.

"No, it was just one of those weird things." I didn't have the heart to tell him about the dream.

"What are you doing here? How did you find me?"

"Your roommate told me where you were."

"Why?" He came over to me and put his arms around me, trying to hold me, but I pushed him away.

"What is it?" He just stood there with his head down and shook his head.

"Anthony, what's up? Is everything okay?"

He looked at me and pulled me closer to him.

"It's your mother. She had a heart attack."

"What?"

"And Tracy is in the hospital. Her husband beat her...badly. She may not make it. Your mom had a heart attack after seeing Tracy in the hospital."

I stood there in confusion. What was he saying? It was almost as if he was speaking another language. I put my hand over my mouth and held my breath.

"I'm sorry. Can you say that one more time?" I mumbled through my hand.

"Never mind." I placed my hand on my head and felt dizzy.

Before I could say another word, Anthony pulled me close and held me in his arms. I could feel my knees begin to give way and my heart beat very fast as if I were about to have a heart attack as well. I wanted to vomit, I felt so bad. I ran to the bathroom and leaned over the toilet just in time. Anthony walked up behind me and rubbed my back while I threw up. It occurred to me that I needed to get home and fast. I started to panic.

As the thought entered my mind, Anthony solved the problem for me. "I bought you a ticket to go home. It leaves this afternoon. I figured that would give you time to get back and get packed. If you want me to go with you, I will."

My body felt numb. I just wanted to sit down and pretend that he hadn't said any of those words. When my body gave me a break from vomiting, I sat beside the tub and cried while Anthony packed my things. When he finished, he came and sat on the bathroom floor beside me. I cried and he just held me. "We need to get going." He calmly picked me up off the floor. Anthony took care of everything. He got me checked out of the hotel and onto the next ferry back to LA. The entire time all of that was happening, I never thought about Dre. I could only think about my mother and what I was in store for. Life suddenly seemed too complex. I wanted to stop and pretend that none of this was happening, but I couldn't make it stop.

When we arrived back in LA, Anthony helped me get to the airport just in time for my flight.

"I'm here for you," he said. "Just call me." I was going to turn and walk onto the boarding bridge, but instead I turned and ran to him.

"Everything is going to be alright, Jade," he whispered in my ear.

I held him tighter and whispered, "Thank you. I'll call you as soon as I land." I walked toward my gate, turned around, and looked back at Anthony standing there, watching me.

I sat in a window seat so I could try to hide my pain from the chipper chick sitting next to me.

"Hey, where ya headed?" she gleefully asked.

"My mother had a heart attack after seeing my sister's badly beaten body. You got anymore fucking questions 'cause I ain't got shit to say."

Chipper chick turned away.

As the plane pulled away, my mind struggled with going home. My heart was filled with so much confusion that it felt like it was bursting out of me. The ride was long and I thought about the last time I had talked to my mother and my sister. Anthony said Mr. Gregory didn't give him any details about what had happened, but this made my pity party over Dre seem really stupid. Anthony had become so much more to me than I ever thought he would be. He had become a new part of my life, nurturing me mentally and physically no matter the situation.

Broken Soul
Monica

The fight that Shawn and I had took a few months to blow over, but we were able to make it through. He apologized, as did I. He said that he'd had an anatomy test that day and was extremely stressed from it. He'd been so worried about me meeting his mom and dad. He just wanted everything to be perfect. So we made up and had been together every moment of every day since.

Jade's step-dad, Mr. Gregory, called me, trying to get ahold of her and told me what happened. I immediately booked the first flight to Houston. I hadn't talked to Jade and I didn't know how to get in touch with her, but I knew she would need me there. Ms. Hall and Jade weren't on the best of terms either, but Ms. Hall was like a mother to me. I didn't want her to be alone in case Jade didn't show up.

Jade and I had been through everything together until recently and I couldn't imagine her dealing with this without me. I wished I could take Shawn, but I knew that would only cause a fight if he met my homeboys. He wouldn't understand them, so I arranged to go on my own. While I was packing, Shawn came and sat on the bed.

"Hi, baby. Are you going to miss me?" he asked.

I stopped packing and stood between his legs.

"Yes, I am." I held his face and looked at him. He looked as though he was about to cry.

"When do you come back?"

"I'll be back Monday morning. I have class and then I'll be home right after that." I kissed his face. Against my desire, I had enrolled into nursing school.

"Can I come with you? I don't know if I can go days without you."

"Honey, you won't want to hang around my little brother and his hood friends."

"Are you going home to be with Jade or are you going to see some dudes?" he asked, and I knew that he was going to take this out of context.

"No, I'm not. I'm going to spend time with Jade and her mom. I'm saying that you may not enjoy my eight-year-old brother and his friends' type of conversation, that's all."

"Well, let me give you something to go away with." He put his hand up my thigh and slipped into my panties.

"Can I finish packing first?"

"No." He shoved his index finger inside of me. I jumped, not expecting that. I didn't want him to feel like I didn't want him, so I gave in and let him have me. That time was unusually rough. He kept thrusting so hard and each time he would say, "You're mine, you're mine."

Just as he seemed to be really enjoying me, he turned me over, threw me face down on the bed, and began to take me from the back. It's not like we hadn't done that before, but it was like he was somewhere else.

That night, after he dropped me off at the airport, it felt sort of refreshing watching him drive off. I walked inside and headed for the first convenience store I saw. I went straight to the counter.

"Hi." I set my bags aside and pulled money out of my purse.

"Hello, how are you?" The lady at the counter smiled.

"Tired. I need a pack of Virginia Slim Lights."

I hadn't smoked a cigarette a day in my life until after the abortion. The cashier passed them to me and I gave her the money. I shoved them into my Gucci purse.

"Do you have matches?" I turned back to ask.

Before I could even finish my sentence, she was holding them up to me.

"Thanks."

I wanted to go outside and smoke, but I figured I should get on the plane and wait until I landed—just to make sure Shawn hadn't followed me or anything.

"The smoking area is out the door to the right."

"Oh, I'm going to wait 'til I get to Houston. I don't want my boyfriend to see me."

As soon as I said it, I realized what was coming out of my mouth. When did I turn into this girl who was afraid and weak? Why had I given up my dreams for someone who treated my dreams as optional? When did I begin living in so much fear? The look on the cashier's face said everything I was thinking.

When I checked in for my flight, a part of me felt like I was running away and I couldn't wait to get to my destination. I was happy to be dressed in the finest clothes, but I wasn't happy. I was afraid of every corner that I turned. I didn't like that feeling. I knew my friends and family wouldn't recognize me on the outside, and I didn't recognize me on the inside. Shawn was so good to me materially, but mentally he exhausted me.

Shawn had purchased me a first-class ticket. I couldn't wait to see what that was like. I had always passed through, of course, but I never thought I would be able to sit in first class. I couldn't wait to get on. The flight from L.A. to Houston was just long enough that I'd be able to get the warm brownie that I heard people get in first class.

I made my way through security and into the terminal. Just being able to look other people in the eye was something I hadn't been able to do since Shawn and I began trying to work things out. When it was time to get on the plane, I held my head up high to let others know that I belonged there. Shawn's father traveled extensively and he was well known everywhere. When I sat down, the flight attendant came bouncing and bubbling over.

"Oh, hello there," she said as she reached for my hand, smiling from ear to ear. "You must be Shawn's fiancée."

"Yes, I am. And you are?"

"Mr. Devereaux and Shawn are frequent travelers. They always call ahead when they're traveling, so when Shawn called and told me that his future wife was going to be flying with us, I promised to take personal care of you."

"Oh, how sweet," I said, but I was really thinking that I couldn't escape Shawn, even on the plane.

"If there's anything you need, just let me know and I will take care of it for you."

"Well, thank you very much."

I was seated in an immensely comfortable window seat. I got myself situated and pulled out my favorite tabloid magazine. Just as I got comfy, a tall, cream-skinned, hazel-eyed man with muscles from head to toe and dreadlocks to his shoulders sat next to me.

This was the first time in a long time that I felt butterflies in my stomach.

"Hello. How are you?" he asked.

I had to snap out of my dazed thoughts to respond.

"I'm good, and you?"

"Tired, but it will be refreshing sitting next to such a beautiful young woman."

Just looking at him was making me blush. His eyes were as inviting as his smile. His complexion was perfect and clear. His eyes told me that he was older, but he had taken care of himself. Part of me was uncomfortable sitting next to him; the other part of me wanted to enjoy the company of this mystery man. From the moment he sat down, we started talking as if we had known each other forever.

"So what takes you to Houston?" he asked.

"My best friend needs me. Family emergency."

"Sorry to hear about that."

"Yeah. it's pretty bad."

"I'm an attorney," he said, pulling a business card from his breast pocket. "I'll give you my card. I know a lot of people so if there's anything I can do, let me know."

The bubbly flight attendant came by and gave us each a heated damp washcloth. I accepted it and then waited to see what my mystery man did with his. I'd learned from being with Shawn to follow other people's lead when I was in a situation where I didn't know how to act. He wiped his hands with it and I quickly followed suit.

"What brought you to LA?" I asked.

"I had a visit with one of my clients."

"Oh, that sounds interesting."

"Believe me, it's overrated."

Looking at him made me feel like a Catholic schoolgirl experiencing her first crush.

"So, I'm sure a beautiful woman like yourself has a man, or is it my lucky day?"

"Yes, I do have a boyfriend," I replied, almost pissed about it.

"I hope that he treasures you."

I blushed again. I realized at that moment that he could have asked me what day of the week it was and I probably would have blushed.

"That's debatable," I said, thinking about how Shawn really treated me.

"Well, it would be a waste if he didn't."

"It is."

The flight attendant came over and took our drink and dinner orders.

"I hope this doesn't offend you, but why do you wear so much weave?"

I couldn't tell him the truth, which was because Shawn wanted me to. "That's an odd question."

"I'm sorry. It just doesn't seem like you. Your vibe seems a little different than the way you look physically."

"It's funny you say that, because I don't think anyone will recognize me when I get home. I was always known as the earthy girl."

"And now you've let L.A. turn you into a plastic pincushion?"

I had to laugh because he was right. His vibe was so strong and sexy that it was turning me on. He reached over and grabbed my left hand in search of a ring.

"Well, he hasn't made an honest woman out of you, so he's not that smart."

The feeling of his hand in mine sent a surge of energy up my arm and into my chest.

"Well, not yet," the flight attendant chimed in as she leaned over to set my Coke down in front of me. Then she turned and walked off.

I hoped that she didn't just mess up my half-assed attempt at enjoying a new face.

"Do you know her personally?"

"No, but we fly a lot and she probably remembers me. I'm not sure," I explained, trying to figure out how to change the subject and the tone from what the flight attendant had just done. "So, I didn't catch your name."

"Patrick."

"Hi, Patrick, I'm Monica."

He lifted my hand and kissed it. "It is my pleasure, Monica."

The three-hour flight to Houston wasn't long enough. We spent the majority of the flight talking and laughing about all kinds of stuff. It helped to take my mind off of what was really happening.

As the plane descended, I couldn't help but think about how great this had been just to chat with someone freely.

"Call me while you're here. If there's anything I can do, let me know. Maybe we can see each other again." He smiled. I stuck the card in my pocket. I'd hoped that I would be able to see him again, but I also knew that wasn't possible.

I made my way to the baggage claim to pick up my bags and continued to enjoy a great conversation with Patrick. We smiled as our eyes met. I knew I could never make anything out of it, so instead I tried to focus on waiting for my bag to come out. When it finally arrived, I quickly said my goodbyes, grabbed my things, and rushed toward the door.

As I walked toward the exit, I saw a man dressed in a suit, holding a sign with my name. I stopped dead in my tracks. This was just another way for Shawn to keep track of me. I had told him I would take a cab to the hospital. I still hadn't had my cigarette and I wanted to get away from Shawn and his control for just a minute. I walked past the driver and headed straight for the door.

As soon as I was outside, I sat on the first bench I saw and lit up. I felt liberated just sitting there. With each exhale, I relaxed, knowing that I didn't have to answer to anyone for at least the next few hours. I dreaded going back inside to the driver, but I knew I had to. Just as I nearly finished my cigarette, a black Range Rover drove up.

Patrick.

"Need a ride?"

I looked from side to side, afraid, and then I remembered that Shawn was over a thousand miles away and I was grown. I could do what I want. I eagerly stood up.

"Yes."

Patrick stepped out and opened the passenger door for me. He took my luggage and placed it in the back.

"What hospital are you going to?" he asked as he drove away.

"St. James," I responded. "But I was hoping to grab a bite to eat."

"Hmm, let me think."

Just as I was getting comfortable with my freedom, my cell phone rang. I knew it was Shawn. I didn't want to answer it but knew I should. I pulled the phone out of my pocket.

"I'd better take this. I'm sorry." I placed my finger over my mouth, signaling him to be quiet. He smiled and nodded.

"Hello?"

"What took you so long to answer the phone?"

"I'm sorry. It won't happen again."

"Are you alone?" he demanded.

"Of course I am. Why wouldn't I be?"

"I just want to make sure."

"Honey, you're worried about nothing."

"Where are you?"

"I'm in a cab, on my way to the hospital."

"Why did you take a cab? So you're not alone. You're with

some random cabdriver. I sent a fucking car for you. I sent the driver a picture of you. He said you walked right past him."

"Huh?"

"You heard me. Tell the cabdriver to turn around and take you back."

"But I'm almost there now."

"Do it, Monica!" he yelled. The loudness of Shawn's voice embarrassed me even more.

"Shawn, I'm not doing that."

"Kelly called and told me how you were flirting with some man on the plane."

"Shawn, I'm hanging up now."

I put the phone down and turned toward Patrick, putting on a fake smile. "I don't think I can go to the hospital just yet. I need a minute."

"Where do you want me to take you?"

I couldn't hold it in. I just broke down in tears and started spewing all of the bad shit that Shawn had done to me.

He listened and kept driving.

"Do you think it's safe for you to go to the hospital?" he asked.

"I honestly don't know. I know I need to. I feel like he's always following me."

"Maybe you can get a good night's rest and I can take you in the morning. I know you don't know me but you're welcome to come to my house."

"No, I should go to the hospital."

"Technically visiting hours are over."

I nodded in agreement.

"Are you sure you don't mind?"

"Not at all, and if you feel like you still want to go, I'm happy to take you."

I nodded again.

For the remainder of the ride, we both remained silent. We arrived at the gate to his condo, and it was stunning. Once again I asked myself what was I doing. I didn't know this man. He could be a serial killer. Well, if he was, he was a sexy one and at this point, he couldn't be any worse than Shawn. He drove into the garage and parked. Soon he put the car in park, took my hand, and tugged me slightly toward him.

"You deserve better."

He let my hand go and got out of the car. I sat there for a minute, thinking about those three simple words, and he was right. I opened the door to get out and followed him into the condo. He removed his shoes at the entry and so did I.

"Red or white?" he asked as I continued following him.

"Huh?" I wasn't listening. I was so afraid of what would happen to me once I went back to Shawn.

At the end of the long hallway was a grand kitchen.

"Red or white wine?" he asked again.

"At this point, I'll have anything. I don't really care."

He opened the wine fridge and pulled out a bottle, then went to the cabinet to reach for two wine glasses.

I let out a sigh of pleasure since it had been a long time since anyone had been that attentive to me. He poured a glass of white wine and passed it to me.

"Cheers."

"Cheers to what?" I asked.

"Freedom." He turned around and headed to the fridge. "You needed this little getaway."

I wanted to be frustrated, but I knew he was right.

He opened the fridge and collected various fruits—papaya, mango, apples, and kiwi.

"I probably should have told you that I'm a vegan, so if you're in need of fried chicken, I'll have to order you some."

"No, whatever you're making already looks delicious."

Patrick was becoming more and more the type of man I wanted to be with by the minute. When he placed the fruit on the counter, he leaned in toward me.

"When's the last time you were kissed?"

I smiled at his question and just shrugged my shoulders.

He leaned in and gently kissed me on my lips. With his right hand he grabbed my waist and hoisted me against his chest. His kiss was the most passionate kiss that I had felt in a long time. It was gentle, soft. Just as the kiss was about to intensify, the house phone rang. The answering machine came on after several rings and played a computer-generated greeting in a male voice.

"We are unable to take your call. Please leave a message."

A woman's voice followed. "Hi, baby, it's me. Listen, I know that you're on your way back and I thought that maybe I could come by. Call me. I miss you."

I stopped kissing him and looked at him. "Are you still—"

He pressed his index finger against my lips. "No, I'm not, but my ex hasn't figured that out yet. She leaves me messages like that all the time and I keep ignoring them. Come on, let's relax."

"No, I think I should go."

"Why? Is your boyfriend going to jump on the next plane out here?"

"I wouldn't be surprised."

"Then you definitely don't need him."

My phone rang again.

"You better answer that."

"I'm grown. I don't have to answer it if I don't want to."

"That's up to you."

I looked at the phone and held down the end key, then powered it off.

"So, tell me why a good-looking man like you is single?"

"My wife of fifteen years cheated on me," he said very matter-of-factly and passed me a glass.

"Oh wow. How did you find out?"

"She told me she was leaving me because she was in love with him. She did and then he left her."

I walked over to him and stood close enough to smell the wine on his breath.

"Well, for now, let's just pretend there are no ex-wives and no ex-boyfriends."

"Oh, he's an ex now?"

"Well, no, but he will be when I get back. And I'd love to be able to see you again. I like you, and I'd like to get to know you better. Besides, I came here for something really important that I need to take care of."

"True, and hopefully you'll take care of yourself while you're here. If I do see you again, I'd like to see the girl underneath the weave, nails, and Gucci."

He put his glass down, smiled at me, and leaned in for a kiss. I could feel myself getting wet. I knew I would pay for this with Shawn, but Patrick was different. There was a sweetness about him that Shawn didn't have. I reminded myself that I didn't come here to hang out. I came to comfort Jade's mom.

"I'm sorry. As much as I'd love to continue this, I really have to go. Would you mind taking me to the hospital?"

"Not at all."

When we got in the car, he held my hand the entire ride. I enjoyed the silence and the peace.

A Broken Heart
Jade

The last twenty-four hours had been pretty rough. It had been so many years since I'd been home. I hadn't talked to Mother in months and I think I was twelve the last time I heard from Tracy. I was so afraid of what I would find when I got to the hospital. Mentally and physically, I was exhausted and not all that sure how I would be able to handle this. My relationship with Mother was a rocky one, but I didn't want anything to happen to her no matter how often I prayed for her death. She was still my mother and I cared about her, despite her faults.

Things got even harder when Tracy passed away. They said the trauma to her brain was too much. I felt like I hadn't known her. I wished Monica was here to hold my hand and I was disgusted with myself for not calling and telling her what was going on with Mother. It was complicated, but I had to accept that. That moment led me to think about how or why I

185

managed to run off the people who loved me the most, yet I'd kept trying to hang on to the one man who didn't love me at all.

When my plane landed, I took a cab straight from the airport to the hospital. During the ride, I longed for the days when the most pressing issues of my day were choosing what color shoes I would wear, whether to eat at McDonald's or Burger King, or what new movie to see—pointless decisions, instead of having so much shit to deal with all at once.

The cab stopped at the entrance of the hospital. I sat back. I was scared to get out. No one was there to help get me out of this. There were no distractions, no Crown Royal to kill the pain, no way to know what my mother would look like. I knew that I needed Mother to know how much I loved her and needed her in my life. I didn't know what I was going to face, but I needed to be strong. Hesitant, I peeled my legs out of the cab and headed for the entrance.

I hated hospitals, especially the smell of them, like rotting flesh with bleach on top. Anthony had given me the room number and I headed straight to the elevators. As I reached for the door handle, I heard someone call my name.

"Jade."

Monica. My heart jumped.

I ran toward her and she ran toward me, arms open. The embrace from my best friend was exactly what I needed. We hugged as if we hadn't seen each other for ten years.

"I'm so glad you're here," I cried.

"I wouldn't be anywhere else," she sobbed.

I couldn't stop the tears as they rolled down my face and onto the back of her shirt. When we finally pulled away, the tears in Monica's eyes made forgiveness critical.

"I love you, Monica."

"I love you, too, Jade."

Monica held my hand and we walked to Mother's room.

As soon as Mr. Gregory saw the two of us, he did his best to rise quickly, but his sixty-three-year-old body slowed him down. He held onto the chair for support and hobbled over to us as quickly as he could.

"Hey, baby," he softly spoke. "Come on in, come on, come on."

Even though he wasn't my dad, Mr. Gregory had been married to my mother for over fifteen years and he was all I really knew as a father. He was the most stable person Mother and I had.

"So glad you here. Lil Mo. Hey, baby, how you doing?" He hugged Monica with an equal embrace.

"I'm good, Mr. Gregory. Thank you for calling me."

"Well, I know Ms. Lori-Ann would want you here. You just as much a daughter to her as Jade."

In the corner of my eye, I noticed a little girl sitting in a chair, watching cartoons on TV. She swiveled around in the chair and looked at me with curiosity.

"Who's that?" I asked Mr. Gregory.

"Maya, Tracy's daughter."

I didn't even know Tracy had a child.

"Y'all come on outside for a minute," he said. He turned to Maya. "I'll be right outside the door, okay?"

"K," she replied and swiveled back in the chair.

We walked outside the door and Mr. Gregory explained as much of the story that he had been able to put together. Apparently, Tracy had been viciously pistol-whipped by her husband when she was attempting to leave him. Thankfully, Maya was at a friend's house when the attack happened. Tracy's husband had taken a baseball bat and beat her. He must have thought that she was dead when he turned the gun on himself. When Mother left the hospital, she was supposed to pick Maya up from school, but she never made it. She passed out while driving and swerved into oncoming traffic.

I walked back into the room and reached for a chair to sit by Mother's side. I sat down and lowered the bar of the bed. I gently took her hand and placed it against my face. The tears could no longer stay inside of me. For the first time in a long time, I prayed. I prayed that God would spare Mother's life and I promised that I would cherish her from that day on.

Tiny fingers touched my lower back and a small voice said, "She's going to be okay."

I lifted my head to a precious little face.

"Thank you, Maya. I need to believe that."

I let go of Mother's hand and gave my niece a big hug.

"Did you know my mommy?"

"Yes, I'm your mom's sister."

"My mommy's dead," she said nonchalantly.

"I know and I'm so sorry."

She didn't say anything; she just walked away, back to the chair, and started watching TV again. I turned my attention back to Mother. I reached for her hand and held it tightly. The identification band on her right wrist caught my eye. I tilted her hand so that I could read her name. For some reason, I didn't believe it was her. Seeing her name on that wristband erased all doubt that it really, truly was my mother. I turned my head away and my gaze fell upon little Maya. She was really there. This was all too real. In complete disbelief that this was my life, I glanced up to see Monica had come back into the room.

"Are you okay?" Monica gently touched me on her shoulder.

"I just can't believe Tracy is dead."

Monica shook her head in disbelief. "He killed her."

I shook my head, unable to deal with that either. Mother looked so peaceful lying there. I had never seen her look as serene as she did at that moment. I didn't think anyone ever thought about these moments—when we see our parents in a weak or vulnerable state.

No one can adequately prepare for that. I sat there, holding her hand and counting the beeps from the heart monitor. I'd never thought about the sounds of the beeps or its importance before.

It was strange, but I caught myself praying that it kept on beeping.

"I'm going to take Maya to the cafeteria to get some lunch," Mr. Gregory said. Maya held onto him like he was life itself. Monica went with them. I wanted to say something to my mother but didn't know if she could hear me, and even if she could, I didn't know what to say.

"Hi, Mom. It's Jade." I took a deep breath. "I don't know what to say to you except that I am so sorry. I'm so sorry that I've been distant and ignoring you."

The door squeaked open and an unfamiliar voice behind me said, "Oh. Hello."

I turned to see a handsome, golden-brown man with salt and pepper hair wearing a meticulously pressed white overcoat. He was about 6'2" with a short curly afro and tired eyes, and his neatly trimmed hairline, sideburns, and beard were shaped to complement his face. His dark brown eyes were calming and complemented his inviting smile. He extended a well-mani-cured hand toward mine and introduced himself.

"Hi, I'm Dr. Hill. You must be Jade."

Breathlessly, I stood and shook his hand. "Yes, I am."

"It's nice to meet you."

Energy passed between our hands and I finally let go to refocus my attention on Mother. "So can you explain all this to me because I really don't understand what's going on?"

"Sure. Outside of the car accident, your mother has a condition called acute stress cardiomyopathy, which is caused by intense emotional or physical stress. It can cause rapid and severe heart muscle weakness that mimics a heart attack. Now, there are a lot of triggers for it. I'm sure the news about your sister is what triggered this," he explained confidently as if I understood the explanation. I stood there frozen.

"Basically, her heart is broken."

"Oh, okay, thank you. I'm sorry. This is a lot for me to take in all at once. Is she going to make it?"

Without hesitation, he said, "There're never any guarantees but I think she'll be coming out of it pretty soon. Have some hope. It's a way for her body to rest. I can have the neurologist talk with you more about that." His pager went off and he looked at it. "Listen, I have to go, but here's my card. If you need anything, you can get in touch with me right away."

"I will. Thank you."

He hesitated before walking away and peered into my eyes. I gazed right back into his as long as I could.

"Okay, well, I have to go, but I'm sure I'll see you around."

"Okay, sure," I replied.

"Ms. Lori-Ann, I'll be back in a little bit to check on you." He touched Mother's hand gently.

"Can she hear you?"

"Yes, she can. She can hear you, too."

His touch soothed my shoulder.

"See you soon." He turned and walked out the door.

As I looked at her, I realized that my mother had once been a young woman in love. I wondered if she had handled things the way that I had. My memory returned to that dreadful day at Mr. Frank's house. Was it possible for another woman to love a man as much as I'd loved Dre, and was Mr. Frank my mother's version of Dre? How could I move on and not have a broken heart?

With a massive hangover still lingering, I sat down in the chair. Exhausted, I dozed off for a moment and didn't leave Mother's side for the next three days.

Surreal
Jade

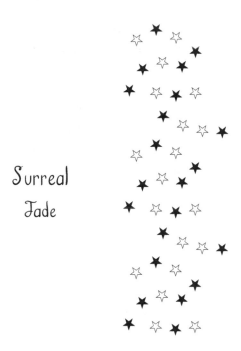

On the fourth day at the hospital, I awoke to a rustling at Mother's bed. I opened my eyes to see Dr. Hill standing over her, listening to her heart with his stethoscope. He was so handsome that I couldn't help but stare. Looking at him helped me understand the word "debonair." There was something about him that intrigued me.

"Good morning, Jade. Your mother's doing great," he said without looking up at me.

"Oh, good," I replied, unaware of what he'd just said.

"She needs a lot of rest until her heart heals."

"My mother has a broken heart." I laughed. "That's quite a pill even for me to swallow."

"It's actually more common than people think. It's a good thing she's here in Houston."

He walked over to where I was sitting and kneeled in front of me. "I've been studying broken hearts for many, many years."

I avoided his eyes, hoping he didn't see that my heart was broken, too.

"I've learned to recognize the signs of a broken heart. I think it's hereditary in this case." He tapped my nose with his index finger. I could feel my eyes blink a little slower and I took a deep breath, trying not to smile. "Are you going to stay at the hospital again tonight?" he asked as he stood up.

"Yes. I'm staying 'til she wakes up."

"That's a normal reaction, but you need to take care of yourself. When's the last time you showered?"

"Oh God, not since the day I got here. I probably smell like a wet dog."

"No, not a wet dog. More like a sweaty puppy, maybe."

I laughed. "Thank you, but you're not making me feel any better."

"True, but I made you laugh," he said, flashing his perfect smile.

"I'll go to the house and take a shower later today. I promise."

"Well, I'm about to end my shift and I won't be back for three days, so I'm happy to give you a ride if you need one."

"That's sweet, but no thank you." I kindly refused with a smile on my face. I licked my lips with the thought of his on mine.

"Well, just text me if you change your mind. It's about 1:30 now. I'll be leaving in another hour."

"Okay."

As he walked away, Nita picked up his scent. I hadn't yet figured out what the cologne was, but it was inviting and there was a slight tingle in my spine. As soon as he left the room, my body odor hit me like a ton of bricks. I decided to take him up on his offer, so I hurried out the door, hoping to catch him.

"Dr. Hill," I called.

He stopped and turned to me.

"I think I'll take you up on that offer. I really do need a bath."

"I have an idea. How about you come to my place? I'll have my chef make you a meal you'll never forget and I can have my massage therapist give you a well-needed massage."

"A massage therapist? At your house? I didn't realize doctors made so much."

"They don't, but I'm the director of cardiology and I invested well."

"Well, Director, if you don't mind taking a dirty, stinky girl with you, I can certainly use a massage. I've never had one."

"All the more reason you need one," he said. "I'll be ready in about thirty minutes. I drive a green Ford F-150."

"Let me get this right…you have a massage therapist that comes to your house with just a phone call, but you drive an F-150?"

"Priorities," he said as he walked away. "I'll meet you downstairs."

When I turned around to go back to Mother's room, I saw Monica coming off the elevator, but I barely recognized her. She didn't have any weave in her hair, her fake nails were gone, and she had on a free-flowing dress with a crazy pattern on it, just like she used to wear.

"Monica, where have you been?"

"I'm sorry. I just had to take care of something."

"I haven't seen you in two days."

"I broke up with Shawn."

"Why?"

Tears swelled in her eyes. "Because I don't want to end up like Tracy."

"What do you mean?" I asked.

"Shawn has been…I just can't do it anymore. He's angry right now because I stayed more days than I had originally told him I would. He told me if I didn't come back that he would drag me back."

"Mo, why haven't you told me any of this?"

"I was embarrassed."

"You don't have to be...just look at me."

We hugged.

"I'm so proud of you."

"Oh my God." She pulled back from me.

"What?"

"You smell like ass and shit."

We both broke out laughing.

"I know. I know...I'm actually glad you're here. I was just about to leave and go shower."

"Good, and be sure to wash your ass!" We both laughed.

"Stay with Mother until I get back."

"I will."

"Okay. I'll see you later."

I went outside and waited for Dr. Hill to drive up. I lit a cigarette while I waited. I had some time to think. I wanted to be a better person. I wanted to have a better relationship with myself, my mother, and my friends, but how did I start? I wanted to stop focusing on Dre and focus on myself for once. If I could take half the energy I'd spent on Dre and put it into being a better person, I just might live a better life. My mother's situation and the death of my sister were teaching me about the true value of life. I was wasting it on thoughts of Dre. I prayed that I would never see him again.

I had just finished my cigarette when I saw a rusted green F-150 pull up. It was Dr. Hill and I vowed not to entertain the thought of sleeping with him. My mission to hurt people was stupid and it was time to let that go also. He put the car in park and got out to escort me to the passenger side.

"Hi there. Are you ready?"

"Yes I am, thank you." I got into the truck. He closed the door like a gentleman and went back to his side to get in.

"What kind of food do you feel like eating?" he asked.

"Uhm, American?"

He laughed. "Have you ever tried anything other than American food? Like Japanese or Indian maybe? You know, there's more to life than McDonald's."

"I don't eat fast food all the time. I try to eat pretty healthy, but I haven't tried Japanese or Indian." I wanted not to feel so young and stupid, so I pretended that I didn't eat fast food on a daily basis. Truth is, I only ate fast food and I hadn't eaten out since Dre.

"I will tell you that I'm tired, I'm sweaty, and I need a bath. So I don't really wanna stop anywhere that I'm going to have to get out of the car, but chicken parmesan sounds good if we can get it to go."

"Don't worry, I'll take care of you," he said.

He took his cell phone out of his pocket and made a call.

"Hi, it's Dr. Hill. I'll need chicken parmesan for two and a bottle of '08 Syrah wine, with salad and breadsticks. We'll be there in about forty-five minutes. Okay, thanks." He hung up. "So, Jade, tell me about yourself."

"Wow…that's a broad question and a narrow one all at the same time. All I can really tell you is that I'm no good."

"What does that mean?"

"I'm going through a lot right now."

"I believe that we only go through what we put ourselves through."

"True, but I'm scared of being like my mother—a bitter and brokenhearted woman."

"Your happiness is up to you, Jade, and no one else."

"True." I looked out the window, trying to keep the tears from flowing.

We drove for maybe an hour. The truck ride was so relaxing that I took a short nap. When I felt the car stop, I opened my eyes and stared at a huge house. The gated two-story home was bigger than any house I had ever seen or been inside of.

"Welcome." Dr. Hill got out of the truck and walked around to my side, opening the door for me to get out.

"I'm bad about cooking for myself so I have a guy that comes by once a week to make a bunch of meals for me. He's pretty good. Trust me, the chicken parmesan is going to be finger-licking good. If I didn't have someone cooking for me, I'd eat all wrong or starve to death."

As we approached the double front doors, a woman dressed in a maid's outfit opened the door.

"Good afternoon, Dr. Hill," she greeted him as she reached for his coat.

"Good evening, Estella. This is my friend Jade."

"Good evening, Ms. Jade. May I take your coat?"

"Sure," I said as I passed her my rusty brown leather jacket.

"If you don't mind, take your shoes off and leave them right over here," he said as he took his shoes off.

"Why?" I asked.

"So that the germs we've dragged around all day stay where they belong…on the shoes and not in the house."

As I stooped to take my shoes off, I noticed the dual winding staircase and the huge balconies that went around the entire second floor.

"Estella will take you to a room where you can get yourself cleaned up. I have to answer some emails. Estella, grab her a shirt and shorts from my room. Just call me when you're all done and ready to eat."

"This is so sweet of you. Thank you so much," I said before following Estella up the staircase. She took me into a room that was decorated like Hawaii, tranquil and relaxing. She showed me around and gave me everything I needed to take a nice long bath. I decided to take a shower. When Estella left the room, I peeled off my clothes. They smelled so bad that I wanted to throw them away.

Inside the shower, there were dual shower heads and a bench. I sat down on the bench, and as the water ran across my naked body, I felt the need to release my fears and frustration. I sat there and all I could do was cry. I thought about Mother, Monica, Tracy, Maya, Slim the Bartender, Curtis the Cutie, Luis the Linguist, Rob the White Guy, Troy the Trucker, Keith the Kappa, Ben the Blanket, Charles the Cashier, the Virgos, the Scorpios, Anthony, and Dre. I thought about all the pain I had caused them and myself. I hated myself for being that way and I wanted the water to wash all of it from me. I wanted to shed my old skin and start fresh.

After my tears filled the shower, I made my way to the bathtub to relax. There were candles lit and music coming from speakers in the ceiling. There was even a bottle of water next to the tub and a bowl of fruit. I couldn't believe that I was here, but I was thankful. When I finally got out of the bathtub, I had five outfits on the bed to choose from. I chose the most comfortable—pajama-like pants and a T-shirt. I made my way downstairs, feeling relaxed and ready to eat. I didn't have to lift a finger. The table was set beautifully.

"Dr. Hill, this is wonderful. Thank you so much."

"You're welcome, Jade, but I insist that you call me Kenneth."

"Okay, Kenneth. So do you treat all your patients' relatives like this?"

"No, but I can't resist a beautiful woman in need."

I hadn't felt beautiful in a long time.

"Thank you." I smiled.

After a delicious dinner, Kenneth invited me outside to the patio where we enjoyed wine and chocolate. We talked until the sun went down. Kenneth was a divorced father of three and was about to turn forty-seven. He had plans to go boating at the Houston Yacht Club over the weekend and wanted me to go with him for the jazz brunch. I was still worried about Mother, but he reassured me. We sat outside talking. I must have been extremely tired or the outdoor couch was intensely comfortable because I fell asleep.

The next morning I woke to the fresh smell of pastries baking.

"Good morning, beautiful," he said, still sitting in his same spot.

"Oh my God! Have we been here all night? Did you go to bed?" I asked.

"No, I usually stay up the first night I'm off. How did you sleep?"

"I don't remember, but I guess pretty good. Thanks for letting me rest."

"Of course." He smiled. "Breakfast is ready if you want to eat and then I'll take you back to the hospital."

"That would be great."

When we arrived at the hospital that morning, the nurse advised that I needed to wait a few minutes because Mother was coming out of her coma, but Kenneth walked me right in. Mr. Gregory, Monica, and Maya were standing there with a look of joy. Mother had revived, just as Kenneth said she would. He gave Mother instructions to stay in the hospital a few more days before being discharged. I didn't go to the yacht club with Kenneth that evening and he didn't go either. Kenneth stayed with us for a few hours, talking and watching Mother's progress.

Over the next few days, Mother slept a lot, sleep she probably truly needed. By the third day of her recovery, Mother asked to talk to me alone.

"Come here," she said. I had to lean close to her to be able to hear her talking to me.

"Mom, don't try to talk too much."

"But I have to tell you something," she stuttered.

"I already know, okay, and you're going to be just fine."

Whispering and stuttering, she said, "Shut up and listen to me." She took a deep breath and a tear fell from her eye. "Jade, I'm sorry."

"Sorry for what?"

"Sorry for not telling you sooner that you are my greatest accomplishment."

That had to be the kindest thing that my mother had ever said to me from the day I was born.

"Life is about love, baby. I love you, and I'm sorry I never told you that growing up. I just didn't know how. I didn't know how to love you or Tracy. So I need you to love Maya. Give her the love that I didn't give you or your sister. My sweet Jade, you are so amazingly strong. You've always been my strongest one, and I'm just so proud to be your mother. I don't want you to be like me. I don't want you to let people—men—hurt you so bad that you stop loving like I did. Don't be like me, be better than me," she said as tears rolled down her face. "You are the best of me and thank you for loving me."

She took another breath, looked up at the ceiling, and said, "Oh, wow."

The exhale never came. Her mouth hung open from the inhale, her head tilted to the side, her eyes slowly shut, and the beeps stopped.

On October 3 at 3:28 p.m., my mother passed away.

Mother had signed a living will that included a do-not-resuscitate order.

I made the decision to have my mother cremated. I spent the next several days on autopilot to get things prepared. I had to be strong for Mr. Gregory, Maya, Monica, aunts, uncles, cousins, distant cousins, play cousins, play aunts, Mother's friends, coworkers, neighbors, the grocery store attendant, the mailman, and everyone else who knew Ms. Lori-Ann. I ordered the flowers, picked the urn, picked the sermon, picked the sermon, wrote the poem, picked the songs, ordered the food, and approved the pictures. I wanted Mother to be remembered as a beautiful woman and honor her the best I could.

On the morning of October 11, I held a burial service for my mother. The woman who may have never known love. Anthony flew down to be with me, but I was exhausted after the funeral and didn't want to see anyone. I just wanted to find a moment alone. I had held up pretty well during the wake and the funeral itself, but by the end of the day, I was ready to collapse.

I dropped Monica off at the airport and headed straight for the pharmacy. Kenneth had called in a prescription of Xanax for me and I truly needed it. The only moment that I could find to be alone was on the drive there. I drove my mother's car and cried the entire way. I put on my super-large black sunglasses to cover my red, puffy eyes and walked into the store, feeling a bit dazed by the events of the day. I think I had been in a trance since the moment I watched my mother pass away.

I made my way to the back of the store and waited in line. There was a woman in front of me who had to be eighty-eight-years-old taking forever. Why was she able to live so long and my mother died so young? I knew there was a message in all of this for me, I just wasn't sure what it was. Finally, Ms. Eighty-Eight moved on and it was my turn.

"Hi, can I help you?" the pharmacist asked.

"Hi, prescription for Jade Hall," I said, my head down as I searched my purse for my wallet. Thoughts of Kenneth and how supportive he had been through all of this came to mind. I thought about Anthony and how concerned he was. I thought about the things that Mother had told me and I wanted to make sure that I lived up to being the woman that she knew I could be.

Mother was right. Life is about love and I wanted to love again, only I wanted to love someone who would love me back, and maybe that was Anthony. I prayed that God would help me live through this.

From where I stood, I was able to see the cars waiting in the drive-through. The death of my mother, thoughts of my purposeful damage to men, and my continuous effort to throw away Dre were buried with my mother. I was ready to extract a moment of joy out of this and I actually found some happiness in watching the couple in the drive-through. They seemed so in love. I could see them kissing and laughing. The girl looked happy and content. There was no pain in her face; she had released her power and by the looks of that smile she was enjoying every day of pleasure she was given.

I wanted that same look. Kenneth was so much older than me but there was something between us that was different. It was comforting and peaceful at the same time. My mind drifted to thoughts of Kenneth. I decided to give it a real chance with him to see if love was in the cards for me.

While I was looking for my credit card, the pharmacist pressed a button to the drive-up window that activated the speakerphone to the pharmacy.

"Yeah, I'm here to pick up a prescription for Darnell Scott. It might be under Andre Scott." The man's voice stung my eardrums and psychosis was about to set in.

I looked at him. He looked at me.
Breathe . . .
Breathe . . .
Breathe . . .
This was not a dream. It was him.
Breathe . . .
Breathe . . .
It was Dre.
Breathe . . .

Breathe
Jade

I inhaled deeply, then ran off toward the entrance. My heart pounded. I felt my blood boiling inside my veins. My teeth were clenched together so hard that I could feel my jaw tightening along with every other muscle in my body. Suddenly I couldn't breathe.

It felt like someone had sliced my heart with a razor blade and poured alcohol laced with salt inside of it. I felt each hair that existed on the back of my neck standing on end. As I ran toward the front door, I pushed an old man with a cane out of my way. Thank God someone had just passed through the sliding door and it was still open, otherwise I would have ran right through that fucking door. My legs and feet moved at what felt like superhuman speed. My brain had blocked all rationale and only fed on anger, deceit, and hatred for that motherfucker. I saw the car headed toward the street and I pursued. I wanted to make sure that he knew it was me, and I wanted to be sure that it really was him.

My radar had that motherfucker in reach. Just as I ran down the sidewalk toward the back of the store, I saw his candy apple red BMW drive off and head toward the street, but not before I saw his face again. I knew it was him. Dre, my nemesis, my lover. I slung my unpaid for water bottle toward the car like a rocket. My usually uncoordinated aim was right on target.

BAM!

My water bottle bounced off the trunk of his 318i and I continued my chase without missing one step. The impact of the bottle made her turn around. And there she was, just like Anthony said. She was blonde, WHITE…and BLONDE, BITCH!

That glimpse allowed me to burn her fucked-up-looking face into my brain. I ran to the other end of the parking lot, barely able to breathe. The sound of his tires squealing enraged me as I watched Dre's car turn out of the parking lot and onto the main road. The smoke from his tires hit me like a sack of potatoes. That didn't stop me; I think it increased my speed. Just as I ran out to the main road, a sudden lack of oxygen to my brain overwhelmed me and I had to stop and gasp for air.

As I gripped the front of my thighs for support, it happened.

HORNS   BLOWING…GLASS…SHATTERING FIBERGLASS…blood . . .

SNAPPING…CRACKING…blood . . .

BREAKING…SHATTERING…warm blood . . .

SCREECHING…SEVERING…RUPTURING . . .

SPLITTING…FRACTURING…BLACKNESS . . .

White lights…cold blood…sirens . . .

Breathe…breathe…breathe . . .

Beep…beep…beep…beep…beep…beep . . .

I awoke and was unable to move a single muscle in my body. The first face I saw was Kenneth's. On the other side of me was Mr. Gregory.

"What's happening?" I was afraid.

"Jade, listen to me now. You stay calm, sweetheart. You were in an accident. You're in a hospital," Mr. Gregory said softly.

"I can't move."

"Jade, you're in a body cast, okay? Just calm down. It's going to be alright. You're okay. Just listen to me," Kenneth said with a firmness in his voice.

I listened as he explained.

"Why? I don't understand."

"I don't know why, baby, but you ran into the street." Mr. Gregory's voice was shaky.

"Kenneth, I can't feel my legs."

"Jade, you may not be able to feel anything right now. You're in a body cast. It's normal to feel nothing. Now I'm not going to beat around the bush. You were hit by a car traveling about forty miles per hour and because you were at a standstill, you were thrown up and forward about twenty feet from where you were originally hit. You broke your back and there's fluid on your spine, which is not good. Both of your legs are broken as well as your left arm and your elbows. You have three cracked ribs and four that are broken. Your nose is broken and your skull has five fractures."

"I'm fucked up."

Aside from all the physical problems, I had one other major fucking problem. Mr. Gregory questioned me about the accident but I had no memory of the incident or anything prior to it. Kenneth said they called it retrograde amnesia.

"Will I get my memory back?"

"Eventually, yes, but right now you need to focus on looking ahead. You have an extraordinary road to recovery, my friend, and it's going to be a very long one."

"Leave please," I said.

"Jade . . ." Mr. Gregory tried to get my attention.

"EVERYONE OUT AND NO ONE COMES IN UNLESS I ASK FOR YOU. I WANT ALL OF YOU OUT!"

I spent the next ten days in total silence. I didn't talk to anyone. I didn't turn the TV or radio on and I refused every phone call and visitor. I spent most of those days trying to make my mind tell me why I was standing in the middle of the street. I did have use of my right hand and I'd asked the nurse to get me a pen and paper.

On Day 11, I wrote:

```
Dear Jade,
    What is love? I don't know, but it's a mess.
Now what?
    ~Jade
```

Day 23

```
Dear Dre,
    When we met, I had never encountered anyone like
you before. From that day on, my life has been turned
upside down and inside out. I have gotten off the path
of the woman that I wanted to become and now I don't
know who I am. All I wanted to do was try as hard as
I could to be all that you would ever want and need,
but I forgot about me in the process. When we were
together, I felt weak yet beautiful, I felt stupid yet
```

loved. That combination was deadly and I just didn't know it. You became my greatest joy and my greatest sorrow. The fact that you're able to just walk away from me told me that you were never the one for me, but it took losing everything to know that.

The morning you left, I felt thrown away like a finely rolled cigar—snuffed out and left in an old ashtray. There's just no way to negotiate this love that we had to make you and me happy.

I'm not even sure I know what happiness means to you, but I know that it's different for me. I would be happy just having a piece of you. You have no idea how painful it has been for me to get over you. The night we first made love was so hard for me because having you inside of me was exhilarating and joyous, to put it lightly. I wanted to cry because I had never experienced feelings like that. I opened my heart to you. There's no man that can do to me what you did to me and that terrifies me. I am exhausted from feeling my body awaken to your touch. With each stroke and each kiss, I had become anchored to you and at the same time afraid of wanting you all the time. I wasn't sure how to balance that.

There's something that connects you and me together, something that neither of us can explain. I had hoped that it was more than sex, but I guess it really isn't. I was ready and willing to throw everything away just for you and I almost did. You'll never know how much I sacrificed to live in the hope of being with you. There was a part of me that wanted to pretend that it was just sex, but the other part wanted you to know that it wasn't just sex. I wish I knew what I

did to deserve this, but I can't figure it out. I don't
know if there was anything that I did. It's just who
you are and I love me more than I like who you are.

~Jade

Day 38

Dear God,

Today they removed most of the cast and some of the
tubes plugged into my body like a surge protector. I
can feel my toes but not all of them. I guess 7 out
of 10 is better than none. What is my purpose? What
is your plan for me? I've lost everything. I don't
want it to be like this, and I can't live like this.
I pray that this pain will go away. Mother was wrong
about some things but there was one thing she was
right about. Cinderella is a fairy tale. I don't want
to live in this dream anymore. So far, it sucks, and
I think my nurse Sheila is putting roaches in my food.
I'm not going to eat when she's on duty.

~Jade

Day 49

Dear Dre,

There was a time when I wished to find a peaceful
place that I could reside with you, although I don't
know how to define that and I don't know if that place
exists. There's no way to be with you without being
hurt and deceived. There's no way to ever have you

in my life and know if you have any feelings for me. Meeting you was all a big mistake and I've got to figure out how to get you out of my heart again. Funny thing is that when I first heard about Shelly, I wanted to beg you to give us another chance, but getting with you would be like watching a car slam head-on into a brick wall at 150 mph—a wall we both knew was there and yet we kept pressing the gas pedal. I hate you.

~Jade

Day 55

Dear God,

The probing is getting to me. I hate all these needles. The dreams are getting worse. I scream, but there's no sound coming out of my mouth. I wanna go home, but where is home? Where am I? Who am I? Does anyone care? Do I?

~Jade

Day 57

Dear Dre,

You're the only man that I've ever loved. I would have sold my soul to be with you. You were a part of me that I couldn't let go of. You gave me life and you took it from me all within minutes. We were like two peas in a pod and it's hard for me to believe that you've forgotten all of that. I don't know how long it will take for me to accept missing the love and heal from the hurt, because I made a fatal mistake in tying my love up in you. Truthfully, I don't know if I ever will. I hope I never see you again.

~Jade

Day 59

Dear Dre,

I don't want to ever see you again. When you and I were together, I tried so hard to watch every word that I said. The woman in me told the scared little girl to sit down and shut up. The woman in me is standing up to say…never again. I don't have to do that. I won't bother going into detail with you about all that I'm going through, but when you left, I waited. I waited and waited by the phone, just hoping that you would call and say something. Say, "Hey you. Where do I meet you, when, what time?" Just so I could hear your voice, I kept the last voicemail from you for years. I'm tired of checking Facebook for the various names that you might be under. I was waking up in the middle of the night, checking my phone to make sure I hadn't missed any calls from you and then it hit me…I'm jocking Dre and he couldn't give a damn as long as I open my legs. Am I, me, your Jade, who can have any man I want, really running behind someone who treats me so optionally? Meanwhile, I've made you a requirement to my personal happiness. Well, there's something wrong with that. I realized that there's something terribly wrong. This is not good for me. You…you are not good for me. All the time I thought it was me, the fact is that it isn't me. It's really you. You are toxic for me and you have destroyed every area of my life that you possibly could. I had this perfect picture of you when the truth is you're not perfect. Just hearing your voice made me smile from ear to ear. Now, when I see anything that even remotely reminds me of you, I'm annoyed and would rather swallow my own vomit than look at you. You probably think that your dick is what makes me happy. Well, it's not just that, Dre. I was happy with you. I enjoyed you. For me, the truest moment we shared was when you looked at me and said, "I love you." That moment meant more to me than you will ever know. That's because I know it was real, but for some reason the power that I held at that moment made you afraid. I saw it in your eyes and I'll never question that moment, but I can't live on that moment forever. I'm a woman who wants respect and honesty. Your name shouldn't be Dre, it should be Destruction.

~Jade

Day 68

Dear Dre,

From this day on, I'm not going to let you pull and push me anytime you want. I guess that's why I feel like I need to say goodbye now. You and I really are not meant to be together. I need more than you could or would ever give to me and maybe you wanted more from me than I could give you. No doubt, you have a part of me that no one can get to. It might always be yours, but not in my life. I will spend the rest of my life trying not to regret you and what you've done to my heart. I will cherish you because you were my first and you've taught me how to give, how to take, and how to let go. I cherish every beautiful moment that we've shared and I wouldn't trade them for anything, but I need to love you only in my heart; it hurts too much on the outside.

~Jade

Day 71

Dear God,

Today I'm being transported to Kenneth's house to recover. Mr. Gregory couldn't take care of me as much as he wanted me to come home. Journals fill the tables in my room. All I can do is write in my journal, even though most of my thoughts are centered around why Dre doesn't love me as much as I thought he did and wondering if everyone goes through the same thing. Do all women have the same issues, or even similar issues, with men? How do they get over it? I'm not sure, but I have plenty of time to think about it. So far, this is the only thing I can do to keep what little sanity I have. I write on days I'm angry, on days I'm sad, on days I'm horny, on days I'm happy, and some days I just cry. There are no words. If I don't get rid of these emotions, they will eat me alive or I will die with them.

~Jade

When my dosage of morphine became lower, it was only then that I was able to fully realize what had happened to me. My body healed slowly, and by day seventy-one I was going stir-crazy. I asked Kenneth if I could stay at his home. He, of course, agreed and I left the hospital. Anthony had brought all of my things to Mr. Gregory's house. Weeks had passed and I still hadn't returned any of Anthony's calls. Eventually he went back to Los Angeles and I was glad because I wanted to start over. I needed to start over and move on.

For some reason, Anthony and Dre were one and the same to me and I just wasn't ready to go there. The more I wrote in my journal, the more I discovered about myself and just how much of whom I had been was centered on Dre. Writing in my journal was really helping me deal with my mother's death and my relationship with him.

I agreed to talk to another therapist as long as she didn't share anything with Kenneth that I told her. The therapist, Dr. Yang, had gotten a copy of the report from my school about my little run-in with Nadia, my previous hospital visit, and the reported damage to my dorm bathroom. Those incidents and the addition of the car accident are what led to the "Is she trying to kill herself?" conversations my therapist seemed to be focusing on. I chose to write about how I felt mentally and physically to try to piece all of the incidents together. So far the only thing I could come up with as a constant was Dre and my lack of direction.

I stayed in my room at Kenneth's house and kept writing until I wrote it all out of me. It seemed to be the only way I could come to terms with the fact that Dre was no good for me. He only caused me pain. Why should I love a man who caused me so much pain? Why would I give myself to someone who had hurt me? I wasn't sure of the answers.

I had finally written him out of me. I had to stop thinking about him, talking about him, hoping for him, wishing for him, praying for him. I knew Dre wasn't coming back and while I wasn't sure if he'd heard about my accident, I knew deep down that he wouldn't care even if he did. He didn't love me, so I figured it was time that I learned how to love me.

Because of You
A Poem by Jade Hall

Memories used to haunt me when I see the color red
Parts of my soul were still with you, dried but dead
My memories reminded me of pain
My life gave me hope that there are no more strains
To cause me more of the same, an unworthy struggle
to let go
I prayed every night for more of you to be gone
Never mind the fact of right vs. wrong
No longer stripping me of my soul
Thoughts of you now rotted and spoiled
Like cheese in desert soil
I am free
I am new
I no longer desire or lust you
I am whole, I am true
I am free to be one
I am free to be
All done with you
So I thank you for teaching me
That the dreams of me
The dreams of me now
Have come true

All because of you
Breathe.
Dear God,
I want to live.

~Jade

Time to Leave
Monica

When I returned to L.A. after Ms. Lori's funeral, I stayed in Jade's apartment for a few days. I didn't call Shawn and tell him that I had returned. Patrick paid to switch me to a different return flight. I knew that Shawn had a class at 4:30 on Tuesdays so I waited until half past five to go to his house, hoping to sneak in unseen. I tried to get on the pill but when Shawn found them, he threw them away. It made him think I was cheating on him. I was pregnant a third time by Shawn, but this time I wasn't going to abort the baby. I had no plans of telling him either.

A big part of me was still afraid of Shawn and I didn't want to live like that. I didn't want to be the next Tracy. As sweet as Shawn could be at times, I just couldn't handle the mental and physical abuse anymore. Patrick had shown me that I didn't have to. Shawn was so focused on me being his whore that he never took the time to learn that I liked jazz music, practicing yoga, and hiking. It's funny that I didn't realize how much I'd given up of myself until I dressed the way I wanted again. I had tried so hard to make it right with Shawn that I had given up all of my friends and family. I became a recluse from my own life.

I was able to get into the house unnoticed and quietly made my way upstairs to the bathroom. I started to put a few items in my purse when I heard the sound of whimpers and sniffles. I stood completely still and held my breath. The cries turned into a full burst of bawling. Without thinking, I ran out of the bathroom to the next room to find Shawn sitting on the floor crying. I stood in the doorway, shocked at seeing him so upset.

"Shawn?"

My voice startled him. He flinched but continued to cry uncontrollably.

"Shawn, what's wrong?" I ran toward him and knelt down. He looked at me and for a moment I was afraid that he would become angry. Instead, he leaned into my chest. I put my arms around him.

"Oh my God, are you okay? What's going on?" I asked. "What happened?" I rubbed his back and squeezed him tightly. He mumbled a few words I couldn't understand.

"My mother's dying."

"What do you mean?"

"She has stomach cancer. The doctors said she only has six months to live."

"Oh Shawn, I'm so sorry."

I was ready to leave him and now this. What do I do? Suddenly he sat straight up and looked at me with snot dripping from his nose.

"I can't do this without you." He put his arms around me and held me tight.

"Shawn—"

He interrupted me.

"Let's get married next weekend while she's still able to get around and hasn't started chemo. She's got all her hair. She can see her only son get married."

I gasped.

"Today is Tuesday."

"Okay, then the following weekend. I'll pay for everything. Anything you want. I can fly all your family and friends up. I'll pay for their hotels, their food—you just make the list."

"Shawn, we can't put together a wedding in a week and a half." The words that came out of my mouth were not what I meant to say.

"Yes we can, baby. Money's no object. I will fly you to New York, London, anywhere in the world right now so you can find the perfect dress. Just say yes. Next weekend. Say yes."

I lowered my head and two thoughts crossed my mind. If I said no, the baby and I would have a hard road ahead of us financially. If I marry him now, I would be doing it with no prenup.

"Yes."

He exhaled a sigh of relief.

"I can't wait to tell Mama. She'll be so happy. I love you, Monica."

"I love you, too," I said, my head still hanging low.

He grabbed my face, kissed me, jumped up, and ran down the hall. "I'm getting married!" he shouted.

I sat on the floor in disbelief. I needed to call Jade. I got up off the floor and walked toward the telephone beside the bed. I called Mr. Gregory's house and when he told me that Jade had been in a serious car accident, I dropped the phone and ran downstairs.

"Shawn, it's Jade. She's been in a car accident and they don't know if she's gonna make it. I have to go back."

"Monica, you can't leave me now! Why would you do that? What are you talking about? What are you saying? Monica, you just got back. We have to get this wedding going. Why are you doing this to me? My mother's dying."

"My best friend could be dying," I argued.

"I understand, but can you just wait 'til after the wedding? I'll go with you. I'll make sure she has the best of whatever she needs. Just don't leave me." Tears welled in his eyes. "I need you, baby."

I inhaled deeply and nodded.

That night, I called back to check on Jade but she wasn't able to speak. Mr. Gregory promised to let Jade know that I had called and keep me updated on her recovery. Within hours, Shawn and I told his mother the news that we were getting married. Her excitement surprised me. That next several days flew by so fast but every day I worried about Jade.

Shawn had hired an assistant for me. Wendy was a beautiful twenty-two-year-old Brazilian exchange student studying marketing who followed me everywhere. I didn't have much to do other than make decisions. Besides, I would have never dreamed that I would have a wedding that cost nearly eighty thousand dollars. The day of the wedding, his mother was ecstatic. She was certainly happier than I was. I barely remember what happened. I showed up, put on a dress, and said "I do" knowing that I didn't love this man. My only thoughts were of the child I was carrying. I had considered having another abortion, but I didn't want to put my body through that again.

Since Shawn's mother was becoming rapidly ill, we didn't go on a honeymoon, and that was fine with me. After the first trimester, I finally told him I was pregnant.

"Oh honey, that's perfect."

I was surprised by his response. "It is?"

"Yes. If Mama knows that her first grandchild is on the way, that will put some fight into her. She won't want to miss that."

All I could do was smile, thinking that now I had become some kind of magical fairy making all of Shawn and his mother's dreams come true.

"You know what would be really great?"

I couldn't have imagined what he was about to say.

"Mama will soon be needing 'round the clock care, so I was thinking with the nursing classes you've taken that maybe you could be there for her here at the house. That way you can get some rest while taking care of my baby. Plus my dad travels so much, he can't take care of her like she needs. What do you think?"

I was thinking I'm gonna cut my fucking throat, but instead I replied, "I think that's a great idea."

Over the next several months, my life became a living night-mare. His mother quickly turned into a bitch from hell. She would vomit and cuss me out all in the same breath. She made it clear that she was determined to see the baby born and all I could think about was her death. I had become a prisoner, trapped in Shawn's world.

I often called to check on Jade but she refused to talk. I would call Mr. Gregory when I could. He said her recovery was slow and she wasn't dealing with it well. I was worried, but there was nothing I could do.

The amount of care that Shawn's mom needed was exhausting. I was having a hard time managing the stress of it all and went into labor early. Devon Devereaux was born on a Friday morning weighing a healthy seven pounds, eight ounces. Shawn missed the birth because his mom had to have a chemo treatment. We had agreed to name the baby Shawn Jr., but since he didn't care enough to show up for his son's birth, I figured I would name my child what I wanted.

I stayed in the hospital for two days and Shawn had a driver pick me and the baby up. When we arrived at the house, he wasn't there. When he finally did arrive home, he came marching upstairs and I could tell by the pounding that he was angry.

"Monica!" he yelled.

I snuggled the baby close to me just as he burst through the door.

"Devon? Who the fuck is Devon?"

He came over to me and grabbed me around my neck and shoved my head up against the headboard.

"I'm going to have this baby tested and if he's not mine you will regret it, bitch."

He let go of my neck and walked out, slamming the door. I lovingly looked at my son and remembered why I had done this. I knew Devon was his son, but I wished he wasn't.

Two months after Devon was born, Shawn's mother passed away and I was happy as hell. With her out of the way, I didn't have to stick around any longer.

The day of the funeral, Shawn took it pretty hard. On our way back home, he didn't say a word in the car. When we arrived home, I put Devon down for his nap and crawled in bed next to him to rest. I kept the baby in the bed with me to make sure that Shawn didn't do anything crazy. As soon as I had lay down, Jade crossed my mind and I thought I would try to give her a call.

"Hello."

"Jade?"

"Monica? Why are you calling me now? Let me guess…you need something? Well, guess what, I'm not available for your crisis right now, the same way you weren't available for me."

"Jade, let me explain."

"Explain what, Monica? That you're a selfish bitch? Well no thanks; I'm busy right now."

"Can I get a word in?"

"No, fuck you and your explanations. I haven't talked to you in months. I guess it's because you're so fucking jealous of me, it's insane. I never thought it would come to this, but guess what? I'm happy. I don't need you."

"Jealous? Of what?"

"That I'm happy and you're not."

"Jade, can you just shut up and listen?"

"Listen to what? Shawn finally damn-near killed you, so is that why you decided to call me? Well don't bother calling me for sympathy. Where was the sympathy when I needed you? You weren't there like I thought you would be. You've been so busy putting Shawn ahead of me that I know where I stand. So now that he's beat your ass, I guess you decided to call me."

"Jade, are you kidding me?"

"When Dre left me, I needed you. I really needed you, and you left me for some fake-ass, flossy brother who beats you. You want to be like Tracy, huh?"

"Jade."

"You're about a year too late for an apology. Tell me why! Why should I jump through hoops for you? Kenneth cares about me and he's the best thing that ever happened to me. Do us both a favor. Stay out of my life you selfish bitch."

"Jade, you always think you're the only one going through something. You want the whole fucking world to stop when you say stop. Well, I'm not at your beck and call, and I'm sick of this one-sided so-called friendship."

I heard the phone slam down and I slammed mine down too. It took a minute for me to realize that I had just thrown out my friendship.

The next day, I took the baby in for his two-month checkup but I got my days mixed up and had to go back home. On the drive back to the house, I decided that I would tell Shawn I wanted a divorce. We had been married for almost a year and I should have been able to get at least enough in the divorce for me and the baby to live comfortably. That night I contemplated telling Shawn that I wanted the divorce. It was hard for me to sleep and around three in the morning Devon was being fussy. He had an ear infection and that made it hard for him to sleep as well.

I got up to feed him and realized that Shawn wasn't in the bed. I picked up Devon and headed toward the kitchen. As I passed Shawn's office, I heard a strange sound. The door was closed and I didn't see any lights on. When I opened the door, I noticed another light coming from the bookcase. Almost from behind it, like a trapdoor. I wondered where the hell did that come from? I peeked inside the door and there was Shawn, bent over a dusty table allowing a mechanical dildo to pump him in the ass. I opened the door in utter disbelief.

"Shawn?"

"Monica." He panicked.

I turned my back to him and walked away. He came after me and grabbed my arm. I yanked away from him. "Don't touch me. Don't you ever touch me!"

"Monica, what's wrong with you?"

"Are you gay?"

"I'm not gay. It's just something I like to do."

I couldn't believe my eyes. I turned away to walk out and he grabbed me by my hair and I almost fell. With Devon in my arms, I tried to stay on my feet but he yanked harder. Losing grip of my son, my entire body fell to the ground. The baby landed on top of me but rolled off my chest. I screamed and Shawn dragged me down the hallway toward the staircase. He let my hair go and started to stomp on my stomach, kicking me in my rib cage. Out of the corner of my eye, I could see my baby and prayed to God he wasn't hurt.

"Shawn, stop it!" I yelled. We tussled and I managed to get back to Devon. I cradled him as blood poured from my mouth. I looked up and looked for the first thing I could grab. There was a lamp on the hall table. Holding my baby in one arm, I threw it at him. He ducked and charged at me. With his fist balled up, he came at me and punched me in the face, and I fell still clutching onto Devon but he fell from my arms. I felt Shawn pick me up by my arm and throw me against the wall. The photos on the wall clattered from the impact. He wrapped his hands around my throat and I started to kick and scream like a wild pig. All I wanted was my baby. I struggled to breathe as my feet lifted off the floor.

"I will kill you and him!"

I kicked him in his nuts as hard as I could and he lost his grip around my neck. I felt my feet hit the floor. I scooped up Devon and ran down the stairs as fast as I could. When I reached the bottom, I looked up and saw Shawn standing at the top of the stairs.

"Fuck you, Shawn!" I screamed. "You will never see me or this baby for as long as you live."

"Get the fuck out, whore."

That's exactly what I did. I headed for the door as fast as I could, but my car was parked around the back of the house. I had to run farther to get to my car and my body ached with pain.

When I reached my car, I put the baby in his car seat but I didn't bother to strap him down. I got in, put the key in the ignition, and unexpectedly heard a loud pop. Then shards of glass rained all over me.

"Get away from me!" I yelled.

Shawn started to punch me in my face like a boxer in a street fight. I tried to shield myself with my arms, but he was too strong. Devon started to cry and I threw the car into drive and mashed the gas pedal. Shawn fell backward and I ran over the flowers planted alongside the driveway. I had never been so terrified in my life. As I sped away, I was shaking so badly that I drove about three miles without stopping. Feeling safe that Shawn wasn't behind me, I turned into a parking lot to strap Devon in his car seat. But when I stopped the car, I felt something warm between my legs. I looked down and there was blood soaking through my light blue shorts.

"Shit."

I looked around me and God was on my side; I saw a sign for a hospital. I headed straight toward it. When I arrived, I took the baby out of the car and carried him inside, but my body started to feel weak. A man walking toward me saw all of the blood on my pants and my face.

"Ma'am."

I shook my head, passed the baby to him, and collapsed.

Revelation
Jade

After several weeks at Kenneth's house and intensive therapy, I was starting to feel a little better about my life. I was at least out of the body cast and now just in a wheelchair. If it hadn't been for Kenneth, I would have gone stir-crazy. When he suggested that we go boating, I was ecstatic. I couldn't wait to get out of the house to go somewhere other than the hospital. I wheeled myself toward the front door and waited anxiously for Kenneth to get home. As soon as I saw his truck drive up, I opened the door and went out on the front porch.

"Well, look who's up and about," he said.

"Hey, I'm ready!" I was excited.

"I see that. Let me just put my stuff down and we can go. Did Estella pack food for us?"

"Yes, and I helped."

"Wow…getting your strength back, I see."

"Yes, and I'm doing much better at standing for almost half an hour."

"Well, you know when you're with me, there's nothing you need to do but smile."

He puts his stuff down on the lounge chair and picked me up, carrying me to the truck. Kenneth was a real life Prince Charming who I finally felt I deserved.

"Are you comfortable?" he asked.

"Yeah, thanks," I replied.

"Okay, then off we go." He put the car into reverse. We drove to the Houston Yacht Club and made our way to Kenneth's boat.

He was there for me hand and foot. I was so content to be there with him. As we sailed out to sea, I relaxed and enjoyed the morning air. He talked to me about sailing and the peace he felt at sea.

"How often do you come out?" I asked while the breeze lifted my hair.

"Not as often as I'd like, but I've been thinking about retiring."

"Really? Retire and do what? Sail all day?" I joked.

"No, but that'd be part of it. Of course, I'd want someone to share the next chapter of my life with." He winked and seductively strolled over.

"Is that right?" I asked, sitting forward in my chair.

"Yes, that's right." He leaned over, looked into my eyes, and tenderly kissed me. I hadn't been kissed in so long that I was looking forward to this moment. His lips leaned in toward mine and the electricity could be felt a mile away as he kissed me softly. The connection sent a gush up my spine, reminding me that I hadn't had sex in a very, very long time.

"So, what do you think about that?" he asked.

"About what?" I replied, having totally forgotten what he'd asked me.

"Being that someone I could share the next chapter with," he responded.

He strolled over to the cooler. I wasn't sure what to say, but from therapy I knew I needed to be honest, and so I was. I took a deep breath.

"Kenneth, I really like you, but I've been through so much with relationships and I don't think I'm ready to talk about commitment. I don't think I'm good at that whole relationship thing. I'm pretty unlucky in that area." I put my head down, hoping to miss connecting with his gaze.

"I can respect that and I'm not trying to rush you, but I do want you in my life. I've enjoyed these months together with you," he said as he opened his beer. He came over to me, bent down to my eye level, and lightly wiped away the tear that I had accidentally let escape. "Hey, it's okay. I'm not going anywhere. Take all the time you need—unless you want to have babies. Then we might have an issue, since my clock is short. I'll be forty-seven next week." He laughed and took a swallow of his beer. "Which reminds me, I definitely want your input on my party."

Kenneth used his index finger to tap my nose. He stood up, reached for his wallet, opened it to pictures, and passed it to me.

"You'll get to meet my son and his wife. I haven't seen him in almost fifteen years." He took another sip of his beer. I took the wallet from his hand and looked at the picture of his son.

SHIT...Breathe...Breathe...Breathe . . .

It was Dre.

Poetic Interlude: Unbalanced
A Poem by Jade Hall

I loathe myself
When I look into a mirror
And I see you.
I daze myself
When I look into a crowd
And I look for you.
I startle myself
When I listen to a song
And I hear your voice.
I dumbfound myself
When I catch a scent
And I smell you.
I frighten myself
When I dream
And I dream of you.
I enrage myself
When I realize how much
I still want you.
You are, I am, still unbalanced.

Unbalanced

Jade

I thought my first reaction to seeing Dre would be rage, but instead, I took a deep breath and held it for a few moments. I exhaled and decided to release Dre from my life. It was time to repair Cinderella. She had been shattered through no fault of her own, but I knew that I was the only one who could put her back together. Some of the last words that Mother spoke to me were about love and I didn't want to die of a broken heart like she did. I may never know who the Dre in Mother's life was, but I knew who the Dre in my life was and I had to let him go or die.

I had spent many of my nights in recovery alone, and in those nights, I thought a lot about the kind of woman I wanted to be. I didn't want to be a bitch, I didn't want to be bitter, and I didn't want to hold onto a man that didn't want me. Like Monica once said, "There's no sense in wasting a precious heart on someone who didn't cherish it enough to even say goodbye to it."

Sure, I had fun with Dre, but Dre wasn't good for me and deep down inside, I really knew that. Maybe it wasn't Dre leaving me that hurt; maybe it was that, for all I thought I was to him, he didn't think I was anything. Not to mention here was Kenneth, a well-educated, strong man who not only liked me but loved me. Discovering that he was Dre's dad was going to complicate things a little bit. We can live in truth or we die in a lie. I had to stop living for Dre and begin living for me. If I didn't, I knew I would die inside. I struggled thinking if I should tell Kenneth at that moment about Dre and me, but losing Kenneth wouldn't be worth it. I decided that I would deal with that when I have to. Right now, I wanted to enjoy spending time with Kenneth. So, without hesitation, I gently grazed my thumb over the photo as if I were wiping a speck of dirt off it, then smiled and passed the wallet back to him.

At that moment, a gentle breeze washed over me.

"He doesn't look anything like you," I said.

"No, but he looks just like his mother. She and I were married as teenagers." Kenneth sat down next to me in the reclining chair. His sigh let me know that he had a heavy heart about seeing Dre for the first time in nearly fifteen years. He gazed out toward the sea and shook his head in disgust. It almost seemed like he still had some pain inside, and I completely understood that pain.

"We got married at eighteen. I was so young and didn't know how to really be a man. I was a kid. I tried so hard to stay with her because I loved my kids, but we just couldn't make it work. Then one day I came home and she was gone with the kids. She changed their names and moved across the country." He shook his head as if he was back in that moment—the moment he walked up to the door and realized they were gone.

"So I threw myself into school and work and pretended it never happened. Then one day, I decided that I wanted to find them, so I hired private investigators, and they found Andre. He's my oldest." He smiled as he took a sip of his beer. "I've only talked to him for a few minutes, but he'll be here for my party. I think it will take some pressure off of him in case he's nervous. You know, in a mix-and-mingle session; that way it's not awkward for him or his wife. What do you think?"

"I think that's a good decision," I said, still struggling with the word "wife."

"You're probably too young to know what it's like to have everything you know, everything you love, taken from you and there's nothing you can do about it, but I know," he said, almost getting choked up. He turned his head toward the open sea and seemed to gaze off again, back to that moment. I placed my hand on his thigh to comfort him.

"Actually, I do know. I lost someone very special to me." I let my head hang down. "Someone I really loved and who I thought really loved me," I said, nearly bringing tears to my eyes. He put his hand over mine and squeezed.

"Well, then maybe we were brought here together to share that pain of losing someone we both love," he said.

"Maybe." There was a quiet and calmness in the air. With his other hand, he touched my chin. I tried to lift my face, but it was too late. Tears had already started to escape my eyes, racing toward my lap. Why was I still crying over him? I thought I had let Dre go, but maybe I hadn't fully let him go yet, or maybe it was the complexity of the situation.

Kenneth put both of his hands up to my face and wiped away my tears. I just needed to let go of the pain that I still had in my heart. At the moment our eyes met, I saw Dre and quickly put my head down, imagining that it really was him and I spewed my soul's burning questions.

"I just...I just don't understand why?" I sniffled. There was a part of me that felt as if I were talking to Dre and this was my chance to just say it. Even if I never got the answer to my question, I was at least able to say it out loud. Somehow that gave me relief to know that we had both been hurt by Dre and we both wanted to forgive him and let go of the pain we felt from losing him.

"Why wasn't I good enough? Wasn't I pretty enough? Wasn't I sexy enough? Wasn't I all that you needed? I mean . . ." I stuttered as I whimpered. My whimpering turned into a full-on outburst of crying and uncontrollable sobbing as my body collapsed into Kenneth's arms. "I'm angry, I'm depressed, and I want revenge, but all of this feels so miserable. I feel like my soul is missing and I just want to get it back. Sometimes I don't know if I can. I can't go on anymore just being mad. It's easy for me to be pissed, but I don't think I've allowed myself to be just hurt. To just miss him. I miss him, I miss us…I miss the laughing, I miss the fun, I miss the love. I miss the way he held me in his arms and the way he touched me. I want to get over that, but no one can tell me how."

I closed my eyes as my face pressed against his chest and imagined for a moment, just that moment, that it really was Dre and that he really was holding me. I even prayed that for one moment God would let me feel Dre hold me. I hoped that my heart would heal in that instant, but it didn't. I clenched my eyes, grinded my teeth, and I prayed intensely, but I knew my wish wasn't going to come true. Dre was never coming back to me.

I don't know how much time passed, but I just sat there with my head in Kenneth's arms crying.

"If he didn't know how special you are, he didn't deserve you," Kenneth said and I felt his hand stroking my hair. As I rocked back and forth, I felt sprinkles of rainfall on my face and I was reminded of all that had happened. The first day we met, the day I gave all of myself to him, the days we spent together in each other's arms. The last day I saw him, the day he left, the day I lost the baby, the day I lost my mind. Thoughts of Mother and the day she died flooded my mind, as well as the day of the funeral, the day of the...the day of the accident.

The accident.

I remembered.

It had been Dre! I'd seen Dre at that store and I'd ran after him and he'd driven away. I was sitting in this wheelchair with a broken body and a broken soul over a man who watched me get hit by a car and drove away.

My tears stopped.

I sat up, looked Kenneth in the face, and leaned in to kiss him. The rain was falling and I couldn't tell the difference between my tears, his tears, and the rain itself. Without notice, Kenneth lifted me in his arms and carried me to the deck below.

Entering the bedroom, he gently placed me on the bed and lay beside me. Overwhelmed by his scent, my mind shifted to determining what my limitations were, considering I was still recovering. I lay there on my back, stretching my body out as straight as I could.

"I'll give you anything you want if you'll be mine," he said as he tenderly kissed my lips.

"I'm already yours," I confessed without realizing what I'd said. He kissed me with an intensity unlike any of the other kisses.

"I was hoping you'd say that." He opened the drawer again and pulled out a little baby blue box with a white ribbon around it.

"What is that?"

"It's for you." He opened the box and inside was a pair of Tiffany diamond-encrusted earrings.

"They're only two carats, but I thought they looked beautiful, like you."

My mouth fell open as I stared at the earrings like I had just seen the Holy Grail. I'd heard about Tiffany diamonds but I had never touched or seen one up close. I stared at the earrings and smiled.

"Kenneth, you didn't have to do that," I said, feeling breathless.

"I know, but I wanted to. I want you to know that you're special to me. Here, let's try them on," he said as he took them out of the box. Still speechless, I removed my five-dollar Rue 21 hoops and sat there with my hands tightly clasped together. The look in his eyes told me that this was exactly what he had planned. He put the earrings in my ears and I could see the joy in his face. When they were both in, he leaned back to see if they were straight. "There, my princess," he said, smiling. Then he leaned over and kissed me. I didn't know what to do. He stood up and headed to the bathroom. He returned holding a mirror and gave it to me.

"Here you go."

I took the mirror, but I was still speechless. I looked in the mirror at my ears and let my head drop.

"What's wrong?" he asked. "You don't like them?"

"No, it's not that at all. I love them," I said, trying to muster up a fake smile. "I've just never had anyone do anything like this for me." It scared me how much Kenneth cared for me.

"I want to do so much more for you, if you'll let me."

I cringed in pain and pushed my head back.

"What's wrong?" He stood up.

"It's my back." I winced.

"You want your medicine?"

"Yeah, could you get it for me? It's in my purse." I laid my head against the rail and let out a sigh of relief. He brought my purse over and sat it beside me.

"I'll get you some water," he offered as he hurried to the kitchenette. I dug in my purse for my medication and when I found the bottle of codeine, I quickly popped three of them, even though I was only supposed to take two. When Kenneth returned with the water, I grabbed it from him and swallowed the pills down. He sat down on the bed and pushed a piece of hair out of my face.

"You get some rest," he said.

"Goodnight baby."

Lost

Monica

When I woke up, I was in a hospital bed and I panicked. I didn't know where my baby was.

"Nurse! Somebody! Hey!" I yelled, not realizing that a nurse was standing in the room.

"Hey now, calm down, your baby is just fine. I'll have a nurse bring him in."

She pressed the intercom button on the wall beside her.

"Yes," the voice on the other end answered.

"Can you bring baby boy Devereaux in? The mom is awake."

"Sure," the voice replied.

"Is he okay?" I asked.

"He's fine. But how are you? Looks like you got into a fight with a doorway and lost."

My stomach ached with pain and I was afraid to think about what my face looked like. All I could think about was my son. I wanted to hold him in my arms and smell his baby skin.

As I lay there thinking about him, a nurse entered the room empty-handed.

"Where's my baby?"

"Your husband came and picked him up. He said his mother would watch him."

I ripped the IVs from my arm and tried to get out of the bed despite the pain intensifying in my stomach. The pain I felt now was deeper. The nurses came running over to me.

"Wait, Monica. What are you doing?"

"His mother is dead you stupid fucking assholes! I have to leave, I have to go get my son!"

The nurse grabbed me and looked me square in the eyes with a look of desperation.

"Let's call the police. You have three broken ribs. You were hemorrhaging when you got here and if he did this to you, you may come back dead. So just calm down and let's call the police, okay? Just stay put."

I started to cry, worried about my son. Scared and angry all at the same time, I asked God to forgive me now for murdering Shawn because when I found that son of a bitch, I would kill him. Then I heard a click of the door and Patrick entered the room carrying a bouquet of flowers.

"Hi, beautiful."

The look on my face gave it away. He dropped the flowers and ran to my side.

"What's the matter?" he asked as he sat on the bed.

"Shawn came and took the baby. I don't know where he is and I don't know what to do. He could be anywhere. He's got so much fucking money he could have my baby in Brazil or somewhere by now."

"Okay, wait, I don't understand. What happened? How did he get the baby?"

"They just gave him to Shawn. They're calling the police but Shawn is so evil, he would hurt Devon just to hurt me.

"Don't worry, we'll find him."

"You don't know him like I do."

I leaned against the pillows and turned my head. Tears flowed from my eyes. He kissed me on my forehead.

"I'm going to go make a few phone calls and see what I can do."

"There's nothing you can do. You don't know Shawn. You don't know what he's capable of."

"I'll be back in a few minutes. Try not to worry, okay?"

He walked out the door and I cried, feeling helpless and scared. The nurse tried to comfort me with her hopeful words, but I could barely hear her. I wasn't listening because all I could think about was Devon, and I prayed that he was okay. I thought I'd be doing Devon and myself a favor by getting a big portion of Shawn's money, but no amount of money is worth the pain I felt, not knowing if my baby was safe.

The police finally showed up and took my statement. For the next hour, they grilled me on every detail of what Shawn had done to me. When Patrick returned, I was ashamed to allow him to hear all the details of the abuse I had endured, but he didn't seem to be bothered at all. He just kept caressing and kissing my hand gently. The officer assured me that they had already dispatched others to Shawn's home. It had been nearly two hours when a different officer opened the door and peeked his head in.

"Excuse me, Officer Stanton, Officer Kingsley? Can I see the two of you for a minute please?"

The two officers stepped out into the hallway. I could see them talking and it was making me even more afraid. I saw a smile come across both officers' faces and that made me eager to know what was happening. One of the officers stepped back into my room.

"Mrs. Devereaux," Officer Stanton said.

"Ms. Thompson," I corrected him.

"Your baby's safe and in police custody. They're bringing him here now."

"What? Are you sure? What happened? Oh thank God. Is he alright?"

"He's perfectly fine." The officer smiled.

"What about Shawn?"

"We arrested Mr. Devereaux for assault and kidnapping."

"Thank you, thank you so much."

The officers excused themselves from the room and Patrick embraced me in a hug that was both comforting and relieving.

"I told you it would be alright."

"I know, but I won't believe it until he's back in my arms. Thank you. How did you . . .?"

"Well, let's just say that playing poker with the chief of police and the mayor makes getting things done faster a lot easier."

"I don't know how I can ever thank you."

"Divorce him and come with me."

I gasped.

"I've got a big ole house and no one to share it with. You and the little man can make it your own."

The door opened and there was a female officer holding my baby. I clapped with excitement and reached my arms out to Devon. When she placed him in my arms, I felt at peace. I checked every inch of his little body looking for one single hair out of place, but Devon was perfect.

I appreciated Patrick's offer to move in with him, but honestly I didn't know him well enough for that kind of decision. I barely knew who I was anymore. I needed to be in a place that felt

242

safe and where I could focus on getting myself back together. I wanted peace, I wanted calm, and I wanted to disappear.

There was one place I knew I could call always call home. That morning, we left the hospital and I took a cab to Mr. Gregory's house.

Knock, Knock.

I stood at the door. The door cracked open slowly. I leaned down.

"You must be Maya. I'm Monica and this is my son Devon."

"I know. Papa G told me you were coming. Come in." She motioned to me.

The moment I stepped in, I felt safe. Mr. Gregory lived on a forty-acre farm south of Houston proper. For as far as the eye could see, there were rows of trees, cows feasting on grass, chickens, and horses. I had forgotten how magical this place was. I brought our things in and settled in. Maybe if I called Jade from Mr. Gregory's phone, she'd answer.

"She invited me to some big party she's having in a few weeks. You want to go?" he asked.

"I can't focus on that right now," I replied.

"Well she'll be by here soon enough. You rest up." He patted me on my back.

"Can I hold the baby?" Maya asked.

"Sure." I passed her Devon.

"I know what to do. Did you know I had a little brother?"

I was stunned and not really sure what to say. I looked at Mr. Gregory for approval. He nodded and I knew it was okay to say yes.

"Can he be my brother?"

"I think he would like that. He doesn't have any sisters."

Mr. Gregory showed me to the room that Devon and I would stay in. I put down my backpack, its contents the only things I had to my name, and smiled. I looked back at him.

"It's perfect."

"Well if it wasn't, ain't nothing I can do to change it. Ain't much you can do to change anything that's already there. You can only change what's ahead of you."

He walked toward the door then stopped and turned. "You and Jade can change your friendship tomorrow. Today is gone," he said.

I hoped so, because I really needed my best friend. But first I needed time.

Connect
Jade

The next morning, I awoke to a beautiful sunrise beaming inside the yacht window. Ocean waves that had gently rocked me asleep gently awoke me. I could hear the wails of seagulls feasting. As I rubbed the sleep from my eyes, I was amazed as I looked around the room to see that it was filled with pink and white miniature lilies. It took an enormous amount of strength to pull my body up to a sitting position and peek out the small window. Zooming like a flurry of bullets raining from the air, I could see the seagulls diving for fish. There was an unfamiliar scent in the air that was there the night before. Taking in a slight breath, I allowed a smile to tug at my lips. I quickly wiped my eyes to find that I wasn't dreaming and I really had diamond earrings in my ears. I reached over to the dresser where my purse was and grabbed my pen and notebook.

The Kenneth-Dre connection was eating away at me and I

didn't know what to do about it. Unlike the other men that I had met in my life, I felt like I needed to protect this relationship and the trust that Kenneth had in me. He really wasn't like any other guy that I had ever known. There was something truly special and genuine about him and I didn't want to let Dre fuck that up by being in my head. I heard a slight knock at the door and it slowly opened. Estella carried a breakfast tray as she walked in.

"Sorry. Did I wake you, Ms. Jade?"

"No, not at all, Estella. I was just getting up," I said.

She walked over toward the bed and set the tray down on the nightstand. "Dr. Hill will be down to join you in a moment."

"Thank you."

"Is there anything else?" she asked politely.

"No, I'm fine, thank you."

As I sat looking at the room I was in and thinking about the fact that I was on a boat with a man who had just put two carats in my ears, I recognized that I was in a very unique place in my life right now. Another knock at the door and this time it was Kenneth. He stood there looking like a breath of fresh air on a Sunday morning.

"Good morning, beautiful." He closed the door behind him. "Mind if I join you?"

"No, not at all."

He sat on the edge of the bed.

"Have you ever been fishing?"

"Fishing?"

"Yeah, you know…rod and reel? Throw out the line…reel it in?"

"No, I haven't. Why?"

"Then it's time you learn. It's what I do when I need time to be silent. You have to be really calm and quiet to fish. That gives me time to get clear about what my next moves are going to be in my life. It's where I discovered my feelings for you."

He leaned over and gave me a long, passionate kiss. His caress of my face in his hand felt safe and complete. We shared a delicious breakfast and then he carried me above deck to teach me how to fish. It was the most calm I had experienced in a long time. While it was quiet, a part of me wanted to tell Kenneth about Dre, but a bigger part of me didn't want to, so I just stayed quiet and waited to catch my fish. Maybe I had already caught it. We sat there calmly, quietly, waiting. I had never been so still. I treasured the silence and realized that there had been so much noise in my life, that I had created the noise.

We sat for hours, just waiting for a tug. The tug never came but the smiles and delicate kisses we shared were genuine and pure. Just as quickly as the sun rose, it set and we made our way back to land.

In the car, we discussed his upcoming birthday bash: a Mardi Gras-themed party with an invitation list that included the elite population of Houston's finest. Kenneth wanted the party at his house and was working with his longtime party planner extraordinaire, Richard, who affectionately liked to be called Dick. Dick had more plans than a damn flight instructor. He made sure that everything was on track and in order. It would be a black-tie affair and everyone would have custom designed Mardi Gras masks.

I had plans of my own for Kenneth's birthday party. He was always worried about how hard I was working during my physical therapy but I wanted to get my body as strong as I could and had about five weeks until the party. I called and invited Mr. Gregory to the party, but he was still adjusting to his new life with my niece, Maya. He told me that Anthony had been calling, but I didn't have time for Anthony. I didn't owe anyone an explanation of where I was or who I was with. Plus I didn't need any more distractions. I liked this place of calm and safety.

Kenneth hesitated about having sex with me for fear of hurting me inside. It was sweet that he considered that, so I was determined to make sure that it was going to be special when we finally made love. I knew that we would not just be making love; we would be making a real connection, something I'd never had before with anyone on my lover's list, including Dre.

Finally the day came and like every morning, I peeked out the window to see Kenneth doing his usual laps in the pool. Dick had helped me select the perfect outfit for this moment that I knew was finally here. I put on a black, tight-fitting, sheer maxi dress and a long black robe. I wanted some really sexy stilettos but I wasn't completely healed so Dick bought me a beautiful pair of Jimmy Choo sandals that were more comfortable. I was tired of walking around in old people shoes for the arch and spine support. I stood in front of the mirror for a few moments and reveled in thanks, grateful that I was no longer in those dreadful casts.

I made my way out to the pool area, the morning air flowing toward Nita. My crotchless panties awakened her and I could feel her preparing herself. The closer I got to him, the wetter Nita became. Lap after lap, I could see the water glistening over his muscles with each stroke. He didn't notice me coming out to the pool walking toward him. I opened my robe and stood there, waiting patiently until he reached the end and popped his head up. He didn't say a word, staring at me as if he'd just seen me for the first time. I dropped the robe, pulled the sheer dress up as I squatted down, and opened my legs wide so he could see my crotchless panties, giving Nita full exposure. He looked stunned and mesmerized. He lifted his glistening body out of the pool and immediately took a lick as if he was licking ice cream before it starts to drip. He knew that I was dripping for him. He grabbed me around my waist, picking my slender, ninety-five pound body up, and placed me on the edge of the pool. I hadn't planned on putting my Jimmy Choos in the pool, but I didn't care. I was sacrificing my Jimmys for his jimmy.

He placed his hand over my heart and pushed gently, encouraging me to lie back. I felt his cold, wet hands glide down my body toward my legs. He carefully placed each of my legs on his shoulders and after twenty insatiable minutes of his pleasing Nita, I exploded. He was able to anticipate when that would happened since he gave Nita attention at least two times a day, if not more. My stomach churned and Nita clenched. I wanted him inside of me and I had prepared my body for this moment. I lifted his face to meet my eyes.

"I have a gift for you," I said.

"Really?"

"Yeah. I do."

"What is it?" he asked.

"Me."

With the softest voice, I then said, "Come inside me. I want you." I didn't think about anything else except him. It was the first time in my life that I wasn't worried about if a man should or should not be wearing a condom.

He started to object. "But your body—"

"My body is ready for you. Happy birthday, baby." I pulled him to me. He kissed my breast. I could feel that he was ready to enter me and I couldn't wait. Finally he made his way in and I groaned with each unhurried and deliberate stoke. I groaned until I cried out his name.

"Kenneth, fuck me," I panted as my heart raced. My legs lingering in the pool, I wrapped them around his body. He picked me up and with a steady serving of his anatomy, he pleased me. Nita was ecstatic and I felt my second orgasm rise. He turned us around so that he was sitting on the edge of the pool and I was straddled across him. I gave him five short strokes and then a long and slow deep thrust, followed by another five short strokes.

"I'm cummin', baby," he said, and I didn't mind at all.

"Cum inside of me."

When the explosions were over, I rested my chin on his shoulder, facing the patio doorway to the house, and opened my eyes. My gaze met with Dre's standing in the doorway. The instant we made eye contact, I froze. Nita froze. Time froze. Dre turned and walked away.

"What's wrong?" Kenneth looked at me, but I couldn't look him in the eye. I fell off of him and fumbled around for my robe sash while pointing at the house.

"I think…uhh…your…your…son." I giggled, still trying to find the words. I stood there in my robe and soaked Jimmy Choos.

"Oh shit!" Kenneth jumped up, grabbed a nearby towel, and ran toward the house.

Karma is a bitch and right then she was wearing Jimmy Choos.

I could only chuckle as I sauntered over to the patio table, sat down, lit a cigarette, and propped my feet up on the chair next to me. I felt a strong sense of accomplishment and shame. I knew that I had to say something to him but I didn't know where to start. Kenneth came back to the patio.

"I guess that's not a really good intro to a fresh start, seeing your old man getting busy," Kenneth said.

I walked over to him. "Baby, there's nothing old about you and I do mean nothing." I removed thoughts of being open and honest with him from my mind and focused on what I wanted. I couldn't fathom telling him the truth. I knew the truth would cost me everything and I loved everything that we had. In that moment, Dre didn't mean that much to me.

Kenneth and I made love for the next three hours outside in the pool area, and with each orgasm there was a tiny part of me that felt like Dre was leaving me and I wanted him to be gone.

The party was scheduled to start that night at eight but as each minute ticked by, I suffered knowing that Dre would be returning. The man I had waited to return to me was now here and for the first time, I wanted nothing more than for him not to return. I knew in my heart that I needed to tell Kenneth, but every time I found the breath to speak, I would look at his smile and change my mind.

Kenneth kept trying to call Dre, but he didn't answer. I hoped that maybe he just wouldn't come to the party, but deep down, I knew he would. At four o'clock, the makeup artist and hair-stylist arrived, ready to make me beautiful. I sat in the chair as they prepped and tugged at my face and hair. My custom-made Versace dress was a halter-top number with a "V" in the front that stopped at my navel. A string of diamonds connected the backless top to the waist of the dress. It was spectacular hanging on the back of the door, still in its package. Dick swirled and twirled around me trying to give me a crash course in everyone who would be in attendance. I knew they were the elite of Houston but I didn't measure up to their status. The more he jabbered on, the more I forgot every word he said. All I could think about was what to say when Dre walked in that door. I started to feel like I was drowning and couldn't get any air.

How was I going to measure up to the elite of Houston. Why had Kenneth chosen me? Was I out of my league? My mind plagued me with questions that I couldn't answer. As the layers of makeup were applied to my face, I felt the layers of lies that I had piled up inside of me about to explode. My truth became like a wild caged animal and had to be set free.

Once my hair and makeup were done, it was time to slip on my dress, and despite all the flurry of activity happening to make me beautiful, I felt ugly and disgusted. Then Dick showed me the Mardi Gras mask that he picked out for me, a half-face mask with gold glitter trim and black feathers. When they put the mask on me, I knew then that I had found a place to hide.

"Did you want a little something to drink?" Dick asked.

"Yes!"

"Champagne?"

"Rémy Martin with a splash of champagne," I replied.

He looked at me strangely and agreed.

"I've never heard that mix before but okay."

"They call that a Biggie. Like Biggie Smalls," I explained.

"Okay, be right back."

My armpits were filled with sweat, my heart pounded, and Nita was clenched tightly.

Dick returned with a glass and I quickly downed the entire drink.

Kenneth had asked Dick to let him know when I was on my way, so I sent Dick with a message once we finished perfecting my hair.

The winding staircase was perfect for any woman to make an entrance. As I stood at the top of the stairs, I scanned the crowd, initially looking for Dre, but I didn't see him. Relief washed over me. Maybe he didn't come. I did see Kenneth staring at me as I made my way down. He stopped in his tracks and watched me descend. He joined me halfway down and held my hand to let everyone know that he was my man and that I was his woman.

"You look stunning," he said.

"Thank you." I beamed right along with him.

He gave me a kiss on the cheek before guiding me toward the dance floor.

"Listen, there are so many people who want to meet you, but we would be here all night trying to meet everyone. I think I can make this simple," he whispered.

"Okay."

We made our way to the stage where the DJ was and Kenneth asked for a microphone.

"Hi everyone. May I have your attention, please?"

Everyone, including me, looked at him, wondering what was going on. I held his hand tighter.

"I just want to take a moment and thank you all for coming out tonight and celebrating my birthday. I also wanted to introduce you to a very, very special woman in my life, Ms. Jade Hall. Everyone kept asking me when she was coming out, but as you can see, this beauty is well worth the wait."

He extended my arm to show me off and I smiled bashfully. The crowd applauded, sharing his joy.

"Now, if you all can bear with me for a few minutes, I have a modification to the plan that my very special woman doesn't know about," he said. He motioned to Dick. I know the confusion showed on my face as I clenched his hand even tighter. Suddenly the lights dimmed and the crowd parted as male and female dancers came out in matching outfits of various shades of pastels.

Each man carried a rose. The band began to play an instrumental version of Stevie Wonder's "Ribbon in the Sky." I watched the dancers as they seemed to fall in love with each other right in front of me.

Everyone in the room seemed to be clued into what was going on except me. Within moments of the song starting, Kenneth took my hand and guided me to the dance floor. A vocalist started to sing and her melodic version was incredible.

"What's going on?" I whispered in his ear.

"Just enjoy it," he replied.

I sank into the moment as the song came to a climax, resting my head on his shoulders, and he whispered, "Jade, I love you. Unlike any woman I have ever known."

I looked at Kenneth and just over his shoulder, there he was. Dre. I refocused on Kenneth and tears swelled in my eyes. I couldn't speak.

He backed away from me and placed me in a chair that I didn't even notice was there. The male dancers then came and lay one white rose each at my feet, posing before moving away. Somewhere around the sixth or seventh rose, I turned to my right with the intention of looking at Kenneth, but caught a glimpse of Dre standing there with a white blonde next to him. I turned my attention back to Kenneth, reminding myself he was really important to me.

By the end of the song, there was only one girl and guy dancing together. I watched him spin her around in the air with a ribbon trailing behind her. The melody continued and Kenneth knelt down on one knee in front of me. At that point, the tears that had swelled in my eyes escaped, because I knew.

Kenneth pulled a ring out of his pocket that was absolutely stunning. Crafted in white gold, the ring held a blinding five-carat princess-cut diamond. I pressed my hands over my open mouth, in awe of the most beautiful ring I had ever seen. The crowd was in awe.

Kenneth grabbed my left hand and placed it in his hand. One tear fell from his eye as he said, "My beautiful Jade, the first time I saw your face, I knew." He tried to smile, but his chin trembled and he squeezed my hand tighter. "I just knew. I knew you were the woman that my heart had dreamt about. You give me a new reason and a new purpose to wake up each day. I want to wake up every day and see your face. I want to hold you every night. You taught me how to love again, and I can't imagine another day of my life without you. You have given me more than I even knew I wanted and I adore you. Will you marry me?"

Perfect Fit
Jade

When I realized what Kenneth had said, I answered without hesitation.

"Yes, yes, yes—I'll marry you!" The crowd erupted in applause. I looked directly at Dre after I said yes and he looked like he had just shit his pants. Kenneth dropped the microphone, swooped me up out of my chair, and swung me around in his arms like a doll. I was free of my feelings for Dre and I knew that Kenneth was the man I wanted to spend my life with. I closed my eyes to savor the moment I had been waiting for all my life but didn't know it.

"She said yes!" he shouted and then hugged me tightly. "I love you, baby," he whispered in my ear.

I closed my eyes even tighter and said with confidence, "I love you too, baby." I opened my eyes, smiled, and then gazed at my ring and smiled even more.

Releasing me just enough to kiss me, Kenneth did so as if it was our first time he had ever given me a kiss. "I also ask you all to welcome my son, Andre. Come on up here son."

I glanced back over at Dre and felt sorry for him. I was a good woman and wanted to be a better woman. All of my dreams had come true and even some that I couldn't have dreamt for myself. Mother would have been so proud of me. I was proud that my feelings for Dre were no longer eating away at me. I was free of him mentally and physically. I saw him shake his head slightly but I didn't care what he thought.

Turning away from him, I couldn't help but admire my new five-carat engagement ring.

"I have an engagement gift for you," Kenneth said, "but you have to come outside to get it."

I couldn't imagine how it could get much better, but it did. I nearly ran to the front double doors, flung them open, and gasped at the sight of a brand new, black-on-black Mercedes. I screamed and ran toward him and leaped into his arms, hugging and kissing him as if there was no one else in the room.

"I'll give you anything and everything you'll ever want," he said.

"Maybe after our guests leave."

He smiled then whispered in my ear, "We can break it in really good."

"Mmmmm, that sounds good. I love you Dr. Hill."

"I love you Mrs. Hill." We turned and faced the crowd.

"Let's get this party started!" I yelled.

The music was jamming and drinks were flowing. I was so happy that I danced and danced and danced, feeling no pain. Soon we started to toast one after another. Two glasses of Cristal, two tequila shots, and a variety of wine later, I was a little more than loose. Somewhere in between all the liquor, Kenneth pulled me aside.

"Hey, come meet my son," Kenneth said.

I knew that moment was coming and all the liquor I had ingested suddenly seemed to disappear and I knew I had to tell him. He deserved the truth. He took my hand but I stopped.

"I need to tell you something," I said, my voice shaking, my breath quivering, my hands clammy, my mind racing. I knew if I didn't tell him, Dre would. I couldn't take that risk.

When moments like this happen, there's always the good side of truth that tells you what to do and then the second-guessing starts. *What if Dre doesn't say anything? What if Kenneth leaves me? What if I lose him?*

"What's the matter, baby?" he asked. I wanted to say it right then. I could feel the words on my tongue but I swallowed them.

"What if he doesn't like me?" I said, and as those stupid ass words rolled out of my mouth, I wanted to slap myself.

"It wouldn't change how I feel about you," he said and continued to walk toward Dre.

I held onto Kenneth's hand tightly and strolled over to the spot where Dre was standing, holding the hand of a tall long-legged white woman. I wish I could say she was ugly but she wasn't. She looked kind and very, very pregnant.

I averted my eyes by adjusting my mask over my face. He stood there expressionless as I walked up.

"Andre, I want to introduce you to my fiancée," Kenneth said as he smiled.

"Well, nice to meet you. This is my wife, Shelly." It took my mind a few minutes to process the words "wife" and "Shelly" in the same sentence. I extended my hand to Shelly first. "Nice to meet you. I guess now I'll be your mother-in-law."

I laughed as I wiggled my new diamond in her face. The look on Dre's face was filled with barely-checked anger. I could see a vein protruding from the side of his temple and suppressed a snicker. I extended my left hand and reached out toward him, but he opened his arms to hug me. It had been years since I had been that close to him and I was afraid of what that feeling might do to me, to Nita, to Kenneth.

I pulled away as quickly as I could. "It is so nice to finally meet you." I tried to adjust my volume to accommodate the blaring music. The passing waiter's timing couldn't have been better. I quickly snatched a martini from the tray and took a drink.

"Didn't know my father liked them so young," Dre said.

"How long have you two been married?" I asked.

Dre looked as if he wanted to interject, but he was cut off by Shelly before he could get a word out.

"Two years, but together since high school." She smiled and gazed at him. A forced smile showed fear in his eyes. A look I had never seen before. He was married when we were together and I'm guessing she never knew about me.

"Hmph, well that's a long time."

"Shelly's a model, right?" Kenneth says.

She nodded bashfully. "I am, but I missed Dre and it was time for us to start a family."

An awkward silence fell amongst us, my eyes locked on Dre's in a battle of chicken. Judging by the look on Shelly's face, I could tell then that maybe I didn't need to say anything. Maybe Dre had his own life and heart to protect. In that silence, it was as if he and I agreed that some things were better left unsaid. I didn't know if he was happy, but I was and exhaled a sigh of relief.

"If you all will excuse me, I'm not feeling well." I turned to Kenneth. "Honey, I think I need to rest for a few moments."

"Jade was in a hit-and-run accident not long ago. Just down the street not far from here," Kenneth said.

And just when you think that you're out in the clear, truth still finds its way to shit on your front door.

Shelly paused and looked at Dre, then at me, then back at Dre. Tears swelled in her eyes and her pregnant ass lunged at me. Martini glasses went flying and our bodies landed on the floor with a thud. I wasn't gonna let her get the best of me. She was screaming and slap boxing but I was ready to whup her ass.

We wrestled and no sooner had I gotten started, I was completely lifted up off the ground, but the wrong thing to do was to grab me around my stomach and hoist me up into the air. I kicked violently, landing several kicks toward Dre, who was desperately trying to shield Shelly. The person who'd hoisted me into the air squeezed tighter. I felt a wave of nausea just before the contents of my stomach erupted all over them both.

"Jade, what's wrong with you?" Kenneth yelled, looking me directly in the eyes. I pulled away from him, turned, and saw a pool of blood on the floor, gushing from Dre's face.

"Somebody get me a towel," Kenneth said, beckoning.

"I'm fine. Let's go." Dre sternly turned to Shelly.

"You bitch! It's you, isn't it?" Shelly yelled.

"You are damn right I'm a bitch, but to you it's Mrs. Bitch!"

Dre grabbed Shelly by the arm and forced her toward the front door.

The entire room was amazed at the display they'd just seen. The space was completely silent. I looked around at everyone gawking at me. I wanted to be embarrassed, but I stood up as straight as I could, adjusted my dress, pushed a few hairs into place, and walked toward the stairs wearing one heel. I didn't know where my other shoe was, but I didn't care. I kept on walking until I made it up the stairs. I stumbled up to the bedroom and passed out on the bed.

It had been a long time since I had been this drunk and I

hoped that Kenneth would check on me soon because I had to pee but didn't have the balance to move.

When I heard the door open softly, I smiled that he had come to check on me. I felt him sit down on the bed and softly caress my back. As I lay on my stomach, it felt like my body was sinking through the bed into the floor. My head was hurting and there was a high-pitched tone in my ears. I sighed contentedly that he was there to comfort and take care of me like always. I felt the soft breeze of his breath on the back of my neck. I tried to turn my body over but it was nearly impossible with the weight of his arm on me. I felt him untie my dress and I helped as much as I could to wiggle out of it. He turned me over and I eagerly spread my legs waiting to feel him against me. He leaned toward my ear.

"I need you." His voice made my body tremble.

"I'm all yours," I replied.

I felt his fingertips traveling across my arms as he reached around and caressed my breast with his lips. He shifted his weight to remove his pants as I eagerly anticipated how ready his manhood would be for me. I felt his smooth hands open my legs which told me that he would be giving attention to Nita. As soon as I felt his tongue move up and down her lips, I wanted to explode. The pleasure that he was giving to Nita sent my mind into a euphoric orgasm and my body trembled at his touch unlike anything I had ever felt before. Just as I felt that I could take no more, he used his hands to turn my body back onto my stomach. His tongue glided slowly over my skin, up my spine. When he reached the back of my neck, he grabbed my arms and put them above my head, holding them with one hand.

"Kenneth," I moaned.

He didn't say a word as he entered me from behind. The tossing and turning made me feel dizzier than I already felt but each thrust gave me a deep pleasure. The strokes were slow, going in and slowly pulling out, but they were perfect. Each stroke went deeper and deeper and I wanted to scream.

"Fuck me," I begged.

My eyes slowly opened and I spotted Kenneth standing in the doorway. Rage covered his face.

In a hazy spin, I rolled over onto my back as he stormed over to Dre.

"You motherfucker!" His left fist swung out and slammed into Dre's face, then he turned and came to me. Terrified, I backed up against the wall.

"Get...the fuck...out...now," he growled, grinding his teeth. "I hope you die and I never see your face again." His face was bright red and tears welled in his eyes, but I couldn't move. I was frozen in horror.

"The truth Jade. Just tell the truth!"

I was startled by the shaking of Estella, Kenneth's maid.

"Ms. Jade. Are you alright?"

I looked at my hand; the ring was still there. Morning had come and I had survived another epic wave of dreams that felt all too real.

As I walked down the long spiral staircase, each step closer to the door was harder and harder to take. Everyone was gone. The room was empty. Dre's blood was still on the floor along with fragments of my broken glass. I lingered a fraction of a second before walking toward the kitchen. Unsure of what I would face when I saw Kenneth, my head was pounding and I couldn't think. Parts of my body ached, my Versace dress was torn, and blood was splattered on my arm. I foolishly attempted to wipe it off but it had dried against my skin. I turned the corner to see Kenneth sitting at the table.

"Morning," he softly said.

"Morning," I replied.

The glimmer in his eyes wasn't there and I wasn't sure what to make of his facial expression. He had a look that I hadn't seen before. I wasn't sure if he'd figured out the truth or talked to Dre, but either way, I knew that my time was now or never. He took a sip of his coffee, snapped his newspaper, and tipped his head, signaling me to sit down.

I slowly walked toward the table and at the opposite end of the table. He took a spoonful of his oatmeal and a bite of his toast. I sat there frozen, unsure of where to start.

Estella brought a glass of orange juice and placed it down beside me.

"Can I get you anything, Ms. Jade?" she calmly asked.

"Maybe she'd like a cup of honest...tea."

I couldn't hold it anymore. I had to tell him.

Like the vomit I had spewed the night before, I told him every detail about me and Dre.

There's a funny thing that happens when you start to tell the truth—it just doesn't stop pouring out. He sat calmly and listened to me explain that when I saw the photo of Dre on the boat, it was then that I realized that Dre was his son.

Kenneth stopped me.

"When you look at me, do you see him?"

I paused, maybe too long.

"No."

He put his head down.

"Estella."

She showed up within seconds.

"Yes, sir?"

"Have the car brought around. Pack Jade's things and remove every trace of her from my house." He stood up and turned to exit the room.

I couldn't say anything. I couldn't move. I sat there as if time had died. As he moved past me, his scent captured my soul and sent me into a hysterical cry. I fell out of my chair to my hands and knees.

"Please don't go. I love you."

He yanked his leg from my embrace.

"You wouldn't recognize love if it was the sun in the sky."

I sat back on my heels and sobbed. I felt empty and hollow. All I could do was cry uncontrollably.

When I heard the front door slam, I knew that he was gone. Kenneth was gone.

Fuck You, Al Green

Monica

From the day I arrived at Mr. Gregory's, he would blast all kinds of sad ass music. From B.B. King to Al Green, he had every record and his record player worked. Morning 'til night, he and Maya would dance to and sing every sad ass song. I was so emotionally drained that I spent nearly a week in bed, barely eating, not showering and not thinking. Plus those sad fucking songs were making my already fucked up view of my life worse. After several days of my sleeping in my own personal hell, I woke up to see a beam of sunlight peering through the curtains, hearing the blaring sounds of Sam Cooke's "A Change Is Gonna Come." Like clockwork, there was a knock at the door. It was Mr. Gregory bringing me oatmeal and toast, like he did every morning. He came in humming that sad fucking song and a poor attempt to hit high notes.

"It's been a long, a long time coming but I know a change gonna come. Oh yes, it will."

"Hey, Mo," he said as he set the tray down. "You know what today is?"

"No, what is it?"

"Today is a good day to die," he said and set the tray down. His comment confused me.

"What?"

"If you're not busy living, you might as well get busy dying. Get busy doing something," he said and walked out the door. I turned over toward the window and thought about what he had said as the trumpets from the song blared. There was a part of me that really wanted to get up and get busy doing something. I sat up in the bed to eat my oatmeal, and when I reached for the bowl, a stench came from underneath my smelly body. The smell was so intense that I felt like my nose was being assaulted. A part of me was happy to be able to smell because I had been numb for so long that I hadn't felt anything. Taking care of Devon was a struggle and Maya helped as much as she could.

As I pulled my dehydrated body from the bed and placed my feet on the floor, I sat on the edge of the bed and lifted my chest and sat up straight. I took a deep breath and stood up. I walked toward the bathroom and caught a glimpse of my reflection in the mirror as I headed toward it. I stopped and stared.

Where did I go? What had I allowed myself to become? Who was I? I was a twenty-four-year-old woman who looked for happiness in all the wrong places. How did I get to this place? There were too many questions and too many unanswered questions. The thoughts in my mind felt cloudy, tangled. I turned and crawled back into bed, pulled the covers over my head, and went back to sleep.

That night I slept better than I had in the past week. Even Devon seemed happier.

The next day, I awoke to the smell of bacon and Al Green's

"For the Good Times," an even sadder song, sounding like an old Negro spiritual with depressing words.

"Fuck Al Green!" I shouted.

I threw the covers back and rushed to the door. I swung it open ready to go and break that fucking record.

There stood Mr. Gregory with my breakfast.

"Morning." Mr. Gregory smiled.

Off-key, he sang, "Life goes on and this world, keeps on turning." He looked at me and shook his head. "You young girls have so much pain so early in life." He put the tray down.

"No one asks for pain."

"And you shouldn't let nobody give you none either. Maya takes care of the chickens and gathers the eggs. I tend to the cows and horses. Could use your help on keeping the place up. My wife used to . . ." He pauses. "Well, she kept it nice and clean in here. She wasn't much for outside. Since she passed, I ain't did much of that."

"Mr. Gregory, did you love her?"

"With everything I had."

"Did she love you back with all she had?"

"Not one bit. But she respected me. Don't reckon you need to be too worried about love though. You can't respect a man if you don't know how to love yourself."

He sang "for the good times" and walked out.

Rather than going to bed, I went to the bathroom, turned on the shower, and listened to the pitter-patter of the water as the steam slowly filled the room. I stood there and watched the steam fill the mirror and my reflection disappeared. I peeled off my pajamas and threw them in the trash. I didn't want to wash them; I wanted it all to go away. I stepped in the shower and let the hot water embrace me. I missed Patrick but I was still afraid of Shawn. I pressed my palms against the shower wall and cried. Regret overwhelmed me and my weak legs gave way. I leaned my body against the wall and slid down as I cried. I soon found myself sitting in the shower with the water beating the top of my head.

"Just let go…just let go…just let go…just let go," I chanted over and over. I rocked back and forth and prayed.

Faintly, I could hear more Al Green, this time "How Can You Mend a Broken Heart."

"Oh, God…grant me the serenity to accept the things that I cannot change, the courage to . . ."

I couldn't continue. I could only cry.

Then I heard a knock at the door.

"Auntie?" the tiny voice said.

"What is it, Maya?"

"I gotta go pee pee."

"Come on in." I heard the door open and saw her little head peek inside.

I peeked from the curtain to see her.

"Why are you sitting in the shower?" she asked. At first I wanted to get angry with her, but then I realized that she asked a valid question. Why was I sitting in the shower?

"I don't know," I replied.

"I sit in the shower sometimes when I'm sad. Are you sad?" She wiggled her pink butterfly skirt up to sit on the toilet. I closed the curtain.

"I am."

"I don't want you to be sad. My mommy was sad and so was my daddy. When people get sad, they die. So can you not be sad?"

"Yeah, I can…can…not be sad."

She started singing, "How can you stop the sun from shining?"

"Does he always play this music?"

"Depends on how he's feeling. I'm gonna flush."

Swoosh.

I screamed as ice cold water rained down on me.

"What the hell?"

"I told you I was gonna flush! Sorry."

I could only shake my head.

"Okay, I'm gonna wait for your but outside. It stinks in here," she said and walked out.

I chuckled.

Oh my God, I actually chuckled and my chuckle turned into a laugh, an uncontrollable one. I couldn't remember the last time I just laughed. I looked at the bush of furry hair on my legs and laughed. I smelled my armpit and laughed. I stood up and started to scrub my body. I wiped away the fog from the mirror fog from the mirror and pulled off my weave ponytail. I popped off my fake nails and pulled off my fake eyelashes. I could finally see myself.

"There you are, Monica. Thank you, God, for Maya. Thank you for Mr. Gregory and thank you God for soap."

By the time I got out of the shower, Al Green's "Tired of Being Alone" was playing and I was tired of it. I was tired of feeling sad and hearing sad songs, and I was over Al Green. Fuck you, Al Green.

Blueberry Blues
Jade

A cab arrived and I was rushed into the car. I reached to close the door, but Estella stopped it and held out her hand. I knew what she wanted. I pulled the ring off my finger and passed it to her.

"Give him time," she said in her broken English and thick Spanish accent.

I could only shake my head.

"Let him come to you, when he ready."

I shook my head in agreement and the door closed. The journey to Mr. Gregory's was a sobering ride that made me realize the mistakes I had made. All of them. There's no reason to give any man that much power and I had allowed Dre to not only control my life but have all my power. And I'd managed to erase the only definition of love that I'd known. I shouldn't have told Kenneth. I should have lied. Whoever said the truth was freeing didn't have what I had.

When I arrived at Mr. Gregory's house, I got out of the car with just my purse. The last thing I had in my possession from Kenneth. Maya came running out the door.

"Auntie Jade, you're here."

"My God, look how big you are."

"Tee Mo is here and my new baby brother."

I looked at her confused as hell. I didn't know what she was talking about until I looked up and there she was. Monica, my best friend.

She walked up to me and I wasn't sure if she was gonna hit me or hug me.

"Do you remember what I asked you the first day we met?"

"Will you be my friend?"

"Will you be my best friend."

We embraced and I held my friend. My best friend. We spent the next few days, laughing like we did when we were kids. Maya came in one night and told us to go to bed.

Monica was there to hold me during the nights I cried hoping that Kenneth would come back to me. There were nights I was there to hold her when she relived the abuse she had suffered from Shawn. If I thought we could get away with it, I might have come up with a way to put him and Dre in the same shallow grave, but that wasn't the answer. The answer many times is to go through the pain and let it heal.

It was hard to tell when the pain was healed, but each time the tears lasted a little less and the sadness went away a little faster. Being able to have Monica by my side to be honest about all my shit was needed because I knew she wouldn't judge me. And I didn't judge her.

It's funny how life can line up what you need and help you move on to the next thing. Just as you think you're getting over one thing, another truth of Cinderella appears, shattering your life.

I sat in the bathroom for twenty minutes looking at that little white stick.

I was pregnant.

How was I supposed to raise a child? Was it a boy? Was it a girl? Do I keep it? Do I have an abortion? Should I tell Kenneth? Could I really do this? Could I be a mom? Could my life get any more disturbing? So many thoughts raced through my mind. It felt like I was spinning in a tornado, and maybe I was because I quickly spun around to pray to the porcelain god. The vomit seemed to never end. Monica knocked on the door.

"You okay in there?"

"No."

She quickly opened the door.

"What's the . . ." She glimpsed at the stick on the sink. "Oh shit. Is that . . .?"

"Yeah."

"We're having a baby!"

"Yeah."

"I'm gonna be an Auntie!"

"Why are you excited?" I angrily replied. "This isn't what I want for my life." I stood up, flushed the toilet, and washed my hands. "I don't want a baby."

"But…"

"I don't want to be a mother and I sure as hell don't want to be a single mother. Do you know what I should be doing right now? I should be planning a wedding. I should be picking out dresses and colors and flowers and shit. Not picking poop out of a tiny ass. I don't have a job. I don't even have an associate's degree and in case you haven't looked around, this ain't my fucking house. My house is on a hill. I was supposed to be making invitations that said Dr. and Mrs. Hill. That's what I was supposed to be doing but instead I'm here, with you and—"

Monica interrupted. "Well I'm sorry you're here with just me but you know what, there're a lot bigger problems that people have than being pissed about wedding colors. You were the main one telling me not to be so superficial, be myself, and right now, *me* is a mother and a single one. So fucking what. Worse shit could happen," she shouted.

"Really? Like what?"

"Like I could have ended up like Tracy with a bat to my face and a dead child. Or like Maya with no parents and a pretend brother or Mr. Gregory, who stayed with a woman he knew barely loved him. Shit can get worse you know. Look, if you don't want the baby then fine, go have it sucked out of you. But don't make that child pay for your mistakes. Don't look at him or her at thirteen and say, 'Hey, asshole, I should have sucked you out while you were a blueberry in my belly because I wanted Jimmy Choos instead of you.' You fucked up, so now what? You either suck it out or suck it up."

She walked out and slammed the door. I knew then that I would keep the baby.

Monica attended every appointment with me and told me everything I needed to do.

A few months later, I lay on the table having an ultrasound.

"It's a girl!" the giddy nurse said.

"Fuck," I replied.

The smile on the giddy nurse's face went away. "Were you hoping for a boy?"

"Yup! Because I have a boy," Monica chimed in.

"Oh, are you two partners?" the nurse asked.

I burst out laughing. "Honey, the closest I've gotten to coochie was when I came out of my mother's."

"Jade, you could've said we're best friends," Monica replied.

The ride home, I couldn't focus on anything except the fact

that I was about to bring a girl in the world and I wasn't sure how to raise her.

"What's wrong?" Monica asked.

"It's a girl. I don't know if I'm happy or sad. When I think about the relationship I had with my mother, I don't feel equipped to raise a girl. How do I explain this to her? Is she going to grow up and hate me for bringing her into a world with no father? Is she going to blame me? Will she be horny like me? Will she have her own Dre and fuck up her life like me? She's not even breathing yet and already she has baggage from my damage. I'm not ready to be a mother."

"You don't have much choice but you've got a few more months to get ready. It's not that bad. If it was, women wouldn't do it?"

"I don't want her to think of me as a desperate woman. I don't want her to know my past."

"Or you embrace it and make sure that you don't pass on your pain to her, like your mother passed to you."

"I still don't know my father."

"You're making some very concrete decisions about a person you don't know. She might be a scientist or President."

"Or a stripper?"

"As long as she's a good one."

We laughed. A rare moment.

That evening when we arrived home, Mr. Gregory was excited to show us the final touches on the baby's room. He had created a split room design, half for Devon and half for my baby. He hung wallpaper and painted fairies and footballs. He took the time to put the crib together and bought nearly everything for the baby. His excitement was so cute, although it was hard for me to share his enthusiasm.

Ring of Fire
Jade

It's 1:15 a.m.

"Monica!" I cried, sitting on the edge of my bed in a puddle of water. Monica burst into the room.

"Holy shit! It's time."

"Time for what?"

"The baby is coming, dumbass."

"Holy shit! I'm not ready."

"Too late, heifer, let's go."

I tried to stand up but doubled over in pain.

"MR. GREGORY!" Monica yelled.

He hobbled in.

"I thought I heard you in here," he said. "Come on, let's get you to the car."

The walk to the car seemed like a three hour death walk. When we arrived at the hospital, it was right on time. I had dilated three centimeters.

"We're about to have a baby!" Monica said excitedly.

"Why are you excited! I'm in agony, heifer!"

I was at the point where I couldn't handle the pain anymore despite my desire to do this naturally. Somehow I thought having a natural birth would make me stronger, but the contractions were too much.

"Nurse?" I said, nearly in tears as they helped me crawl onto the bed. "I need an epidural please."

"I'm sorry, honey, but we won't be able to give you one," she responded. Her facial features reminded me of Mother and I wished she was here.

"I don't understand. Why not?"

"Yeah, why can't she have the medicine?" Monica scoffed. "Ain't that what it's for?"

"You indicated on the paperwork that you had broken your back and been in a body cast. The trauma you endured from that accident and the damage to your vertebrae was too much."

I wanted to hit her in the mouth, so that's what I tried to do. I swung at her, but I missed. She grabbed my wrist.

"Settle down, Jade. You can do this," Monica said.

I flopped back onto the bed and started to cry.

Monica leaned over and wiped my tears from my face. She then took my other hand and held mine. "Jade, I'm here with you. We got this."

"Just squeeze my hand," she said calmly. "We're going to get through this together, okay?" I nodded.

Another contraction and this one felt like a lightning bolt in my back. The nurse gripped my hand and knelt down close to my face. "Jade, I'm here with you too, okay? And you can do this."

How did she know what I could do? I wasn't even sure of what I could do. She placed my hand close to her heart.

"I'm going to be right here with you," she said, smiling. Tears continued to roll down my cheeks and she wiped them just like Monica had. The doctor entered the room and introduced himself, but I was in so much pain, I didn't pay much attention to what he was saying.

"Hi, Jade. I hear we're ready to have a baby," Dr. Benner said. "Listen to me. Just take deep breaths and follow the sound of my voice."

"I'm scared."

"I know you are, Jade but don't be. Everything's going to be okay. The baby is ready to crown. I'm going to need you to push, okay? Just push when you feel like it," Dr. Benner said, smiling at me.

"But I don't—" I pressed my head against the pillow, bracing against the pain, and just as my eyes began to feel like they were rolling to the back of my head, the nurse captured my attention again.

"Jade, stay with me, okay? Listen to me. My name is Rainy and I'm here for you."

"Rainy, I can't—"

"Yes, you can!" she said confidently. "Now you need to push and push hard!"

Thoughts of my life and pain flooded my mind. All I could do was cry. Not because of the pain, but because this innocent child would have to be stuck calling me Mother.

Another contraction and I clenched my teeth, Rainy's hand, and Monica's hand. I thought for sure I was going to break the stirrups my feet were in.

"PUSH, JADE!" Nurse Rainy said.

I held my breath and pushed with everything I had inside me, but it wasn't enough.

"Again, Jade. Harder! You can do this!" Dr. Benner encouraged.

"My ass feels like it's on fire. Oh God, help me please, please!"

"Come on, Jade," Monica said. "Get that baby on out of there."

The pain had become so intense. It was like nothing I had ever felt.

"PLEASE GET IT OUT!" I shouted. "PLEASE…PLEASE… PLEASE!"

"Jade, you're doing great. Stay with me," Nurse Rainy said.

"What's happening? I'm scared. Oh my God, God, please help me…oh God, please!" I begged for death to take me. The pain was so intense, it was as if there was a ring of fire around the entire bottom half of my body. All I wanted was for it to stop.

"Jade, listen to me. You need to push. Don't hold it in, Jade, push," Nurse Rainy calmly coached.

"Jade, just let it all go. All of your pain. Let it go right now!" Monica said to me, and it was the perfect set of words that I needed to hear.

So that's exactly what I did.

I screamed! I screamed from the depths of my soul, but the scream was less related to the physical pain I was feeling and more closely related to the internal pain I had caused myself. I screamed for the anger I felt toward my mother, her broken heart, and her broken spirit. I screamed for the anger I felt at never knowing my own father. I screamed for my sister. I screamed for her killer. I screamed for Maya. I screamed for Monica. I screamed for Dre. I screamed for Kenneth. I screamed for the countless men who suffered my tormented spirit. I screamed for love. I screamed for hate. I screamed for my childhood dreams and nightmares. I screamed for my fears. I screamed for my loneliness. I screamed for my heart, dignity, and respect. I screamed for my child and I screamed for my life.

"The head is out! One more big push, Jade! Come on, you

can do it." Nurse Rainy cheered with a joy on her face that reminded me of Mother even more.

"SSSSHHHHHHHHHIIIIIIIIIIIIIIT!!"

I took a deep breath in and pushed. I could feel the muscles in the back of my neck, jawbone, chest, and shoulders. I pushed out the pain of hating Dre, the pain of losing Kenneth, the pain of losing me. When I saw the joy on everyone's face, I knew it was over. A euphoric feeling came over me that was to become a new definition of power. All of my power, all of my pain, was finally released. She was out and I felt free. I heard the cry and I cried, reaching for her.

I was exhausted and if I wasn't already lying down, I would have collapsed, but Rainy walked over to me and placed my daughter in my arms. She was the most beautiful creature I had ever seen.

"I knew you could do it," Nurse Rainy said. Looking at my daughter, I couldn't believe that God had given me this gift. I knew my life would never be the same. I looked at my treasure and told her that I loved her. I nuzzled against her brand-new skin and I prayed for her to know how much she meant to me. Tears ran uncontrollably down my face, and I was in awe that I was able to love and care for something, someone, so quickly.

This was it...this was love.

"Thank you for choosing me," I said to her.

"What are you going to name her?" Nurse Rainy asked.

"I hadn't thought about that. I'm not sure yet."

An Old Sweet Song
Monica

The next morning, Mr. Gregory came to the hospital with Devon in the stroller, unbuckled, diaper dirty, face crusty. Maya was pushing, barely able to see over the top of the stroller. She looked like an orphaned homeless child. I think he could tell by the look on our faces that we were not too happy.

"Hey there. How're my girls doing?" he joyfully inquired.

"Mr. Gregory, have you changed Devon's diaper since we left?"

"I'm too old to change diapers."

He sat down in the chair by the bed.

"'Cause I can only see out of my left eye and hear out of my right ear but don't tell nobody 'cause they'll take my license from me."

Jade and I looked at each other and could only laugh.

"Mr. Gregory, I've been meaning to ask you, what's your middle name?" Jade asked.

"Mali, after the country in Africa. That was how my family kept up with where we were from and so all men in my family have the same middle name. Why?"

The nurse was checking Jade's vital signs when she looked up at the woman and said, "Remember you asked me what I wanted to name her? Malia. I'll name her Malia, after my dad."

Mr. Gregory looked up at Jade, instantly teary-eyed. He pursed his lips and pulled a handkerchief out of his pocket to wipe away the moisture.

"That's a good name." He nodded. "Good one."

Despite all that we had both gone through, the birth of Malia was the best thing for all of us. Jade and I were still healing emotionally but we were making the best of life, one day at a time. She enrolled in school for writing and I found the courage to file for divorce. It's amazing how many things can change in just one year.

We celebrated Malia's first birthday with a much needed dinner at Mr. Gregory's favorite restaurant, IHOP. Kids and seniors ate free so it was cheap. The birthday pancake showed up and we sang "Happy Birthday" to Malia.

Mr. Gregory asked, "Jade, Mo, either of you ever want to get married?"

We looked at each other confused by where that came from.

"Yeah, someday, but no time soon. Why?" I asked.

"Well, 'cause I just want to tell you one thing."

"Okay," Jade said with a chuckle.

"I want you both to get married one day. Give these children fathers."

"They don't need fathers, they got you," Jade said.

"I ain't got long."

"Don't talk like that. You could live to be one hundred. That's another twenty-five years from now." Jade laughed.

"When you my age that sound like a death sentence. I don't wanna be delirious peeing on myself." He chuckled.

"I'm just scared that I don't know what real love looks like. How am I going to know? I thought I was in love and look where that got me," I said.

"You won't know. Women never do when it's real love," he said as he poured more syrup on his pancakes. "But he'll know you."

"That makes no sense. I've had plenty of men who loved me," Jade countered.

"That's 'cause you tried to marry the man who you loved. Marry the man that loves you." He sipped his orange juice. "That may not make sense to you now, but when it happens it will. I loved your mother and I still do. I miss her," he said as he shuffled his fork around the pancake.

"I miss her, too," Jade echoed.

We arrived home that night. We each took a sleeping kid out of the car and put them to bed.

Mr. Gregory woke Maya. "I'm going to bed now but I love you."

"I love you, too, Papa G," she sleepily replied. He shuffled toward the door. "Papa G, can you make me pancakes in the morning?"

"With blueberries or chocolate chips?" he asked.

"Both," she replied.

"Ray Charles or Al Green?"

Jade and I both interjected. "Ray Charles!"

"I'm going to bed now. I'm tired." He passed out kisses to everyone.

"I love you, Dad," Jade said.

"Love you, too, baby girl," he acknowledged.

"Love you, Mr. G," I added.

"Love you more." He chuckled.

From the other side of the door, we could hear him singing, "Georgia. Georgia, the whole day through, just an old sweet song, keeps Georgia on my mind."

"Well, we know what song he'll be playing in the morning," Jade said.

The next morning an eerie silence filled the air. I looked at the clock and it was 7:13 a.m. I went to Mr. Gregory's room only to find him cold and stiff, Ray Charles' album on the floor beside him, a picture of him and Jade's mom by his bed stand.

We buried him quietly and tried to keep life normal for Maya's sake. She took it the hardest. Every morning while getting dressed for school, Maya would put on a different record that she enjoyed with Mr. G. Jade and I gradually figured out farm life and were doing okay.

Is Less More?
A Poem by Jade Hall

Less passion is not exciting, to me.
Less desire is not tempting, to me.
Less breath is not sensual, to me.
The more you give me less,
The more I lose my breathlessness.
My dreams become desireless.
Never lowering my speechlessness but using my volume, to say,
That I will always want more from you, not less.
Because I am more, I will never step to you with regress.
For you I have cheated, for you I have lied, only for you I have cried,
I tried to hide from the rage that lived inside my veins.
Disturbed that I could no longer wait to masturbate
Desire for you to saturate me, bad-bitch is how you rate me
Even if I am your bitch,
Can you be less of a dog?
To me.

One

Jade

Life without Mr. Gregory was hard and I missed him, but having Monica around helped me a lot to deal. We had developed a schedule like an old married couple and it was my day to pick Maya up from school. She begged me to go to the park and I didn't feel like fighting the Houston traffic, so I agreed. When we got to the park, I let Maya play while I tried to get a little homework done. Malia was in the sandbox and tried to stand up but her wobbly legs gave way and she fell, startling herself. When she started crying, I picked her up and cradled her in my arms. She rubbed her eyes, a signal that it was time to go home. I packed up the stroller with all of the usual play toys and called out to Maya, who wasn't ready to go.

"Five more minutes." she yelled.

"No more minutes, let's go. Malia is sleepy."

"Ah man," she whined.

"Ah woman. Let's go," I urged.

As we walked down the trail toward the car, I saw a man jogging toward me who looked strangely familiar. He had on black shorts, a blue sports shirt, a hat, and sunglasses. My heart pounded and my feet felt like I was caught in cement.

"What's wrong Auntie?"

Kenneth.

The slowing of his pace told me that he recognized me. He stopped a few feet away. We stood there for a moment, and it felt eerie staring at each other silently.

"Hi," he said

Hearing his voice made my heart pound even faster.

"Hi."

The silence continued for a few seconds that felt like hours.

"How are you?" he asked, panting.

"I'm good. How are you?"

"I'm okay." He removed his shades.

Silence.

"Is that Maya?" he asked.

"Yeah."

"Wow, look how big you are?"

Maya smiled and swung her leg, holding onto the stroller.

"Auntie, can I go slide one more time?"

Maya took off running back toward the slide.

"Sure."

"Is this your daughter?" he said, pointing.

"Yeah. This is…this is Malia. She just turned one."

"Wow, has it been that long?"

"Yeah, I…I guess so," I stuttered.

He knelt down and looked at her. Watching him look at her, I knew in my heart that he knew.

"Hi, Malia." He extended his hand to her and she reached for his face. The smile on his face gave me joy.

"She's beautiful."

"Thank you."

Silence.

I wanted to touch him.

"Well, I have to get back to the hospital. It was good to see you, Jade."

All I could think was, *Say something stupid!* But nothing came out. I just stared at him. I'm pretty sure my mouth was actually open but there were no words coming out. I was stumped.

"You too, Kenneth."

Just saying his name made my heart flutter.

He tapped Malia on her nose and started to jog away. "Bye, Jade."

Like a fool, I watched him jog away.

How could I stop him? I didn't want to see him leave. I wanted him.

I loved him.

I loved him.

"Kenneth, wait!"

I pushed the stroller as fast as I could to catch up to him. "Kenneth!"

He stopped and turned around. When I caught up to him, I felt like I was out of breath.

"I umm...I . . ." I could hardly speak as tears surged in my eyes and my heart was in my throat.

"Jade . . ."

I interrupted because I knew if I didn't say it now, it would never come out and God only knows if I would ever have this chance again.

"Kenneth, I miss you and I'm sorry. I'm sorry that I was stupid and childish and drunk but I never meant to hurt you. I never wanted to hurt you. I wanted to spend my life with you. I *still* want to spend my life with you. I never knew how love *looked* or *felt* until I met you and I didn't know how to love myself but I do now and I need you to know that I'm not perfect but I know that you…you are the only man who's worthy of my love. And even if you walk away right now, I promise that I will wait for you until the day I die because you are…you are the man I was designed for. You are the man who my dreams were made of. You are why women believe in Cinderella, and I got to touch it, smell it, and feel it. I know that love is more than just sex and lust and control. I know that it's none of those things. It's being vulnerable and open and honest and true to yourself. You taught me that. If you ever gave me another chance, I wouldn't take you for granted. I would love you and honor you and cherish you. But if you walk away right now, I understand, as long as you know that you…changed…me."

I tried to wipe my tears and snot when he reached in his pocket, pulled out a towel, and wiped my tears away. Feeling his touch sent quivers from the top of my head to the soles of my feet.

"Jade." He stared into my eyes, cupped my face in his hands, and kissed me. "There are so many things that I've asked myself about what happened to us. There's not a day that I haven't woken up and wanted to hold you, reach for you, smell your skin, or feel your touch. There's very little I regret in life but letting you go…that is my greatest regret. I didn't want to lose you and I started to question if I was too old for you but your face was burned into my mind and everywhere I would go, it was as if I could see you. I realized how lonely I was without you. Sitting at the table alone, walking alone, felt like death because you…you gave me life. I love you."

As he wrapped his arms around me, it felt like a warm blanket on a cold winter night. I was scared, I was happy, I was full, and if this moment, just this moment was real, I knew that I could die and be able to say that I knew what true love felt like.

I embraced him. I was ready to surrender my heart to him and only him. I didn't want to let him go and I didn't want him to let me go. He took a step back and reached down behind his neck and started to unclasp a necklace hidden underneath his shirt. When he pulled it from around his neck, I recognized what was on the end of it. My ring. The ring he had given me the night of the proposal.

"I've never let you go, Jade. Do you think we can try again?"

Speechless.

"Yes, yes...yes...I will."

Two weeks later, Kenneth and I went to the justice of the peace and were married with only Monica, Devon, Maya, Malia, and Estella present. Monica and Patrick reconnected when a pregnant Asian girl washed up dead on the coast. Her husband, Shawn, pled not guilty to two felony counts of murder with premeditation. Monica's testimony secured her full custody of Devon and helped put Shawn away for two consecutive life sentences. Monica and Patrick married three months after the trial ended.

Dre and Kenneth hadn't spoken since the night of the incident. Dre moved to Paris with his new wife but left her for a French photographer. I went back to school to study English and now write an advice column for the *Houston Chronicle* called "Sex & Soul Ties." I focus on helping people heal from toxic relationships. I still work on my poetry, only now it has meaning and purpose.

The Untethered Soul
A Prayer by Jade

Today, I have untethered the ties to my soul.
Known or unknown
Remembered and forgotten,
Today, I have unhitched my heart
Today, I have loosened my nature and tightened my
nurture
Today, I am free of my mistakes,
Free of my mistakes
Free of my self-hatred
Free of my greed
I have forgiven myself for all of it
I have not forgotten the pain
But I have not held it.
I have untethered my soul from yours
Now, until my breath is no more
I am free.

Book Club Discussion Questions

1. Which characters in the book did you like most?

2. Which characters did you like least?

3. Share a favorite quote from the book. Why did this quote stand out?

4. What songs does this book make you think of?

5. Create a book group playlist together!

6. Did the characters seem believable to you? Did they remind you of anyone?

7. Have you ever been in love with anyone the way Jade was?

8. How did Monica's story affect you?

Acknowledgements

To my Mom, I miss you dearly! To my Daddy for always loving and supporting me. I want to give a shoutout to my brothers, Scott and Kyle Whitley (and their families). A SPECIAL Thank you to Steve Harvey and Monica Barnes for launching "The Delusion of Cinderella" on the Steve TV show and for your continued support.

In addition, I want to give a special thank you to Tom Joyner and The Tom Joyner morning show family, I love ya'll. Sybil Wilkes for your wholehearted support and my radio partner Sherri Shepherd for your encouragement to keep writing. Thank you, Vivica A. Fox, for support. To Rushion McDonald, thank you for pushing me to excel. Thank you to my Village, you know who you are and I couldn't do this with our all of you. I love you guys for life.

Stephanie Proctor, I can't thank you enough for loving, guiding and watching Joshua. Shavone Terry and Earlene Gray for all that you do to keep my life together.

Christie Dawson, I can't "Thank You" enough for never giving up on me and forcing me to sit down and just write. I love ya girl! Carla Civil, you brought the cover to life like no other. You were patient with all of my annoying tweaks but never once complained—Thank you. Joe Fox, what can I say? You put up with emails and text from me to get the book cover layout just right. To Clarence Haynes, you took all my money, but you edited the hell out of this book from the other side of the world. To Nakia Laushaul for the guidance, advice on the nitty gritty details and I love the interior design. To Leroy Hamilton of photographybyhamilton.com. Thank you so much for the beautiful pictures you took of me.

Thank you to all the fans who have continued to support me over the years. sticking with me.

To the greatest person in my life, Joshua. Thank you for interrupting me while I was trying to get the words out. Thank you for being the amazing little boy that you are. I'll let you read this when you are 33. Mommy loves you son.

About the Author

Kym Whitley is one of those rare individuals to whom the phrase "renaissance woman" might be applied. These days, most people know her either from her frequent appearances on Larry David's groundbreaking HBO series Curb Your Enthusiasm or from the Tom Joyner Morning Show, a nationally syndicated radio program. But that's just the tip of the iceberg. Kym is actually a comedienne, actress, activist, author and — perhaps most importantly — a mother.

Originally from the Cleveland area, Kym has been based in Los Angeles for years. She was a schoolteacher in Compton back in the day but always loved performing and, especially, comedy. A chance encounter with the legendary Redd Foxx (who told her she had "the comedic goods") led her to pursue acting more seriously. Her first real job was in the Shelley Garrett play Beauty Shop, which started in L.A. and did a national tour.

Kym's TV career began a few years later. One highlight was when she launched the first female panel talk show, Oh Drama, on BET. Kym has appeared in Moesha, The Wayans Brothers Show and many others. Of the latter series, she says, "My favorite was The Wayans Brothers Show. I laughed through the whole thing!" She was also was nominated for both a Daytime Emmy Award and an Indie Series Award for her portrayal of "Big Candi" in The Bay, The Series.

Kym is also no stranger to the big screen. Her first big role was as "Auntie Suga" in Next Friday. Since then, she has appeared in The Nutty Professor, Along Came Polly, College Road Trip, the upcoming Young & Hungry and dozens of other films. She also voiced the characters "Honey Bee" in Black Dynamite and "Melonee" in the popular computer-animated feature Rango.

As of late, some of Kym's projects have become more personal. She and her adopted son Joshua became the focus of Raising Whitley, which ran on the Oprah Winfrey Network a few years back. She is also gearing up for what may be her most exciting project yet: the novel The Delusion of Cinderella, which goes to print this summer. Although details are still largely under wraps, Kym says the book is "not for the faint of heart!" Indeed, the tag line is "Love and lust feel the same but you can only trust one of them."

In addition to all her work as an entertainer, Kym is a dedicated activist. Her 'Don't Feed Me' campaign began as something she did for Joshua but evolved into an ongoing, high profile project to raise awareness of food allergies for children and adults. Kym holds an honorary doctorate from UVa — Lynchburg, as well as a Bachelors of Science from Fisk University. She serves on the board of directors for both The Special Needs Network of L.A. and The Jefferson Memorial Home for Foster Children.

You can follow Kym Whitley on her official website, www.iamkymwhitley.com; on Facebook, Instagram and Twitter @kymwhitley; and at www.dontfeedme.org.

CPSIA information can be obtained
at www.ICGtesting.com
Printed in the USA
LVHW04s2342191018
594246LV00001B/42/P